THE
Dispatcher

A Novel

RYAN DAVID JAHN

PENGUIN BOOKS

PENGUIN BOOKS

Published by the Penguin Group

Penguin Group (USA) Inc., 375 Hudson Street, New York, New York 10014, U.S.A.
Penguin Group (Canada), 90 Eglinton Avenue East, Suite 700, Toronto,
Ontario, Canada M4P 2Y3 (a division of Pearson Penguin Canada Inc.)
Penguin Books Ltd, 80 Strand, London WC2R 0RL, England
Penguin Ireland, 25 St Stephen's Green, Dublin 2, Ireland (a division of Penguin Books Ltd)
Penguin Group (Australia), 250 Camberwell Road, Camberwell,
Victoria 3124, Australia (a division of Pearson Australia Group Pty Ltd)
Penguin Books India Pvt Ltd, 11 Community Centre, Panchsheel Park, New Delhi - 110 017, India
Penguin Group (NZ), 67 Apollo Drive, Rosedale, Auckland 0632,
New Zealand (a division of Pearson New Zealand Ltd)
Penguin Books (South Africa) (Pty) Ltd, 24 Sturdee Avenue,
Rosebank, Johannesburg 2196, South Africa

Penguin Books Ltd, Registered Offices:
80 Strand, London WC2R 0RL, England

First published in Great Britain by Pan Macmillan,
a division of Macmillan Publishers Limited 2011
Published in Penguin Books 2011

1 3 5 7 9 10 8 6 4 2

Grateful acknowledgment is made for permission to reprint an excerpt
from "Cascando" from Collected Poems in English and French by Samuel Beckett.
Copyright © 1977 by Samuel Beckett. Used by permission of Grove/Atlantic, Inc.

Publisher's Note

This is a work of fiction. Names, characters, places, and incidents either are the product
of the author's imagination or are used fictitiously, and any resemblance to actual persons,
living or dead, business establishments, events, or locales is entirely coincidental.

LIBRARY OF CONGRESS CATALOGING IN PUBLICATION DATA
Jahn, Ryan David.
The dispatcher / Ryan David Jahn.
p. cm.
ISBN 978-0-14-312070-4
1. Police dispatchers—Fiction.   2. Kidnapping—Fiction.   I. Title.
PS3560.A356D57 2011
813'.54—dc23
2011039306

Printed in the United States of America
Set in Warnock Pro

For my father

THOMAS NATHAN JAHN

1949–2004

Author's Note

Bulls Mouth, Texas, does not exist, nor does Tonkawa County, in which it is supposed to be nested. None of the people who populate Bulls Mouth are based on people who populate the real world. While most of the other towns and cities mentioned are real, or based on real places, this novel and accurate cartography are not close friends. They're barely acquaintances. In all instances where the story's demands conflicted with reality, reality came out the loser.

This book, like my first two, was edited by Will Atkins, who helped me cut fifty pages while simultaneously improving all those that remained. In a just world his name would have a place on the cover. Unfortunately, this is not a just world, so he'll have to settle for my heartfelt thanks.

Also due thanks are Mary (always), Seán Costello, Sophie Portas, Sandra Taylor, and everyone at Macmillan.

Finally, thanks to you—for reading.

RDJ
July 2011

If you do not love me I shall not be loved
If I do not love you I shall not love.
Samuel Beckett

What is done out of love always
takes place beyond good and evil.
Friedrich Nietzsche

THE
Dispatcher

ONE

Ian Hunt is less than an hour from the end of his shift when he gets the call from his dead daughter. It's been over seven years since he last heard her voice, and she was a different person back then, a seven-year-old girl with pudgy hands and a missing front tooth and green eyes that could break your heart if she wanted them to, so at first he doesn't know it's her.

But it is.

He's sitting in the dispatch office in the Bulls Mouth, Texas, police station on Crouch Avenue, which, as usual, he's got to himself, though he's sure if he were to poke his head into the front room he'd see Chief Davis leaning back in his chair with his feet up on his desk and his Stetson tipped down over his eyes. An ancient swamp cooler rattles away in the window to his left, dripping water onto the moldy carpet beneath it, though the July heat doesn't seem much intimidated by its efforts. Sweat rolls down the side of his face and he tilts his head sideways and rubs the trickle away on the shoulder of his uniform shirt. He clicks through a game of solitaire on the computer-assisted dispatch system on the desk in front of him. If folks in town knew this was how he spent ninety-five percent of his time they'd shit.

But Bulls Mouth just isn't a big town. Three thousand people if you count everyone in the surrounding area, including the end-timers, revelators, snake-handlers, speed-cookers, dropouts,

3

and junkies, and he supposes you have to count them. Bulls Mouth PD handles their calls.

Despite being the very definition of a small town, Bulls Mouth is the second largest city in Tonkawa County, making up a quarter of its population.

He picks up his coffee mug and takes a swallow of the cold slop within. Grimaces as it goes down, but still takes a second swallow. He must drink three pots of Folgers a day, pouring one cup after another down his throat as he clicks through his hundred games of solitaire.

He's just setting down the cup when the call comes in from a pay phone on Main Street, just north of Flatland Avenue. Probably a prank call. In this day of cell phones, calls from pay phones almost always are. Fuck-off punk high-schoolers trying to chase away midsummer boredom with a little trouble. Growing up in Venice Beach, California, he did the same thing, so he can't really hold it against them.

'Nine-one-one. What is your emergency?' he says into his headset, fingers hovering over a black keyboard, ready to punch in information.

'Please help me!'

The voice belongs to either a girl or a woman, it's impossible to tell which, and it is trembling with panic and out of breath. The girl/woman is gasping into the receiver, which is crackling in his ear like there's a heavy wind, and high-pitched squeaks escape the back of her throat. If it's a prank call the person on the other end of the line is the best pretender he's ever dealt with.

'Please, ma'am, try to remain calm, and tell me what the problem is.'

'He's coming after me. He's—'

'What's your name and who's coming after you?'

4

'My name is Sarah. Wait, no. No. My name is Maggie, Maggie Hunt, and the man who's . . . I was . . . he's . . . he's—'

As soon as he hears the name, Maggie Hunt, Ian's lips go numb, and like a low note plucked on a taut metal cord running through his middle, a strange vibration ripples through him. Nausea in F-sharp minor.

He swallows.

'Maggie?' He inhales through his nostrils and exhales through his mouth in a long trembling sigh. 'Maggie,' he says, 'it's Daddy.'

The funeral was in May, two months ago now. At first he didn't want to have it. He thought it an absurd and ritualistic way of burying a past that was still, and is still, very much alive, and you don't bury something when its heart is still beating. But finally Debbie convinced him that she needed it done. She needed closure. Her shrink, whom she drove all the way to Houston to visit, thought she did, anyway. So they had the funeral and people came and Pastor Warden stood and spoke platitudes while behind him lay a small and empty coffin.

But his words were as empty as the coffin was.

People cried and sang hymns out of tune and dropped to their knees and bowed their heads and prayed. They looked at pictures of pretty little Maggie, from age zero to age seven—up to seven but never older—sitting in a high chair with cake on her face; walking for the first time; sitting before a blue background for her second-grade yearbook photo; sitting on the front step of their house at 44 Grapevine Circle with a bloody knee, a crash helmet on her head, and a wide, mischievous Cheshire grin on her face.

If she were alive she would be turning fifteen in September.

Ian was neither among the hymn singers nor the weepers. He sat silent in the last pew throughout it all. His back was straight, his fingers laced together, his hands resting in his lap. Though Bulls Mouth Baptist was hot, even in May, he did not move to wipe the sweat from his forehead nor that trickling down the side of his face. He sat there motionless, his mind a room without any furniture in it. He only moved when people began to walk up to him and offer their condolences. He shook their hands and said thank you and when someone tried to hug him he accepted their hugs, but he simply wanted to leave. He wanted to go home and be alone.

After everyone else had come and gone Debbie walked over with Bill Finch. Bill was her new husband. He was also police, working out of the Tonkawa County Sheriff's Office in Bulls Mouth, just other side of the county jail from Bulls Mouth's city police station, and a man who started many a jurisdictional argument with Chief Davis over even small issues the city always handled, which usually resulted in a yelling match between Davis and Sheriff Sizemore. Bill was one of only three county police regularly in Bulls Mouth. The main office was up in Mencken. The city PD handled most day-to-day policing on its own, and because of that all emergency calls in the area were filtered through Ian.

Debbie hugged him and thanked him for agreeing to the funeral. He and Bill nodded stiff greetings at one another, but neither offered a hand to shake. Then they went their separate ways. Debbie and Bill headed to their house and their twins, now three, and their two dogs and their backyard with its above-ground swimming pool. Ian to his apartment on College Avenue and his buzzing refrigerator and his piles of regrets.

'Daddy?' Maggie says.

'I— I'm here . . . I'm right here,' he says after a moment during which speaking seems impossible. Then he realizes he has a job to do: 'Tell me where you are. Are you on Main Street?'

Sometimes the location that comes up on the CAD system is incorrect. If someone is coming for his daughter he wants to make sure he's sending a unit to the right place.

'I don't know. I need help.'

'I know, Maggie. Help's coming. But I need to know where you are. Do you see any street signs? Any store names?'

There is a pause. It seems to stretch on forever. Continents sink into the empty space. Then: 'Yeah. It's Main Street. The Main Street shopping center.'

Two months ago she was dead. Her headstone even now is planted in Hillside Cemetery just other side of Wallace Street. Row 17, plot 29. But there is no one in the earth beneath it. The person who in another world would be there is now standing in front of the Main Street shopping center with a telephone to her ear.

And she must be alive because Ian can hear her breathing.

'Good girl. The man who kidnapped you, what does he look like?'

'He's . . . he's big,' she says, 'as big as you, maybe bigger, and he's old. Like a grandpa. And balding. His head is shiny on top. And his nose, it's . . . it's like all these broken veins and . . . oh God, Daddy, he's coming!'

His heart is in his throat; he swallows it back so that he can get words out.

'What are you wearing?'

7

'What? He's coming!'

'What are you wearing, Mags?'

'A dress. A blue dress with pink flowers.'

'Do you know the man's name?'

'It's H—'

But that is all and that is it. That followed by a scream.

Ian can hear the phone on the other end bang against something as it swings on its cord. It bangs again and again as it swings, the space between each percussive thump longer than the one before until the final thump does not arrive and the space is infinite.

Maggie escapes only because of an open door.

If it weren't for that door being left open she would never have tried to get out. Years of imprisonment have caused whatever hope she once felt to grow cold inside her, and now she does not feel it at all. She has not felt it for a very long time. She doesn't know if it's there anymore. Maybe it is: some small spark.

Days and nights she spends in this miserable concrete-walled basement. She is alive but below ground all the same. Buried. Trapped in what she has always thought of as the Nightmare World. Trapped with its moist stink. Trapped with its seemingly living shadows. Trapped with nothing but her thoughts to keep her company.

And sometimes Borden. She'd been here for several days when she first saw him. He was hiding in the shadows, a small, skinny boy in Chuck Taylors and Levis and a red button-up shirt tucked into his pants. He did not have the face of a boy, though. He had a shiny brown coat covering his face between forelock and muzzle and a black mane and shining black horse's eyes and flaring nostrils and large square teeth. Maggie was afraid of him at first, but her loneliness was stronger than her fear. Now he is the only friend she has.

He doesn't talk about how he got here, and Maggie is the only one who knows he's here at all. He hides when anyone opens the door at the top of the stairs, when anyone starts making their way down the wooden steps. Maggie does not hide. It would do no good. They know she's here. They brought her here. Here to this horrible place. It is a small place, keeping you from the rest of the world. Keeping you from the sunlight and the grass and trees and playing with friends.

The only way to remember that the rest of the world even exists is to look out a single rectangular window and see it. All you can do is look. It is too narrow for even a cat to crawl through. But the sun shines on Maggie in the morning and it is bright and warm on her skin. After noon the shadows begin to lay themselves out before her, growing long as the hour gets late. But mornings are hers.

The window is partially covered by a few thatches of weeds growing from the ground right outside, and it is splattered with dirt. Her biggest fear is that the weeds will grow so thick that she will not be able to see outside at all, or stand in the light that cuts its way into the darkness for half the day every day. Most days. If the clouds are heavy all she gets is a hollow gray illumination that for some reason reminds her of having a cold. But this is summer and the sky is clear and the light is bright.

Was bright.

It is now after noon and, though it is still daytime, the sun is on the other side of the house and sinking toward the horizon.

When the sun's light cuts into the room she stands in it. She stands in it as long as possible, moving as the light moves across the floor, but the sun is gone so she is merely sitting on the mattress in the corner of the room with her knees drawn up and her arms wrapped around them. A book sits on the mattress beside her—sometimes Donald brings her books and even gives her lessons—but she does not feel like reading right now.

'Borden?' she says to the shadows, but there is no response.

So she counts. One two three four five six seven eight. She likes to count. When she is not counting all sorts of terrible thoughts enter her mind and make her stomach feel sour. Even reading cannot always keep out the thoughts. But when she counts she can keep them out by filling her mind with numbers. Not at first: the small numbers are too easy, they don't require full concentration, and bad thoughts can still snake their way into her mind between them. But once she counts high enough, two thousand twenty-three, two thousand twenty-four, the numbers are big enough to fill her head and nothing else can squeeze in. Everything goes quiet inside her and she does not feel afraid.

She's only up to three hundred and seventeen when Beatrice comes downstairs to collect her lunch plate. It is sitting empty on the small card table at which she usually eats her meals. Sometimes Borden will sit across from her while she eats and they'll talk about things, though she can never really remember any of their conversations, and he has never eaten any of the food she has offered.

Three hundred and—

The door at the top of the stairs creaks open and Beatrice's large frame fills the doorway. She flips a switch. A yellow bulb hanging from a brown wire in the middle of the basement comes to life. It chases away the shadows, filling the room with pale light. Maggie squints and watches Beatrice make her way down the stairs. First she steps down with her right foot, and then follows with her left, setting it next to the other. Once her feet are side by side again she pauses to breathe. Then she progresses once more with her right foot.

'How are you, Sarah?' she says once she gets to the bottom of the stairs.

'Okay.'

'Good.'

Maggie says nothing.

'Do you want me to brush your hair for a while before I do the dishes?'

'No.'

'Do you want to brush my hair?'

'No.'

'Are you feeling okay?'

'Yes.'

'You sure?'

'Yes.'

'Okay.'

Beatrice walks to the card table and collects the empty plate. It is white with blue flowers and vines decorating its edge. Maggie hates it.

'You ate all your food.'

'Yes, ma'am. Thank you.'

'I wish you wouldn't call me ma'am.'

'I'm sorry.'

'I wish you would call me Momma.'

'Okay.'

'You always say okay, but you never do it.'

'I'm sorry.'

'Okay.'

Beatrice turns around and heads back up the stairs. When she reaches the landing she pulls open the door and turns to face Maggie again.

'We're having meatloaf for dinner. With lots of grated carrots, like you like.'

Then she flips off the light, steps through the door, and pulls it closed. But Maggie does not hear the click of it latching, nor does she hear the sound of the deadbolt sliding into place. She sits and waits and listens, but she hears nothing.

After a moment she gets to her feet and pads barefoot to the bottom of the stairs. She looks up to the top of them. A sliver of light cutting its way into the darkness between the door and the wall. The steps at the top are visible in the light, rounded and worn smooth by shoes sliding up and down them, a few rusty nail heads jutting up.

'Borden,' she says. 'Borden, it's open.'

Something within her shifts. A long eclipse of the sun ends and light comes into her.

Even before she knows what she's doing, even before instinct becomes thought, her heart begins to thump and her mouth goes dry. Her hands form fists on either side of her. The fists grip the fabric of her dress tight within them. She steps up, her bare feet moving one at a time from the cold smooth concrete floor of the basement to a warmer textured surface. The grain of the wood feels good beneath her feet, alive somehow, more part of the outside world than anything else down here.

She takes another step up, gently rolling the ball of her foot onto the wood and then putting her weight upon it and pushing herself up. The step does not moan in protest as it would were Beatrice putting her weight upon it. It accepts Maggie silently. The only sounds she can hear at all: the muffled vibrations of the television coming through the walls and the rhythmic sound of her heart beating in her chest and ears and temples.

She takes another step—oh, God, don't let it make any noise—and that is followed by yet another.

By the time she reaches the top of the stairs her palms feel itchy and her throat constricted. Her breath wheezes into and out of her through a throat like a kinked garden hose.

She swallows.

Then grabs the doorknob. It is cool to the touch and smooth. She pulls. The sliver of light cutting its way into the basement becomes a block of light splashing door-shaped against the wall to her left. The shadow of her arm in relief against the wall.

On the other side of the door she can see scarred green linoleum flooring, dark cabinets, a laminated kitchen counter piled with filthy dishes. The oven is ancient, and while it once must have been white it is now splattered with all manner of food. The window above the sink is water-spotted. The ceiling is fly-specked.

A cockroach scrambles from a stack of plates piled like porcelain pancakes and runs across the counter toward the sink, into which it disappears.

To her left she can hear the television and though she can neither see nor hear them she knows Henry and Beatrice are in there. But then she does hear them. She hears one of them.

The floor creaks just the other side of the wall.

She pulls back from the door and eases it shut but for a crack and continues to peer out to the kitchen. Her breath catches in her throat. Her eyes are wide and feel very dry, but she is afraid to blink. Beatrice enters the kitchen. Maggie's muscles tighten and lock her motionless.

The woman scratches between her legs through the fabric of her dress as she walks to the stainless steel sink. She turns on the faucet. Pipes rattle and moan. The faucet spits a wad of rusted water, and then flows orange for a moment before going clear. Soon the water is steaming, fogging the window above the sink despite the heat outside.

Beatrice squirts orange dish soap onto a green scouring

14

sponge, grabs a dirty plate—Maggie's lunch plate—from a stack of them, holds it under water a moment, and then scrubs at it. Once it's clean she rinses it and sets it into a rusty dish drainer. She grabs a second plate.

Her back is to Maggie. Maggie thinks that if she doesn't get out now she might never get out. The door is unlocked and she's standing at the threshold. She pulls the door open and simply stands in the doorway a moment. She is waiting to be noticed. Her heart is beating so loud Beatrice almost has to hear it. Except she doesn't. With her back to Maggie she continues to wash dishes.

'Get back here before she sees you.'

Maggie jumps and glances over her shoulder.

Borden stands on a step halfway up the stairs, only his horse's head in the light, the rest of him hidden in shadows. His eyes are like great pits spooned out with an ice cream scooper. His mouth is covered with a frothy foam.

Maggie swallows. Then she shakes her head at him. No. I'm not coming back. She turns her back on him. Beatrice is still standing at the sink washing dishes.

'Get back here.'

No.

Though she does not know the layout of the house she knows she cannot go left—the sound of the TV is coming from there—so she turns right and walks as carefully as she can, praying—God, please—that the floor does not creak beneath her feet. One step, two step, red step, blue step.

Beatrice puts another plate into the dish drainer.

Ahead of her and to her right a door opening onto a hallway. Old-timey pictures hang crooked on the wall on the other side of the door. A yellow light splashes across them from somewhere. The light is rippled with shadow and reminds

15

her of light reflected off water. She hopes the yellow light is coming from the sun. She hopes she is that close to outside, to the daylight world.

Another glance toward Beatrice. The woman is picking up a dirty saucepan. It has dried pieces of cabbage sticking to it. Beatrice hums as she scrubs at the pan. Maggie recognizes the tune. Jesus loves me, this I know, for the Bible tells me so. Little ones to Him belong, for we are weak and He is—

A dog barks. Maggie jumps. A squeal escapes her throat. She slaps her hands—both of them—over her mouth, trying to hold it in, but it is too late. It's out on the air where Beatrice can hear it.

She knew there was a dog up here. She has heard its nails clicking on the floor above her head for years. She even knows its name: Buckshot. But until now she has never seen it. It is standing in the doorway toward which she has been walking. It is waist high and the color of tree bark. Its tongue hangs from its mouth and its tail thumps wildly against the doorframe as it wags.

Beatrice has stopped washing dishes. She now stands looking at Maggie. Her shoulders are slumped and her mouth agape. Her hands hang empty at her sides and drip water onto the dirty green linoleum.

Buckshot growls and the growl grows slowly into a series of quick barks.

Maggie jumps again.

From the basement just other side of the doorway Borden whispers loudly to her: 'Come back now and you won't get into trouble.'

'Henry!' Beatrice says. 'Henry, she's got out! Sarah's got out the basement!'

Maggie glances behind her but Henry is not there. He will

be coming soon. She glances to the doorway where Buckshot stands and blocks her way, his tail thumping and thumping against the wall. He is scruffy and scars line his face and the side of his body, but he is not Henry. She runs toward him. As she runs past he licks her hand and his tail thumps against her hip, but he does not bite, nor does he bark again. She glances right and sees the hallway leading deeper into the house. To her left is a wooden door, the top half filled with yellow pebbled glass which allows the light to come in but does not allow visitors to get a good view of the interior. She grabs the door handle and thumbs down a brass paddle. She pulls.

A wall of heat greets her and bright sunlight like opening an oven door and finding an entire universe within. Wind blows against her face.

'Sarah, get back here! She's getting out, Henry!'

She turns back to the open door. Beatrice's fingers at the back of her neck. She runs across the porch and leaps, arcing through the air and down onto the gravel driveway. The sharp gray stones dig into the soles of her bare feet. She almost falls, but does not. She looks around, trying to figure out where her best chance lies. To her left, a grazing pasture in which a few cows stand dumbly working their jaws. To her right, woods of hickory and oak and pine. Maybe she can disappear into them. She runs toward the trees.

Her heart thumps in her chest and her throat feels dry and scratchy, but her skin is hot from the sun, a wonderful feeling, and she is outside outside outside with a hot breeze blowing against her back as she runs, pushing her forward, pushing her toward freedom.

As she reaches the wall of trees just other side of the driveway she looks back over her shoulder and sees Henry running toward her. Running after her. An old man with his big gut swinging back and forth like the pendulum on a grandfather clock, a few strands of gray comb-over hair blowing in the wind, face a grimace, eyes cruel, bulbous red nose bursting forth like an internal hemorrhage about to rupture.

'You better,' he says angrily between great heaving breaths, 'you better stop, Sarah!' Another breath. 'You fuckin' stop!'

She runs into the woods.

And through them. Blades of sunlight cutting through the canopy overhead and splashing across her face and legs and arms. The sound of birds singing, then taking flight as she nears. Breeze shuffling through the summer leaves. She is outside. She has escaped. She glances back over her shoulder but sees no one. She is outside. No walls surround her.

She runs until it hurts to breathe, until the stitch in her side is unbearable, jumping over plants she thinks might be poison oak or poison ivy, ducking beneath thick mustang grape vines that are growing between the tree branches and wrapping themselves around tree trunks. She runs until she has to stop, and then she does stop.

She stands breathing hard, bending over, hands pressed against her knees. Her throat hurts but it feels good too. Clean hot summer air. Lungfuls of it. She tries to slow her breathing so she can listen. She hears nothing. She hears nothing and she sees nothing behind her.

Maybe he gave up. Maybe she really is free.

She walks to a white beam of light breaking through the canopy overhead and she stands within it. An outside observer would see a pale, fragile-looking girl seemingly glowing while everything around her was covered in the shade of trees. An outside observer would see an angel. But there are no outside observers. There is only her and the sunlight and the silence of the woods.

She allows herself a quiet moment, almost allows herself to cry, and then she pulls herself together again, and continues on. She walks at first, but the walk becomes a jog, and soon enough she is running again.

Despite the pain it feels good to run. She has spent years trapped in a place where running was impossible and it feels good to have this much space open before her.

In five minutes she comes to a sun-faded road, cracks twisting their way across its surface like rivers on a map.

She turns left for no reason she can think of and continues on, padding her way along the asphalt. It feels good on the soles of her feet. It is almost too hot, and if she slowed to a walk it would be too hot, so she does not slow to a walk. She keeps running.

Henry is watching TV and sucking at a beer like it's mother's milk when Beatrice calls to him from the kitchen.

'Henry!' she says. 'Henry, she's got out! Sarah's got out the basement!'

'Ah, fuck,' he mumbles to himself. Then gets to his feet, finishes the Budweiser in his hand, showing the bottom of the can to the ceiling, and sets the empty on the coffee table. 'How the hell'd she get out?' he says.

'Sarah, get back here!' Bee says from the kitchen. 'She's getting out, Henry!'

'I'm coming.'

He walks to the kitchen. Beatrice is on the far side of the room facing the open front door. When she hears him she turns around.

'She's got out.'

'Well, goddamn it.'

'I didn't mean to let her.'

'Goddamn it.'

'I told you she was getting out.'

He ignores her and hurries to the front door. Sarah is running barefoot across the gravel driveway. She is running to the woods west of the house.

Henry jumps down the steps and runs after her, feeling sick to his stomach. He's too old for this kind of activity. When he catches up with Sarah he's gonna make her sorry she ran like this. He's gonna make her sorry she made *him* run like this. She'll be *screaming* sorrys, is what she'll be doing. She'll keep screaming them for a week.

As she reaches the line of trees she glances back.

'You better,' he says angrily between great heaving breaths, 'you better stop, Sarah!' Another breath. He feels like he's gonna have a heart attack. 'You fuckin' stop!'

He knows she is afraid of him. He'd like it better if she didn't have to be afraid of him. He'd like it better if she accepted the fact that she was now part of this family. She's had a long enough time to get used to it. It would make everybody's life easier. Including hers. He'd like that; it just ain't the way it is. But she is afraid of him and she does what he says. So when he shouts at her to stop he fully expects her to comply.

But she doesn't. She turns and disappears into the woods.

'Fuck.'

He runs to the woods and into them.

He sees flashes of blue dress between the trunks of trees. He chases after that color. Branches scratch at his face and grab at his clothes. He tries to keep her in sight as he runs, but it's an impossible task. He must pay attention to what he's doing or he's liable to run straight into a tree. He loses sight of her. Then another flash of blue thirty or forty yards ahead. He cuts toward her, but the heel of his boot catches on the root of a tree and he falls face first to the ground, getting a mouthful of composted leaves. He spits and picks himself up. He looks to see if she's still in sight but she is not. He briefly considers chasing after her anyway, but doesn't think he'll catch her on foot. But the woods are surrounded by road, and she'll have to come out of them eventually.

He turns back and runs toward the house.

'Bee, I need my keys!'

A moment later Beatrice arrives at the front door.

'Did you get her?'

'No, goddamn it, I need my keys.'

'Your truck keys?'

'Of course my truck keys. All my keys are on the same fucking key ring. Come on.'

'Okay.'

Beatrice turns from the doorway and disappears a moment. When she returns his keys are dangling from her hand. She throws them toward him, but they land in the gravel five feet shy of their intended destination. Henry curses under his breath, goddamn it, leans down, and snatches them up. He walks to his pickup, a green '97 Ford Ranger he bought used a couple years ago from Davis Dodge—it's got a mushy clutch, but you have to expect that kind of thing when you buy your truck used from Todd Davis, Mr Chief of Police, you just might get pulled over less with a Davis Dodge license-plate frame on your vehicle—and slides into the driver's seat.

A few seconds later he's slamming the thing into first and the tires are kicking up gravel as he takes the driveway north to Crouch Avenue.

He drives west along the old cratered road, squinting left into his own woods, trying to see white skin or a snatch of blue dress between the trees. On the other side of the road is Pastor Warden's place, alive with the sound of barking dogs. It sounds to Henry like a schoolyard during recess. Pastor Warden breeds dachshunds and sells them to pet shops in Mencken and other larger towns. Maybe even to some places in Houston. The goddamn dogs never shut up. Henry doesn't know how Warden can stand it. Then again, after a few weep sessions with troubled parishioners laying their guilt on him, maybe the sound of dogs barking ain't so bad.

He makes it to Main Street without seeing Sarah, but that doesn't really surprise him. She was heading west when she ran into the woods and unless she got disoriented there'd be no reason for her to come out on the north end. He makes a left and drives south, along the western edge of the woods.

The gray strip of road stretches out before him, empty of life.

A tight feeling in his chest, like his heart in a vise.

If Sarah manages to get out of the woods and comes across someone and tells them what happened, that will be the end of his long and peaceful life here in Bulls Mouth. He knows everyone in town and everyone knows him. And mostly they like him. Sure, it's because they don't really know him, because he's always smiling and patting backs and saying give my regards to the missus, Dave, but who really lets the world see their guts? Guts are ugly; that's why we have skin. Take away the skin and what remains? Nothing you'd want to have a conversation with.

As he drives south he looks left, hoping to see Sarah emerge from the trees.

'Where are you, you little bitch?'

And then he sees her. Not in the woods but in the road up ahead, running into the Main Street shopping center. At least he thinks it's her. From this distance it could be anybody in a blue dress, but he thinks it's her. He shifts from second to third and gasses it.

'It's H—'

But that is all and that is it. That followed by a scream.

Ian can hear the phone on the other end bang against something as it swings on its cord. It bangs again and again as it swings, the space between each percussive thump longer than the one before until the final thump does not arrive and the space is infinite.

'Maggie?'

Silence. She is gone.

'Officer Peña, what's your twenty? You ten-eight?'

'Oak Street and Flatland. Good to go.'

'You at Wal-Mart?'

'Not even in the parking lot yet.'

'Get over to the Main Street shopping center. Forty-one forty. Suspect is a tall white male in his sixties, gray hair, balding on top. Victim is a fourteen-year-old girl, Maggie Hunt, blond hair, green eyes, wearing a blue dress. Code three.'

'Ten-four. I'm on it. Did you say the name of the victim was Maggie Hun—'

'It's my daughter,' Ian says.

Then, before Diego can respond, he pulls the headset off and leans down over a trashcan. His entire body is shaking, vibrating like sound, and he is covered in sweat. He feels as though he may vomit, but when he opens his mouth, nothing comes out. He spits a mouthful of sour saliva into the can and stares at a wadded-up piece of paper lying inside. The paper has been torn from a yellow legal pad. There is writing on it, and he knows that it is his, but he cannot remember what it says. It doesn't matter. The only thing that matters now is that his daughter is alive. He stares at the paper for a very long time.

She was kidnapped in the spring. Her older brother Jeffrey was supposed to be looking after her. Jeffrey is Ian's son from his second marriage, Debbie being his third wife. Now his third ex-wife. Jeffrey'd flown down from Los Angeles to spend spring break here. He was fourteen when Maggie was kidnapped. Now he is twenty-two. He just turned twenty-two last month, in fact, on the twenty-seventh. Ian bought him neither card nor gift. For a few years after Maggie was kidnapped Ian and Jeffrey had some kind of relationship, tense though it often was, but eventually it dissolved till there was nothing left. A chess game they were playing over three years ago still sits unfinished on Ian's coffee table. Two unsent birthday cards lie at the bottom of his sock drawer. Happy birthday, son. I love you. Ian tried to call Jeffrey just over two years ago, dialed and let the phone ring, but when his son picked up, hello, he could not get any words out. They caught like fishhooks in his throat.

Maggie was kidnapped in the spring, and, while her kidnapper cannot possibly know it, Ian lost both his children that night, though it took a few years for the second loss to be finalized. It was a slower vanishing, that's all.

But it still began on that spring night. A Saturday with a full moon, bone-white and bloated, floating in the vast dark sea above.

Ian was behind the wheel of his partially restored 1965 Mustang, a car his father had purchased for him when he was seventeen and they were living in Venice Beach. Dad thought they could rebuild the car together. He said it would be a fun project. They'd even made a couple trips to a junkyard in Downy and found a fender they needed, and a primer-gray trunk-lid, and a taillight. Unfortunately, Dad's suicide got between them and their plans. Three months after buying the car the old man decided to smoke a shotgun. Ian found him on the floor in his bedroom when he came home from school.

On this night, this spring night during which Maggie was kidnapped, he and Debbie were in the car with the windows down. The night air was cool and felt good blowing against his face. The radio was on and playing 'Love Comes in Spurts' by Richard Hell. Debbie was wearing a summer dress, and her large breasts were spilling out of the top of it. Ian reached over and stroked the inside of her thigh and she separated her knees slightly.

'I'm glad we did this,' he said as they drove north on Crockett Street, heading from Morton's Steakhouse, where they'd had dinner, toward home. 'It's been a good night.'

Debbie put her hand over the back of his hand and slid it up the inside of her leg until it was under her dress and pressed against her panties. He could feel her heat and her coarse pubic hair poking through the panties' fabric and a pleasant sticky humidity.

He thought of a time when he was eleven or twelve, in Venice Beach, where his dad had a surf shop, when he had headed down to the water to hang out and try to get one of the older guys to let him have a beer and he saw a girl in her twenties whose pubic hair was visible on either side of her bikini bottoms. She was wet and the fabric was molded to her body and he could see the dimpled mound between her legs. It was strange and foreign and exciting. It did things to him that he didn't understand. He went into the water where no one would see him and he masturbated to the mental image while it was still fresh in his mind, and he shot a load into the water, and somehow that was sexy, too. Even now he is able to get excited thinking of that long-ago girl and that mysterious hint of sex he did not fully understand. He cannot remember the last name of the girl to whom he lost his virginity, Jennifer something, and he cannot picture her face, but he remembers every detail of that day on the beach four or five years earlier.

He looked up at Debbie's face.

'The night's not over,' she said smiling. 'It's about to get better than good.'

Ian rubbed her gently a moment before reluctantly pulling his hand from beneath her dress so he could turn right onto Crouch Avenue. Then left almost immediately onto Grapevine Circle. As he drove along he could see Bulls Mouth Reservoir to his right, reflecting the image of the fat moon and the stars like glowing fishes. Then Grapevine Circle bent sharply to the right, and as they made the turn a police car came into view. It was double-parked on the street, lights flashing in the night.

'Is that—?'

'Oh, shit.'

'Stay calm,' Debbie said. 'It's probably nothing.'

'I am calm.'

But even so he screeched along the street at a dangerous speed, then hauled the car to the right and two-footed the clutch and brake simultaneously when he reached 44 Grapevine Circle and the police car already parked there. He killed the engine by pulling his foot off the clutch and stalling the fucking thing, then yanked the key from the ignition and was out of the car. Debbie stepped from the passenger's side.

Beneath the hood the radiator hissed. The sound of traffic coming from Interstate 10. Usually you couldn't hear it, but in the quiet night it became audible. The faint sound of Pastor Warden's dogs barking in the west. A few neighbors were standing on their porches, looking this direction. Their mouths hung open. Ian hated each and every one of them. And himself. And Debbie.

They never should have left Maggie and Jeffrey home alone. Ian had wanted to have a night out with Debbie, and Jeffrey was fourteen, old enough to babysit, but if anything had happened Ian would never—

Jeffrey was standing on the front lawn, within the circle of the porch's yellow light, talking to Chief Davis, who had thought whatever was happening was important enough he should crawl out of his whiskey-induced sleep and come out here himself. Davis was taking notes while Jeffrey talked. Jeffrey's eyes were red and every so often he was wiping at his nose with the back of a wrist.

'What happened?' Ian said as he approached. 'Where's Maggie?'

Jeffrey and Davis both turned toward him, but neither said anything.

'Where's Maggie?'

More silence.

Ian grabbed Jeffrey by the shoulders, fingers digging into the flesh of them, and shook him. 'Where the fuck is Maggie?' he said.

'Honey,' Debbie said, 'don't.'

'Ian,' Chief Davis said and put a hand on his shoulder.

Ian turned on Davis and knocked his hand away with the

swipe of an arm. The old man blinked like an owl behind his glasses and mustache but said nothing. He simply tilted his Stetson back on his head and hooked his thumbs in his pockets and rocked back on the heels of his boots and looked away. Debbie, though, did not look away.

'Don't touch me,' Ian said to both of them and neither.

Then he turned back to his son.

'Jeffrey,' he said, 'where is Maggie?'

Jeffrey looked up at him. Ian saw for the first time that there was something like terror in his eyes. They were alive with it. It danced in them like flame in a night window. Then, once more, he dropped his gaze to his feet. He had on a pair of slippers. They were blue corduroy, darkened by the damp grass. They were one of his Christmas presents from the year before. Deb had picked them up from a drugstore while grabbing a prescription for antibiotics and they'd tossed them into the box they mailed to California with the rest of his gifts, as well as a cordial if distant holiday card for Lisa, Jeffrey's mother and Ian's second wife.

'She's gone,' Jeffrey said finally, staring down at those blue slippers.

'Gone?'

Ian was expecting an injury, a broken arm, fingers burned on the stovetop, a bad cut—but gone? For a moment his mind could not even process the word.

Without looking up at him Jeffrey nodded.

'Gone where?'

A pathetic shrug.

'I don't . . . I put her to bed. I was watching *David Letterman* and . . . and I heard a noise in her bedroom like she was playing around. I yelled at her to calm down and go to sleep. I yelled at her. Then it got really quiet and I started to feel bad about yelling. I went back to make sure she was okay, to say sorry if I'd hurt her feelings or . . .' A shrug. 'But when I went to her bedroom . . . she was . . .' He licked his lips. 'She was gone.' He glanced up once as he finished talking, but quickly looked down again.

Ian walked past Jeffrey and Chief Davis, knocking against Davis's shoulder, and into the house. Walked straight to Maggie's room. To what was Maggie's room. To what is now, in this different world, like that old world but not quite the same, the twins' room: refurnished, repainted, re-carpeted, hardly the same room at all. It was empty. He walked to the bed and put the back of his hand against the dent in her pillow. It was cold. There was no warmth left in it at all. Beneath it, a tooth. Waiting for a tooth fairy that would never come. He walked to the window. It was open and a breeze was blowing against the curtains. The screen frame was still in the window but the screen had been cut out. A few loose strings still hung from the frame. The rest of it lay on the grass just outside. When the wind blew it shifted, looking like a living shadow.

'Ian,' Chief Davis said behind him, 'you really shouldn't be in here. I got Sheriff Sizemore sending down a couple people from Mencken to pull evidence.'

Ian nodded but continued to stare out at the night. The wind blew. The screen shifted. After a few moments of silence he heard Chief Davis leave the room. And after a few more he turned away from the window and followed.

He was thirty-eight then. Now he is forty-five, though he sometimes feels older. Three marriages, one abortion, two children (a son he hasn't spoken to in over three years and a daughter he's feared dead for twice as long), seven broken bones (four fingers, a collar-bone, his nose, and a toe), one gunshot wound, four car accidents, three dead pets, and two dead parents: yes, sometimes he feels older than his years.

When you glance over your shoulder and look at what you're pulling behind you in your red wagon it can be hard not to feel overwhelmed by the weight of it all.

He wakes in the morning with a neck that won't turn and a right hand that's already beginning to feel arthritic, with a swollen right knee that won't bend for the first hour of the day, with a sore back and a mind he wishes he could scrub the memories from. He wakes and showers and dresses. He shaves every other day. He's blond and can get away with that one bit of laziness concerning his appearance. He eats two soft-boiled eggs (and sometimes a piece of toast). He drinks a pot of coffee. He goes to work, where he sits for eight hours and plays solitaire and answers calls. Occasionally he goes out on calls himself if someone needs backup and it's close by (keeps a bubble light in his glove box). He is technically a police officer and wears the uniform every day. But that is the result of the city council not approving the hire of a civilian dispatcher and not a difference of job function. Mostly Ian simply sits in the office and takes calls. Sometimes the calls are ugly: husbands collapsed while feeding the horses, or maybe kicked in the head while changing a shoe; sons who accidentally severed a thumb while sawing wood; wives who spilled two gallons of simmering lye soap down the front of their dresses. And it seems those bad calls come one after another, piling up during the course of a day. Some black luck blown into town on the wind. By the time those days are over he feels hollow as a Halloween pumpkin. He drives to the Skyline Apartments and parks his car. He locks himself inside his apartment. He watches TV. Situation comedies. After a few hours of this, during which he drinks six bottles of Guinness and, if it's Friday, one small glass of scotch (usually Laphroaig), never more, he falls asleep on the couch.

Five or six hours later he wakes and repeats the process.

But not today. Today is different. He would normally leave at four, but today he walks out the door at three fifteen.

He gets to his feet and walks into the police station's front room.

Chief Davis is right where Ian thought he would be, leaning back in his chair with his boots kicked up on his desk, Stetson tipped over his eyes. He has a reputation for laziness, but he's on call twenty-four hours a day, and is often out nights dealing with drunks and wife-beaters, so he catches naps when he can. Ian himself doesn't count that as laziness.

'Chief,' he says.

Chief Davis groans and wipes at a bit of drool at the corner of his mouth.

'Chief.'

Davis sits up and tilts back his Stetson. He knuckles his eyes, pulls his glasses from his pocket, and sets them on his nose. He rubs the palm of his hand down the front of his face, then looks up at Ian, blinking.

'Ian.'

'I just got a call.'

'Yeah?'

'From Maggie.'

'From—' Blink, blink. 'From your *daughter*?'

Ian nods.

'You sure?'

Another nod. 'She called from a pay phone front of Main Street shopping center. She's alive. I sent Diego down just now, and county guys are on the way, but I'm going too. Maybe you could keep point on the phones?'

Davis shakes his head.

'No,' he says. 'You know I gotta deal with Sizemore. Thompson can handle the phones.'

Steve Thompson is Bulls Mouth's other daytime police officer. He's good police, so far as Ian can tell, when there's something happening, but otherwise he tends to wander off. After four o'clock, there are only two officers on duty at a time—one of the three part timers to take calls and a guy in a radio car. And of course they call Chief Davis if necessary. Four to midnight is Armando Gonzales and one of the part timers. Used to be Diego Peña, but Peña switched to days a while back. Went from part time on the phones to full time to days in quick succession. From midnight to eight is Ray Watkins.

Ian nods. 'All right. Where's he at?'

'Out back washing my truck. Tell him to get on the phones and then let's go.'

Ian nods.

'What are you wearing?'

'What?' She looks over her shoulder and can see Henry's Ford Ranger speeding toward her, and behind the glass Henry's large frame hunched over the wheel like a bear over its prey. 'He's coming!' she says.

'What are you wearing, Mags?'

'A dress. A blue dress with pink flowers.'

The truck pulls into the parking lot, tires screeching. Smoke wafts from burned rubber and the foul stink of it hangs in the air. The door swings open, engine still running. She can hear Henry's footsteps behind her. She looks over her shoulder and he is making great steps toward her. He curses under his breath. His hands open and close at his sides as he walks.

Open and close, open and close, open and—

'Do you know the man's name?'

'It's H—'

But that's all and that's it. Henry grabs her around the waist. She screams. Henry puts his hand over her mouth. He pulls her away from the phone. She tries to hold on to it, to maintain her connection to Daddy, oh God, Daddy, please, but her hands are too sweaty and it slips away and swings down on its cord and bangs against a phone book hanging from a metal ring. She tries to scream again but to no end. The hand over her mouth keeps the sound trapped in her throat.

Henry carries her while she kicks and claws at him. She grabs his fingers and tries to pull them away from her. She tries to contort her body so that she can bite him. Nothing works.

'You little bitch,' he says, 'don't you ever run from me again.'

He throws her into the truck through the open driver's side door. She lands lengthwise across the beige vinyl bench seat and hits her head on the passenger door. She pulls herself up to a sitting position and looks around in a daze. She is disoriented and for a moment lost. Everything feels unreal to her. Then she sees the open door and knows once more where she is and what she must do. She crawls toward escape.

Then Henry's large frame fills the opening and he slides into the truck. He pulls the door shut behind him and releases the hand brake. The truck turns toward the street. Maggie looks out the window to the phone. It is still swinging from its cord. Daddy.

She grabs the passenger's side door handle and pushes open the door, trying to jump out before the truck gains speed, but as the truck turns out onto the street, the momentum forces the door shut again. She has to pull her hand away so that it isn't slammed between the door and the frame. Then Henry grabs the back of her dress and pulls her away from it. And slaps the side of her head.

'Stop it, goddamn you! Just fucking stop it!'

Tears of pain and defeat and rage stream down her face.

'I hate you!' she says.

'Shut the fuck up, Sarah.'

'That's not my name.'

'I said shut—*up*.' He punctuates the last word with yet another angry slap at her head.

'No, you shut up.'

35

And she attacks him. She tries to claw at his stupid face. She punches at his chest and neck. He fights her off with one hand while steering with the other. He tries to grab her by the neck. She sinks her teeth into the web between his thumb and index finger. He hollers in pain and yanks his hand away. She spits out the salty taste of his sweat and blood, wipes her mouth with the back of her hand, and goes at him again. He shoves her away with great force and she flies backwards and hits her head against the window.

The truck swerves as they reach Crouch Avenue, travels another fifty yards, weaving back and forth across the two-lane asphalt, and then crashes through the fence behind which Pastor Warden keeps his dachshunds. The chain-link fence peels open where two sections were held together only by baling wire, curling in either direction like a sardine can lid, and there's a great scratching sound. Then the brakes lock, Maggie is thrown against the dashboard, and falls down to the floorboard.

The truck slides along the ground another ten or fifteen feet before coming to a stop.

Henry puts the truck into reverse and backs out to the street. There is more metal on metal scraping, a few serious jerks as the truck rolls once more over the shoulder of the road, and then they are on asphalt again.

Maggie pulls herself off the floor and goes for Henry once more.

Henry shoves her away again, and she hits her head on the passenger's side window for the second time. It hurts and makes her feel dizzy and sick. Her vision goes wonky and she loses her equilibrium. She thinks she might vomit. The skin is split and she feels blood trickling down the back of her head.

She is reaching back to touch the wound when she is hit

again. Henry simply fists the side of her head above the ear. Just behind the temple. He likes to hit her where Beatrice won't see the bruises. There is a strange sensation like sinking into thick liquid, and then there is no sensation at all. Everything goes dark.

Henry puts the truck into gear and gasses it. It gets rolling. He glances in his rearview mirror and sees what must be two dozen dachshunds escaping through the hole his truck punched through the fence. He figures there's a good chance of it coming back to him. His truck is scratched all to hell. If it does come back to him he'll just say he got a little too drunk. He'll smile big and apologize and if it's Chief Davis who comes knocking he'll say, 'You know how it is. Anyway, maybe I'll be trading this thing in now it's not prime no more. Maybe you'll see me down at the dealership. Tell Pastor Warden I'm real sorry. Tell him I'll pay for the damage. You got any good deals, any new used trucks in?' That will, in all likelihood, take care of the situation with the fence. If it even becomes a situation. It might not.

What really worries him is witnesses at the Main Street shopping center. What happened there could not be explained away.

Horizon Video is almost surely nothing to worry about. The kids who work there do nothing but sit in the back and smoke weed and watch pornographic films unless they hear the front door's bell chime, at which point one of them cuts through the curtain of smoke and walks to the counter and stands around while browsers browse. The barber shop is closed Sundays and Mondays, so there was no one there. That leaves the old cobbler who has a shop next to Horizon Video, the dry-cleaning place, and Bill's Liquor. Bill's Liquor is also, unless a customer was in, nothing to worry about. It's possible—just—that no one saw him.

But he can't worry about it. Either someone saw him or no one did. He'll find out which soon enough. Fretting over it won't change a goddamn thing.

Acid bubbles up at the back of his throat and he reaches into his shirt pocket and pulls out a roll of antacids. He picks lint off the top of the roll, peels back the foil, and thumbs two tablets into his mouth. They are chalky and flavorless. He chews them slowly.

Then glances over to Sarah. She's unconscious, head leaning against the glass of the window, a thin smear of blood just above her, a few drops of it splashed onto the beige armrest. As he looks at her another drop of blood splashes onto the vinyl.

'You little bitch,' he says. 'Don't even think I'm finished with you.'

He tongues chalky antacid from a molar and downshifts to second. He hits his turn-signal lever—click-click, click-click—and turns right into his gravel driveway.

The tires kick small stones out into the street.

He carries Sarah into the house. Beatrice is standing over a bowl of raw hamburger, grating carrots into it. When he walks into the kitchen she looks at him, and then at Sarah draped limp in his arms. A worried grunt escapes her throat.

'What happened?'

'She fell.'

'Is she bleeding?'

'Uh-huh.'

'How'd she fall?'

'She tripped. How else do people fall?'

Beatrice does not respond. He walks past her, kicks open the basement door, and carries Maggie down the stairs.

Ian slides into his Mustang and pulls the door shut behind him.

A three-inch plug of cigar pokes from the ashtray. He grabs it, grinds his teeth into the sloppy end, and lights it, sucking on it while watching with crossed eyes as the other end glows bright orange and smokes. He rolls down his window and exhales a thin stream of blue smoke. He spits a piece of tobacco off the end of his tongue, jabs the cigar back into his mouth, rolls it between his teeth, and starts the car.

The radio comes on, but Ian isn't in the mood for music. He turns it off immediately. Then grabs his sunglasses from his shirt, large mirrored things—cop sunglasses, you get them when you graduate academy—and slides them onto his face.

Sweat trickles down his cheek and drips onto his shirt. The white sun overhead imbedded in the blue-glass sky. He reaches down and grabs the shifter, sliding it into reverse, and burns his hand on the knob. He pulls his hand away and shakes it. Every day he does this. You'd think he'd learn. He looks over his shoulder and backs out of his spot, handling the wheel as gently as possible, so he doesn't get burned on it, but it's hard to handle a car with a light touch when you don't have power steering.

He arms sweat off his forehead, shifts, and drives out onto the street.

He's not even sure why he's going to the Main Street shopping center. Chief Davis heading there makes sense. He'll have to liaise with Sheriff Sizemore. The Tonkawa County Sheriff's Department handles any major crimes, with the city police department at its disposal. The county has access to labs, detectives, forensics guys, and can pull strings when necessary. The city has nine cops (three of them part time), three police cruisers bought from Houston when they were taken out of commission there and given an oil change and a paint job, and a police station smaller than most houses, with but a single holding cell.

And Ian hasn't been real police in over a decade, not since he took a bullet in the knee and Debbie talked him into moving them to Bulls Mouth, her hometown, where things would be quieter and calmer than in Los Angeles, where Maggie would be safe and they could live a peaceful life, where he would not have to worry about getting shot a second time.

There will almost certainly be nothing for Ian to do when he gets there.

But that doesn't seem to matter. He wants to stand where his daughter recently stood. He's certain he will sense her presence, like a scent hanging in the air, despite the fact that she was GOA, gone on arrival, when Diego pulled into the lot. He has feared her dead for a very long time, and he wants to feel her presence. To know she's alive.

He drives along Crouch Avenue till he comes to Wallace Street, where he makes a right. He drives past the post office and the firehouse and Bulls Mouth High School, shut down for the summer, and makes a left onto Hackberry. In another five minutes he is pulling into the Main Street shopping center's parking lot, bringing his car to a stop next to Diego's cruiser and behind a sign that marks the spot:

FOR DRY CLEANING PICK UP ONLY
VIOLATORS WILL BE TOWED.

Diego Peña is simply standing in front of the pay phone rolling a cigarette. He's a thin man, half Spanish, half Apache, with wavy black hair and sun-baked skin. He's got a series of tight little knot-like scars running across his face as well, the results of a domestic disturbance call he took five years ago, back when he was working nights.

Jimmy Block and his wife Roberta used to share a house in the south part of town, just off Clamp Avenue. A neighbor called about a ruckus. Diego knocked on the door and Roberta answered it. The lower half of her face was a mask of blood and a purple crescent in the shape of the moon was swelling around her left eye and said eye was swimming in tears. Jimmy was sitting quietly at the dining-room table. Diego went to get him, intent on putting him in jail overnight so he couldn't do any more wife-beating—this was his third call to the house in a month—and Jimmy grabbed a roll of barbed wire he had sitting on the table—he'd planned on fencing in the earthworm farm behind his bait shop the next day, apparently, to make it harder for kids on their way to the reservoir to snatch handfuls of them—and flung it into Diego's face. One of the barbs came within a centimeter of taking out his left eye. Instead of overnight, Jimmy Block was in jail for the next six months.

Roberta used the time to change all the locks in the house and file for divorce.

Ian steps from his car and into the heat of the day. He taps ash off the end of his cigar and jams it back into his face. He grinds it between his teeth.

Chief Davis pulls in behind Ian and parks.

Diego squints at Ian. 'You okay?'

'No. Guarding the phone?'

'Yeah. Thought it might have fingerprints or something on it and figured the sheriff would have county boys coming down from Mencken to brush it.'

'Anyone try to use it?'

Diego shakes his head. 'You wanna come over for dinner? Cordelia'd love to have you.'

'No, I'm not much for socializing right now.'

'Sure you wanna be alone tonight?'

'Yeah.'

Chief Davis steps up beside Ian and puts a hand on his shoulder.

'I'll see what I can see about witnesses before Sizemore gets here and ruins them.'

'I'll come with you.'

He drops his cigar to the asphalt and grinds it out with his heel.

'It's an open invitation,' Diego says.

'Thanks, anyway.'

Then he glances past Diego to the phone. He has a strange urge to lift the receiver and put it to his ear and listen, as if he might be able to hear Maggie's voice once more. She was just here today. She called him from that phone.

'Well,' Chief Davis says, 'let's ask some questions.'

They walk into the shoe repair shop first. Lining the walls are wooden racks on which rest shoes dropped off for repair but never picked up again: white leather loafers with gold buckles, snakeskin cowboy boots, resoled wingtips, resoled ropers.

There are white stickers on them with prices scrawled in blue ink.

Behind the wood counter at the back of the narrow store stands an old man with hunched shoulders and a face like an apple core left in the sun. He smiles, revealing very white un-fitted dentures. His smile is open-mouthed and the top row of teeth starts to slip from his gums, and he slams his uppers and lowers together with a clack and works his jaw, getting the dentures back into place. His hands rest on the counter. Black shoe polish has stained the fine spaces between the whorls of his thumbs and built up beneath his fingernails. A polish-stained rag lies on the counter near to hand, beside a tin and a pair of buffed shoes.

He finishes working his jaw and says, 'How can I help you gentlemen?'

As the cobbler speaks his gaze drops from their faces to their feet, to their shoes, the thing by which, it is clear, he mea-sures all men. His frown makes it clear that neither Ian nor Chief Davis meet his minimal standards.

'A quick polish, perhaps?' he says.

'You hear a ruckus out front 'bout ten-fifteen minutes ago?' Chief Davis says.

'Ruckus?'

'Noise.'

'Scuffle,' Ian says. 'Maybe a scream.'

The cobbler shakes his head.

'Nothing, huh?'

''Fraid not.'

Ian pulls his wallet from his right hip pocket and in it finds a photograph of Maggie. The edges are torn and browned from frequent handling. He looks at it a moment himself, at his grinning daughter's first-grade yearbook photo, and then turns it around and sets it on the counter and pushes it toward the cobbler.

'Ever seen this girl before?'

The cobbler shakes his head without so much as a glance at the picture. His eyes remain dull and unfixed, looking toward some nothing in the middle of the room.

'No,' he says. 'Ain't seen nothing.'

'You didn't even hear nothing?' Chief Davis asks again.

The cobbler shakes his head, then taps the hearing aid hooked around the back of his ear. 'Maybe the battery's dying.'

'Could be.'

'You don't seem to be having much trouble hearing us,' Ian says.

'Well.'

'Look at the goddamn picture.'

'I already told you I didn't—'

Ian hits the counter with the flat of his palm, creating a loud clap, and the cobbler recoils like he's been hit.

'You haven't even bothered to fucking *look* yet.'

'Hey,' Chief Davis says, putting a hand on Ian's shoulder, 'man's got no reason to lie.'

Ian ignores this. He leans on the counter and glares at the cobbler, forcing him to meet his eye. The cobbler looks uncomfortable, but he stares back for a couple seconds before his gaze drops to Ian's chest.

'This is my daughter. She's been missing for more than seven years. The picture was taken before she went missing, so she'd look different now. She's fourteen, fifteen in September. She made a call from the pay phone out front not twenty minutes ago. Now look at the goddamn picture and tell me did you see her.'

The cobbler looks down at the photograph. After a moment of silence he reaches out and touches it with a black-stained fingertip. He touches it gently. Ian has to fight the urge to snatch it away from the man. Instead he puts his hands behind his back. The cobbler's face softens and his eyes find focus as he looks at the picture. He scratches his cheek.

Without looking up he says, 'I didn't get a good look at the girl but this might've been her.'

'Did you see the man she was with?'

'The one who took her?'

'The one who took her.'

The cobbler nods. 'I don't know him. But I only been in town four years and don't meet nobody unless they come in the shop.'

'You didn't recognize him?'

'Not to name,' the cobbler says, 'but I think I seen him at Albertsons a few times.'

'So you'd recognize a picture?'

The cobbler nods. 'Think so.'

'In his sixties, gray hair, bald on top, busted capillaries in his nose, and about my size?'

'He's fatter'n you, but about the same height, I reckon.' He holds his hand up to measure. 'You know who done it?'

Ian shakes his head. 'She told me what he looked like.'

'Was he on foot?' Chief Davis asks.

The cobbler pauses a moment, then says, 'No. I heard a engine running, but I didn't see it. Must've parked to one side or the other.'

'Car or truck?' Ian says.

'He said he didn't see it. He couldn't tell you just by—'

'Truck,' the cobbler says, then nods to himself as if getting internal confirmation. 'Yeah,' he says, 'definitely a truck.'

47

'Thank you,' Ian says. 'You've been a big help. Someone will probably come down with a book of arrest photos for you to look through, and maybe even ask you to Mencken to help reconstruct a picture if you don't recognize him in the book.'

He reaches across the counter and picks up Maggie's photograph. He slips it into his wallet, folds his wallet, and slips it back into his hip pocket.

'And if you see him again,' Ian says, 'I want you to call nine-one-one.'

'Okay,' the man says.

When they get outside Chief Davis says, 'Goddamn, Ian, if you ever get tired of being a dispatcher, I tell you what, I'll give you a job down at the dealership in a second. You can just bully folks into buying cars. I'll sell out in a week.'

'Thanks, Chief.'

Cora Hanscomb at the dry-cleaning place next door claims to have neither seen nor heard anything. She says this without looking away from the TV upon which her gaze is fixed. She sits in a metal fold-out chair behind the counter and moves popcorn from a bag in her lap to her mouth. The backs of her fingers are glazed yellow with imitation butter and several pieces of popcorn lie on the floor around her chair and in her lap.

'Nothing?' Ian says again.

'Huh-uh.'

'Too busy watching the tube to pay attention to a kidnapping?'

'I guess.'

'Can't bother even to look at the people talking to you?'

'Huh-uh.'

'Right,' Ian says. 'Thanks a fucking lot.'

'Watch your mouth.' She says even this without looking away from the TV, her voice a droning monotone.

'Get fucked,' Ian says, and pushes his way out the door.

They walk into Bill's Liquor. Ian glances left to Donald Dean. He's standing behind an orange Formica counter looking bored. A scruffy guy, maybe forty-five, maybe fifty, with oily brown hair and a patchy beard that makes his face look like it was mauled by a large cat. Above the beard, high on his cheeks, acne scars. He's thin as a stick and pale, and his smile, when he smiles, looks like a grimace. Teeth crammed together like he's got a few too many. He nods at Ian and reaches over to a tub of red vines, which is sitting between a tub of pickled pigs' feet and a tub of beef jerky, pulls one out, and chews on it awhile.

Chief Davis walks over to him.

Ian turns right. He walks to the refrigerator at the back, scans the shelves, opens a glass door, which immediately fogs up, and pulls out a six pack of Guinness. The door swings shut behind him as he turns around and walks to where Donald and Chief Davis are standing at the counter.

'—at all?' Davis is saying.

'Huh-uh.'

Davis turns to Ian and says, 'He didn't hear nothing either.'

'Maybe the battery in his hearing aid is dying too.'

'What? I don't—'

'Nothing.'

Ian sets the beer on the counter.

Donald rings it up and says, 'That all?'

Ian scans the shelves behind him, looking just below the rows of hard liquor, to several boxes of cigars and cigarettes.

After a moment he says, 'Gimme a couple of them Camachos.'

Donald turns around and looks for them.

'Diploma?'

'Maduro. Bottom shelf, to your right.'

He grabs them and rings them up. Then he grabs a black plastic bag and loads Ian's purchases into it. Ian knows the cigars will be dry and probably taste like smoking dog turds. The middle of summer and they've been sitting out since the spring. He doesn't care. He's used to smoking cigars past their prime.

While Donald loads the bag Ian pulls out his wallet and removes Maggie's photo from it. He holds it up in front of Donald.

'You remember my daughter?'

Donald nods. ''Course.'

'You didn't see anyone resembling her today?'

'Huh-uh,' he says with his mouth hanging open. Ian can see bits of red vine ground into his molars like wax fillings.

'And you didn't hear anything?'

He shakes his head. 'Like I told Chief Davis.'

'What about a guy in his sixties? Tall, gray hair, balding on top, busted capillaries in his nose. Heavy.'

Donald lets out a strange giggle and grins with his too-many teeth, but when Ian gives him a dead pan the smile vanishes, and he stares down at the counter nervously and scratches at something sticking to it, part of a price sticker looks like, with a dirty fingernail.

'What's funny?'

Donald shakes his head. 'Nothing, it's just, you know, you described damn near half the fat old alcoholics in town.' He looks from Chief Davis to Ian and a smile grows once more on his face. 'Hell,' he says, 'you just described my brother Henry.'

Chief Davis snorts once.

'True enough,' he says. 'How is Henry, anyway? I haven't said much more than hello to him since high school, I reckon.'

'He's okay, I guess.'

'Still working at the community college?'

'Uh-huh.' Donald nods.

'If you see anyone looks like my daughter, I want you to call. I'd rather a false alarm than to miss our chance.'

'I will,' Donald says. He wipes the sweat from his upper lip with a downward swipe of his palm, and then wipes his sweaty palm onto the leg of his pants. 'I will,' he says again.

Ian and Chief Davis step into the daylight. It seems bright even after Ian puts his sunglasses back on. An oppressive wall of heat surrounds them. Ian reaches into his bag and pulls out one of his cigars. He bites the end off, spits it to the parking lot asphalt, plugs the stick into his mouth. He lights it, looking past it to Diego. Diego standing with his arms crossed, watching one of the boys from Mencken pulling finger-prints.

Then the sheriff himself pulls up in the Ford Expedition Tonkawa County provides for him and screeches to a stop. He steps from the thing, all five feet five of him, all two hundred and sixty pounds of him. He walks toward Ian and Chief Davis, belly swinging before him like a wrecking ball.

Ian glances at his watch.

'I'll let you talk to the sheriff,' he says. 'I need to tell Deb. Call if there's any developments.'

'I will. And Ian,' he says, patting him on the shoulder. 'Stop in at Roberta's tonight, okay? You shouldn't be alone through this.'

'I'll think about it,' Ian says, knowing he won't.

Maggie opened her eyes and saw white white white: the ceiling. She tongued the place where her loose tooth should have been, but all that was there now was smooth wet gum and a bloody divot that tasted vaguely of metal.

Someone took it, she thought. Tooth fairy took it and didn't pay. *Stole* it.

Then it occurred to her that maybe the tooth fairy *had* paid. She flipped over in bed and tossed the pillow aside, but the only thing beneath it was wrinkled sheet. There was no green dollar bill awaiting discovery. Not even a lousy quarter. She couldn't believe the tooth fairy would sneak into her bedroom in the dark of night and yank her tooth from her mouth. What a butthole. She briefly considered putting a fake tooth beneath her pillow—a piece of chalk, maybe, or else a white stone if she could find one of the right size—and pretending to sleep so that when the tooth fairy came she could grab him and force him to pay for what he had taken from her.

But then she saw it on the floor. It lay half-buried in the thick carpet. She hopped from her bed and picked it up. She brushed off the dirt specks it had collected and held it up in the morning sunlight shining through her bedroom's open window and looked at it, amazed at how big it was, at how much of it had been buried in her face. It was kind of gross and kind of neat at the same time. She tongued the gap between her teeth. There was a strange flap of skin there that she could flip back and forth. It felt weird. She ran to the mirror on her dresser and looked at herself and smiled. Then she ran into Mommy and Daddy's room to show them.

'Look it,' she shouted as she shot into the room like a human bullet, door swinging open as she pushed it aside and banging against the wall. The curtains were drawn, daylight held temporarily and ineffectively at bay, and there was a strange grown-up smell in the room. It made the air feel heavy and close, like being in a zipped-up sleeping bag.

Daddy groaned and sat up. He cleared his throat. It was a funny sound. Like a monster in a Saturday morning cartoon. He rubbed his red eyes and wiped his mouth and twisted his neck left and right, sending out little hollow-sounding pops, and looked in her direction. But for a moment his face was blank.

'Look it,' she said again and held up the tooth for him to examine.

'Wow,' Daddy said after a moment. He coughed into his hand and yawned. 'Is that a grown-up tooth? It's huge. Have you been out stealing teeth? You know the tooth fairy doesn't buy stolen teeth, Mags. It's a felony.'

'It's *not* stolen. Look.' She gripped her tooth in her right palm, folding three fingers over the top of it, and with index fingers stretched her mouth open wide so Daddy could see where the tooth used to be.

'My God,' Daddy said, 'you could park a car in there.'

'Could you two chatterboxes take it to the living room?' Barely a mumble. 'Mommy needs her beauty sleep.'

'Sounds like someone's got a case of the crankies,' Daddy said, then winked at Maggie and got to his feet. A pair of pants lay in a pile on the floor. He picked them up and slipped into them, hiding his red boxers.

'Come on, Mags,' Daddy said. 'Let's get some breakfast.' He looked over his shoulder at Mommy with a smirk in the corner of his mouth and said, 'Cereal. With *lots* of sugar.'

They headed to the kitchen. Maggie climbed onto one of the barstools lined up before the counter that separated the kitchen from the dining room. She spun around left, catching herself on the edge of the counter, and then spun herself around right, back and forth, back and forth. She liked to go round and round in one direction, she liked the dizziness it brought, it was fun, but once she accidentally unscrewed the stool all the way and the seat fell to the floor and she sprained her wrist catching herself, so she didn't do that anymore. While she played on the stool Daddy went digging through the cupboards.

Maggie caught herself on the counter one last time and said, 'What does the tooth fairy need teeth for, anyway? It's kind of a weird thing to collect.'

'He turns them into stars.'

'Really?'

'Maybe.'

'No.'

'Maybe.'

'Really?'

Daddy nodded, then put two bowls on the counter and poured Froot Loops into them. He put away the box and got out a half gallon of milk and poured that over the cereal. He pushed a bowl across the counter to Maggie.

'Eat up.'

'What about a spoon, silly?'

Daddy picked at his bellybutton and flicked a wad of gray at her.

'What about some lint?'

55

Maggie dodged it, dipping her head to the left.

'*Gross.* Don't. I don't want your smelly lint.'

'It's not smelly.'

'How do you know?'

'I'm sorry.'

'You almost got it in my cereal.'

'No, I didn't.'

'Get me a spoon before it gets soggy.'

'Okay.'

Daddy grabbed two spoons from the silverware drawer and handed her one. Then he dipped his into his bowl and shoveled a mouthful of pink and green and orange into his face. He scratched at his blond stubble. Scooped another bite into his mouth and milk dripped down his chin and he wiped at it with his hand.

'What do you want to do today?'

'Petting zoo!'

'What if they mistake you for one of the goats and fence you in?'

Maggie rolled her eyes. 'They won't.'

'How do you know? You're stubborn as a goat.'

'I don't even know what that means.'

'Shouldn't we wait till Jeffrey wakes up and weighs in?'

'He loves the petting zoo.'

'He's never been.'

'Then we should *definitely* go. He's only here another two days and he needs to go before he leaves town.'

'You have a point.'

'See?'

'Okay.'

'Okay?'

Daddy nodded.

'Okay what?'

'Okay okay.'

'Okay petting zoo?'

'Yup.'

'Really?'

'Really really.'

'Promise?'

'Promise. Now eat your cereal before it gets soggy.'

'You're the best daddy ev—'

'Wake up.'

A familiar voice gurgling up from swampy depths. The stench of onion on a wave of breath. The sound of swallowing.

Something small shatters in a sharp pop. A moment later the stink of ammonia fills her nostrils. Her eyes flutter open. Warm water runs down her cheeks.

Everything is dark and without form. A shadow, like a vaguely human-shaped hole scissored out of reality, before her. Behind it, bright white light making it impossible for her to see anything more than shadow. She closes her eyes and opens them again. Her pupils shrink, adjusting to the room. The shadow grows features, taking on detail and color and a third dimension. It is a man. The man has a name and she knows what it is. Henry. She blinks again and sees him clearly for the first time since waking. He simply stands before her with his arms at her sides, fists opening and closing.

Then he reaches into his shirt pocket, pulls out a roll of something, small white disks, and thumbs one into his mouth. He chews it, swallows.

There's an intense pain in her wrists. She can feel blood warm and thick rolling down her arms. She looks up and sees her wrists tied together with coarse yellow rope. The rope is slung over a large metal hook which has been screwed into a wooden ceiling beam. Her hands above the rope are purple and numb, bloated fingers curled slightly, fingertips touching. She has been here before: the punishment hook. You've been very bad, Sarah. Very bad indeed. Looking at her fingers she thinks of a rhyme she learned in Sunday school. Here is the church and here is the steeple. Open the doors and see all the people.

Her feet dangle far above the cracked gray surface of the concrete floor.

Henry stands and stares. Fists opening and closing, opening and closing. He tongues at a molar. His breathing sounds funny. It gets heavier and thicker and faster.

'I'm sorry,' she says. 'I'm sorry.'

His breathing stops. There is silence.

Then: 'But you're really not, are you?'

'I am.'

'What are you sorry for?'

One two three four five six seven eight.

She looks around for Borden, just to know that she isn't alone down here. Just to know that she isn't alone with Henry. Maybe he's standing in the shadows somewhere. She knows he cannot save her from whatever punishment Henry will be delivering, but seeing him would be a comfort still. She does not see him.

A hand across her face so hard it makes her eyes water and a bruise above her ear begins to throb. She had forgotten about it, that place where Henry punched her earlier, but now it is throbbing with the beat of her heart.

'I said what are you sorry for?'

She looks down at her feet once more. They are filthy, black with dirt, and if she ignores the pain she can pretend she is simply floating above the floor. A crack in the concrete moves left and right beneath her as she swings by her wrists. Just pretend you're floating: above the ground without a care in the world.

He reaches toward her. She instinctively recoils. He slaps at her cheek, a quick whip-crack of his fingertips, then grabs her chin and tilts her head up so that she is looking him in the eyes. An uncaring cruelty floats in them and nothing more: pools of bad water. She hates them.

'You don't know?'

'What?'

'You don't know what you're sorry for?'

'I'm . . .' she says, and licks her lips. They are dry and cracked. 'I'm sorry for running.'

'You're sorry for getting caught.'

'No.'

'Oh, you wanted to get caught?'

She turns her head and looks away. She can feel fresh tears welling in her eyes. She tries to blink them away. She doesn't want to cry in front of him. She doesn't want to be weak in front of him. He is a cruel man and weakness makes him angrier, more likely to attack.

'You didn't want to get caught.'

'No.'

'That is why you're sorry.'

'I don't know.'

'Well I *do*.'

With the last word he puts a fist into her stomach, punching all the air out of her. It leaves her in a single rush. If she weren't strung up by the wrists she would curl into a fetal ball. Instead she swings and gasps for air like a fish on the end of a line.

Henry stands and watches her swing. Fists opening and closing.

'You've made me very angry, Sarah.'

He has always called her Sarah. Both he and Beatrice. Another way of torturing her. Another way of confusing her. Of making her confused about who and what she is.

She is just getting her breath back when Henry grabs her by the hips and stills her swinging. He looks at her in silence.

Then: 'What do you have to say for yourself?'

She breathes in and out, chest heaving. Her stomach is a tight, cramped knot.

'My daddy's coming,' she says.

'What?'

'I called my daddy and told him everything. You better just let me go. If you don't he's going to, he's going to get you and he's going to—'

'Lies!' Violence like a large wave crashing upon a beach. She flinches away but does not break eye contact. 'You're lying,' he says. 'Tell me you're lying.'

She shakes her head. 'He's going to get you,' she says.

'Henry?' Beatrice's voice stumbling down the stairs.

'What?'

'You're gonna be late for work.'

He looks at his watch and curses under his breath. 'I'll be right up,' he says.

He grabs Maggie by the waist and lifts her off the hook and sets her down on the cold concrete floor. Then he unties her wrists and makes four loose loops of the bloody rope.

She looks down at her wrists and sees the shape of the rope imbedded in her skin. She pushes herself backwards until she is up against the wall. She looks up at him, awaiting some final act of violence. It does not come.

He nods to the rusty sink in the corner and says, 'Wash up before Bee brings you supper.' Then trudges halfway up the stairs before turning around again. 'You've broken Bee's heart with your behavior. All she wants is a daughter. She loves you, you know. Even though you're a failure as a daughter, she loves you.' Then he heads the rest of the way up the stairs, turns off the overhead light, and closes the door. A moment later, the sound of a deadbolt sliding into place.

The only light left in the basement is the laundry-water gray of late afternoon coming in through the basement's sole window.

Her hands begin to throb with sharp pain as the circulation returns to them. She cries silently, trying to bend her fingers. It hurts too much, and she knows from experience that it will take several minutes for the pain to recede. And she knows, too, that the tide of pain hasn't yet even fully come in.

But she knows something else as well: she almost got away.

After years in captivity she managed to get out. Hope which she'd long thought dead throbs hot in her chest. Even now, back here in the Nightmare World, there is a new sense of possibility. The world on the other side of the window is not unreachable. She has walked upon its ground. She has run through its woods. She has heard her daddy speak into her ear.

Getting out today was a fluke, she knows that, but if she plans it she can get out again. And this time she will not be brought back.

Henry walks to the fridge and pulls it open. On the top shelf, a brown-bag meal Bee has packed for him. He grabs it and looks inside. A Tupperware bowl with a chunk of corned beef in it and a soup of cabbage and water. Every day he gets the leftovers from the day before. He's already looking forward to tomorrow's meatloaf sandwich. In addition to the corned beef there are two pre-packaged chocolate cupcakes. He folds the bag, grabs the five beers left in a six pack he broke into at lunch, and lets it dangle from a finger by its one empty plastic ring.

He walks out the front door and into the late afternoon daylight. Long shadows stretch out on the ground. He walks down the steps and across the gravel driveway and out to his truck, sliding onto the seat, tossing his lunch next to him, and popping one of his beers from its ring. He opens it and it foams up and spills down the side of the can before he can get the can to his mouth and suck at it. It drips down his chin and the front of his shirt and into his lap. He takes two good swallows before looking down at his Levis.

'Goddamn it.'

Looks like he sat here and pissed hisself.

Then another swallow before resting the can between his legs. It's a hot day and the cold feels good. The heat also means the beer he spilled will be dry by the time he arrives at work. Good thing: one of the office administrators has already complained once about him smelling of alcohol. But he supposes right now that is the least of his worries.

He feels sick about what Sarah said in the basement. That she called her daddy. That she told him everything. If she was telling the truth he will end up in prison. Not jail, where, in his youth, he spent more than one drunken night, but prison, where bad men go.

He starts the truck, puts it into gear, and gasses his way up the driveway to the street.

The first Sarah was born thirteen years ago in Mencken Regional Medical Center. They had not planned on having children. Beatrice was forty-four, and in the twenty-eight years she and Henry had been together they had never used contraceptives, so Henry didn't even think they could have children if they wanted any. But Beatrice got pregnant and when Henry saw how it affected her he was glad. She was happier than he had ever seen her before. Henry had never heard someone sing so much in his life.

When the baby came they named her Sarah. Sarah Jasmine Dean. Weight: seven pounds three ounces. She had a cute oval face and thin blond hair that wisped up from her head in a silken hook. She smiled constantly with her mouth open and her green eyes shining. She kicked her feet and laughed and laughed and laughed.

But then she stopped laughing.

Beatrice put Sarah into the bathtub and left the room to get toys for her—a plastic duck, a ball—and when she came back Sarah was under water. Beatrice told Henry that she was only gone a second or two, but he knew it wasn't true. She had gotten distracted looking for toys and lost track of time.

After the funeral, after they lowered that tiny coffin into the ground at Hillside Cemetery, Beatrice did nothing but sit on the couch and cry. Henry wanted to fix it, to make her happy again, but didn't know how. Sarah was gone and she was never coming back.

But then he got an idea.

He wasn't sure how Beatrice would react, so he held off for a long time, hoping she would manage to pull herself out of the hole in which she was wallowing. She had stood by him for twenty-eight years, through drunken arrests and holes punched in walls, through fist fights with her brother, through slaps and punches that were the cause of the fist fights with her brother, but he didn't know if she would stand by him if he went through with this, and if he went through with it it would be for her.

Beatrice only got worse. She stopped bathing. Sometimes she would urinate or defecate without getting up from the couch. She did nothing but watch TV and eat and cry. The dishes piled up in the sink and on the counter. The house started to smell bad. He took off her clothes as she sat passively, neither assisting him nor trying to stop him, and wiped her down with washcloths, but it didn't help much, and soon she began to develop sores—small round scabrous holes in her flesh like cigarette burns. Some of them got infected. But still she would not move.

It was horrible. He knew he had to act.

So he spent several days driving around, looking for potential Sarahs. He sat in front of a couple daycare centers in Mencken, but all the kids there were too old to be proper replacements. He tried the Mencken Regional Medical Center, but couldn't manage to get past the front desk. Finally he got lucky at an Albertsons. He wasn't even looking for a Sarah at the time. He was there simply to get groceries for the week. But when he saw his opportunity, a baby sitting unsupervised in a shopping cart while her mother fought with groceries in the back of a station wagon, he took it. He walked by and scooped the baby up, walked around a gray Nissan, and made his way back to his truck. He walked briskly but did not run. Running, he knew, would give him away. He glanced down at the baby as he walked. She had an oval face and blue eyes, not green, and a pink ribbon in her hair. Her eyes weren't the right color, but they were close. He slid the baby into the seat and buckled her in and was sticking the key into the ignition when the woman started to scream. He looked up at her through his bug-spattered windshield.

She was standing outside her car with her mouth hanging open and her eyebrows cocked and her eyes wide and glistening with terror. She turned in a frantic circle and said, "Becca? 'Becca!' Then she said, 'Someone took my daughter!' Then she put both her fists into her hair and began to pull at it. 'Help. Someone help. My baby's gone. Someone took my 'Becca!'

Henry put the truck into gear and pulled out of the parking lot. He watched in the rearview mirror as a store employee ran toward the woman, then he made a right onto the street and drove away and could not see her anymore.

Beatrice loved her. Her face lit up and she held her and stroked her face and loved her. She insisted that Henry get rid of all Sarah's 'hand-me-downs', stuff that they did not get for her, the things she was wearing when Henry took her, so he put them in a bag to throw them away, but because he didn't want anyone to find them, he buried them in the woods instead.

Life returned to normal. Life was good, even; they were simply a happy family living a normal life.

But six months later Henry had to put her into the ground next to her clothes. Bee had forgotten to feed her. She said she'd forgotten, but Henry thought she had stopped lactating after the first Sarah died and hadn't wanted to admit it to herself; he'd seen the baby suck at her nipple but cry still hungry fifteen minutes later. Either way the second Sarah was dead.

Bee held on to the corpse for a week, refusing to let Henry take it away from her. She held it and rocked it in her arms and tried to brush its hair, but the hair peeled away with a flap of skin and she put the flap back, pretending to herself that it hadn't happened. Finally when Bee was asleep Henry took it out of her arms and carried it out to the woods and dug a hole. He put it into the hole and tried to say a prayer, one he'd learned in church, but couldn't remember it, so he made something up about children being innocent and please take this innocent into Heaven, amen, and scooped dirt over its face so he wouldn't have to look at it any longer.

Two weeks later he found their third Sarah. She lived five years before Henry spanked her too hard. He felt bad about it, it had been an accident, but she'd misbehaved and she needed to be punished, and if he punished her a bit too much, well, that was as much her fault as it was his. If she hadn't misbehaved in the first place he never would have lost his temper. He put her into the ground beside the last Sarah and went looking for the next.

That one screamed and screamed when he grabbed her and he put his hand over her mouth to silence her. She stopped screaming, but she stopped breathing too.

Then there is this Sarah. He spent a week fruitlessly searching before he finally decided to go up to the petting zoo. It was on the north side of town, near Interstate 10, and mostly people who visited were traveling through. They saw the signs,

BULLS MOUTH PETTING ZOO
PUBLIC RESTROOMS

and their kids bugged them till they agreed to stop for half an hour. Since it was Saturday there would probably be a dozen Sarahs to choose from.

It was a pleasant April day with a breeze just strong enough to make the trees whisper.

Kids were running around looking at all the animals—pot-bellied pigs and rabbits and miniature horses—and reaching through the fences to pet them. Some of them were buying celery and carrots from a woman with a vegetable cart.

Everybody else was there with kids. Henry felt very conspicuous walking alone. He felt like he must stand out, the only giant at a midget convention. But nobody seemed worried by his presence. He was in public and behaved accordingly. A sort of dumb open-mouthed smile pushed up his cheeks, his eyes wide and bright, his hands in his pockets, legs doing a going-nowhere shuffle. Just a harmless old man probably there with his granddaughter who'd run off someplace, maybe to use the restroom.

'Would you care to buy some vegetables to feed the animals?'

'Not today,' he said, pulled out his pockets to display them empty, and shrugged.

'Maybe next time,' the woman said.

Then he saw her, the Sarah he wanted, standing just behind

the woman with the vegetable cart. She was standing beside her daddy and a teenage boy, looking through a fence at an alpaca.

'Look it, Jeffrey!' she said as the alpaca pulled a piece of celery from her fingers.

'I am, dorko.'

'*You're* the dorko, dorko.'

She was the one. Beatrice would love her. Her face was a bright oval, green eyes alive with joy and humor. Beatrice would absolutely love her. He knew she would.

He followed the family around from a distance, waiting for his moment, but her hand remained within her father's as they walked. Eventually they circled the entire petting zoo and headed for the exit.

He followed them out to a dirt parking lot east of the petting zoo and watched them pile into a red '65 Mustang with a primer-gray trunk lid. He got into his truck and followed them out to Crouch Avenue, and then left onto Grapevine Circle. They wound round Bulls Mouth Reservoir, water on their right, a bunch of trees and mustang grapevines and blackberry bushes on their left. By summertime half the houses around the reservoir would be loaded with jars of homemade preserves. They pulled the car into a driveway at 44 Grapevine Circle. Henry drove all the way around the reservoir, made a u-turn when he got to an intersection, and went back. He parked across the street and a few houses down. He had to wait for hours, till her mom and dad left without her, and later still, till the teenage boy watching her finally made her go to bed. He sat and waited, urinating into three beer cans while he did so, setting the warm beer cans just outside his truck on the asphalt, and watching the house. He hummed to himself. He nodded once at someone walking by. Once the little girl was in her bedroom Henry got out of his truck and walked the perimeter of the house. He peeked into her window and watched her change for bed. Little Sarah. He waited till she was asleep before cutting the screen away with a box cutter. He didn't want to scare her before he was near enough to keep her silent.

It was worth it. Beatrice's face was as joyful as he'd imagined it would be when he presented their new Sarah. It simply lit up like sunshine.

Henry hits a red light at the corner of Crockett and Hackberry and brings the truck to a stop. He finishes his beer, tilting the bottom of the can to the sky, tosses it to the floor where it falls among the other dead soldiers, and pulls a fresh one from its ring. To his right he can see one of Pastor Warden's dachshunds digging in a flower garden in front of the Skating Palace, head down, dirt flying up from between its legs and arcing through the air before it falls to the sidewalk. He wonders when—if—someone is going to see how scratched up his truck has gotten and make the connection between that and Warden's fence. There is probably green paint residue on the chain-link fence as well.

The light turns green and Henry's gas-foot gets heavy.

He pulls his truck into the lot on the east side of the small college campus, parks in front of the two-storey building where all classes are held, and kills the engine. The first floor won't clear out till ten, but until then he and Mike will be plenty busy with the second floor, which is not used for classes after four o'clock.

He finishes his second beer, grabs the three that remain, as well as his lunch, and steps from the vehicle.

When he walks into the janitor's closet Mike is already slipping into a blue work shirt. Mike's a permanent fixture, been here three years now, but not technically a full-time employee of the college. If he works more than a hundred and eighty days he becomes eligible for benefits, so Henry has to lay him off for a month every six so that his work cycle will start anew. He hates to do it, but he can never seem to get approval for a full-time hire.

He walks through the door and smiles. 'Hey, Mike. Sorry I'm late.'

'That mean you let me do classrooms tonight?'

'I'm not that sorry.'

'But Doug always accuses me of stealing chips from the rack.'

'Then don't steal chips from the rack.'

'I make six bucks an hour, Henry.'

Henry shrugs: what are you gonna do? Then he changes into his blue work shirt. He grabs his cart and pulls it away from the wall and checks to make sure it's properly stocked: cleaning fluids full up, plenty of trash bags, rubber gloves, paper towels, a couple fluorescent tubes in case he stumbles on any that have gone out. Once he's sure everything is in order he rolls his cart out of there and into the hall.

From now till two o'clock in the morning his job is to get classrooms ready for tomorrow. He likes his work. There's nothing to it but to do the same thing again and again. It's relaxing. You find your rhythm and let the night pass you by.

He walks to the cafeteria, which is closed—it closes from four to six—unlocks the door, and walks to the chip rack. He snags a bag of Doritos and heads out, locking the door behind him. Doug will notice, of course, but it doesn't matter. Henry can just blame Mike.

Ian pulls his car to the curb in front of the house he once called his own. It is nothing special as far as houses go, a brick building fronted by a lawn and a tree with branches like broken fingers, but once upon a time it belonged to him. Now another man sleeps beside his wife and watches baseball on his television and eats food prepared in his kitchen off his plates with silverware he and Deb got as a wedding present from his mom, two years before the lung cancer got her. Bill Finch doesn't even know there's a history there; as far as he's concerned all these things came into existence the moment he got the key to the front door.

After Maggie was kidnapped he spent a long time living in a strange fog, and when Debbie finally asked him to leave the conversation was short. In his mind he supposes he was already gone. He didn't even look away from the television commercial telling him he needed to switch toilet paper brands.

'I want you to move out.'

A pause. Then: 'Okay.'

'That's it?'

He nodded.

'You're not gonna get mad? You're not gonna fight me over this?'

He shook his head. 'No.'

'Do you wanna know why?'

'No.'

'I'm sleeping with Bill Finch.'

'I know.'

Debbie stood there for a long time. He didn't look at her, but he could sense her in his periphery. After a while she simply said, 'Fine,' and walked away.

The next night he slept on Diego and Cordelia's couch.

And a week after that he put the extra TV, some books and book cases, a couch from the garage, Maggie's bed, and his clothes into a truck he rented from Paulson's U-Haul and drove to his new apartment. He could have afforded a house, but did not see the point. Houses were for people with families and expanding futures. He was no longer one of those people. His future was shrinking.

The first few weeks were strange and sleepless. Not because he missed Deb—he did not exactly miss her—but because he was used to having someone sleeping beside him. Soon enough, though, he got comfortable with the absence. His body learned to spread out across the full width of the bed. He stopped sitting up at night to call Debbie's name. He stopped believing she was merely in the next room.

Ian knocks on the front door and waits.

He scratches the top of his head where the blond hair is thinnest, then arms the sweat off his forehead. It's still hellish out.

Debbie pulls open the front door from inside. She's wearing beige shorts and her white work T-shirt with PINK'S SALON written in cursive across the right breast. She manages the place for Vicki Dodd—who's the only reason the Dodd family has any money left at all, her brother Carney being useless—and must have just got home. When she sees

Ian she frowns. It's brief, and the frown is immediately followed by a polite smile, but the frown was true and the smile is false. Ian understands this. As far as Debbie is concerned he can be nothing more than a walking reminder of the biggest loss she's ever suffered. He just looks too much like the daughter she has spent the last seven years trying to forget. She's tried to bury her again and again. He's from a part of her life she no longer wants to think about.

'Ian.'

'Deb.'

'What is it?'

'Have you heard from Bill or Sheriff Sizemore?'

'No.'

'Mind if I come in?'

'Did something happen? Is Bill okay?'

'Bill's fine. I thought he might have called you.'

'About what?'

'I think you might want to sit down for this.'

'What is it?'

He doesn't answer. He simply stands there and waits.

She searches his face for clues, but he gives her none. He keeps his expression blank.

After a moment Debbie steps aside to let him in.

Ian watches Deb as she sits on the couch and looks up at him. Her shoulders are tense, the cords in her neck taut, hands clenching her knees. There was a time when Debbie touched him with those hands, when she caressed him with them. But that was long ago, and he cannot even feel her touch in his memory anymore.

'What is it?' she says.

'It's Maggie.'

Debbie sighs and the tension leaves her body and she relaxes into familiar bad posture.

'They found her body,' she says.

The relief in her voice, the unspoken but nearly audible 'Thank God,' makes Ian want to grab her shoulders and shake her and shout at her. What is wrong with you, Debbie? This is your daughter we're talking about. Your *daughter*. How *dare* you sound relieved when discussing her death?

But he knows what's wrong with her. She wants to move on. The funeral wasn't enough. It didn't provide the closure she thinks she needs. Coffins can't contain memories and dirt cannot cover them. She wants a corpse. She doesn't understand that even a corpse would not give her what she desires. She doesn't understand that the dead don't die until everyone who ever knew them and loved them dies too.

Ian shakes his head.

'No,' he says. 'There's no body to find,' he says. 'She's alive,' he says.

And she is no longer seven years old, no longer frozen in time. She is fourteen, fifteen in September, and she called for help today. Right into his ear.

He won't let her die again.

TWO

Ian opens his eyes. He is lying on the couch, head turned to the right. With one eye he is looking at his work shoes on the floor near the wall opposite. The other eye can see only his out-of-focus shirtsleeve, his arm folded up over his head. One of his shoes is on its side. There is a blackened piece of chewing gum sticking to the heel. He sits up. His neck hurts. Sunlight shines through the dirty living-room window. Six empty Guinness bottles stand like bowling pins on the coffee table, the labels peeled from two of them and stuffed inside like messages floated in on the tide. Near the bottles is a saucepan, the bottom blackened by flame, with a fork poking out of it. Ramen noodles and a small slice of overcooked carrot cling to the inside of the pan. On the far corner of the coffee table, a chessboard with several pieces resting on it, revealing a partially played game. He puts his face into his open hands and rubs at it. Beard stubble against his palms like sandpaper.

His watch's alarm sounds. He looks at his wrist, but his watch is not there. It's on the kitchen counter. That means he must stand up.

'Fuck.'

He gets to his feet and walks to the kitchen and thumbs the watch silent. Then he rinses the ramen pan he used last night, puts two eggs inside, puts enough water into the pan to cover the eggs, and sets the pan on the stove. The turn of a knob makes a clicking sound which is followed after a moment by the poof of orange-tipped blue flames. With that going he gets the coffee pot started as well, scooping coffee into a filter and pouring water into a tank. He presses a button. A red light flashes green. Liquid drips into the coffee-stained carafe. The drops sizzle, dancing on the heated surface.

After pouring a cup of black coffee and peeling his soft-boiled eggs he walks back to the couch and sits down. He pushes the empty beer bottles aside and pulls the chessboard toward him. He looks at the game in progress. It seems ancient to him, some relic of an era lost in time, but he refuses to consider it abandoned. He bought the chess set from a junk store. It's a cheap wooden case, lined inside with plaid fabric, one side of its exterior inlaid with veined marble squares to form a playing surface. The pieces were carved also from cheap marble by an apprentice or an old man with shaky hands, and because of the failing of the pieces the set was especially inexpensive. Both the board and the pieces are covered in dust. Ian hasn't ever brushed them off for fear of disturbing the game, though he has sat and stared at it so frequently, replaying each move in his head, that if knocked to the four corners of the room he could still gather the pieces and reassemble the game in a matter of minutes.

It's his move. It has been his move for three years. For over three years. And he's known what his move would be for just as long. It took him an hour of semi-drunken study to figure it out. Queen to b4. But by the time he did figure it out it was late, even in California where Jeffrey was still living with his mother, Lisa, so he decided he would call the next day. Instead he opened up another twelve pack and drank his way through it, drank till the sun rose and he had to drive to work. Three years ago he was still allowing more than a six pack into his apartment at a time. When he got home from work that day the alcohol was finally wearing off and he was hung-over and did not feel up to calling Jeffrey, so another day passed. And another. Then a week passed. Then six months. And how do you call a son to whom you haven't spoken in six months and say 'Queen to b4'?

He picks up his dusty black queen and moves it to the new square and looks at it. He sips his coffee. Problem is if Jeffrey doesn't know about it the move hasn't been made. Ian puts the queen back and pushes the board aside. Maybe he'll call Jeffrey later today.

He salts and peppers a soft-boiled egg and shoves it whole into his mouth. He chews slowly and washes it down with a swig of coffee.

Strange how the longer you wait to do something the harder it is to do it. You push a task forward rather than pick it up, knowing you can take care of it later, always later, but as it rolls it gathers mass, like a snowball, and what you could once have picked up with one hand and put into your pocket now has to it the weight of planets.

Ian burps and salts his second egg.

He steps onto the elevator.

His apartment building was constructed as a hotel in 1924 by Carl Dodd. For some reason known only to him he thought Bulls Mouth was going to grow into the major metropolis between Houston and San Antonio. But it never happened. He died and left the place, as well as Dodd Dairy, to his children Carney and Vicki, who turned around and sold the hotel to a Houston realtor in 1996. The realtor converted the hotel into apartments for college kids who wanted out from under daddy's thumb, but the conversion consisted of little more than knocking down the old sign and putting up a new one. Certainly a repairman hasn't so much as glanced at the elevator in twenty years or more. Every day Ian steps into it he's certain that today will be the day the cables finally snap.

The doors creak shut and Ian presses a button. The elevator shakes violently, as if the mere thought of movement frightens it, and then begins its descent.

The doors open on the ground floor.

Ian glances at his watch. He has twenty minutes to get to work.

Maggie hardly slept all night. Her thoughts kept turning to escape. Even counting did not help. She kept losing track and having to start over. She tossed and turned and found herself tangled in her sheets. She could not get comfortable and her brain could not find peace.

Now morning is here and she is standing beneath the basement's sole window, on tippy-toe so that she can put her face into a bright beam of morning sunlight. The heat feels good on her skin. She wants to be out there again. She wants once more to feel fallen leaves and soil beneath her feet. To hear birds sing. To hear the still air come to life as a gust of hot summer wind forces itself through the leaves of the trees.

'He might kill you if you try to escape again.'

She glances to the left.

A horse's head poking from the dark shadows, flaring nostrils, a single black eye glistening in the small gray light reaching him from the window while the other is hidden in darkness, the toes of a pair of Chuck Taylor basketball shoes. That is all she can see of Borden. The rest of him in darkness.

'I think he's killed others.'

His mouth does not move when he speaks. The words seem to simply float from his mind, scatter on the air, and reform in hers.

'I think so too,' she says. 'But I can't stay.'

'Don't you remember what he did yesterday?'

'I remember.' She touches the scab bracelets on her wrists.

'Then how can you think what you're thinking?'

She does not respond. She looks back toward the window and lets the light fall upon her face once more.

'It will be worse next time.'

'I know.'

'Even if he doesn't kill you it will be worse.'

She nods silently. And now he has made her picture it in her mind. Hanging from the punishment hook, her hands purple and numb, her wrists bleeding, the rest of her body helpless, defenseless as she swings. She has been there before, at least two dozen times, and it is always terrible.

She can kick. Kicking keeps Henry away, but only temporarily, and when she stops kicking, as she has to eventually, Henry's punishment is even worse than it would have been. The mere thought of the punishment hook has kept her obedient on many occasions when every part of her down to the last cell cried out for rebellion against the horrors of the Nightmare World.

'I know,' she says again.

But with the morning light falling upon her face she does not care. She does care, she is terrified, but even caring and being terrified she believes it will be worth the risk. She cannot stay here any longer. Not after yesterday. It's worth the risk.

'Even if he kills you?'

'Even then.'

'But what about me?'

'You can come.'

'I can't.'

'Why not?'

'I can never leave. This is my home.'

'It doesn't have to be.'

'This is where I was born. I can't live out there.'

'You can try.'

'I know better. I can never leave.'

'Why?'

Only silence in response.

'Borden?'

More silence. Then: 'If you try to leave, I'll tell.'

'You can't.'

'If you leave . . .'

'If I leave, what?'

'You can't leave.'

'You can't tell.'

'I can never leave and you can never leave.'

'You can't tell!'

He steps back into the shadows.

'Borden?'

He does not respond. She closes her eyes imagining herself swinging from the punishment hook, imagining blood running down her arms from her bloody wrists, imagining the terrible pain in her shoulders and hands, imagining the blows she will receive.

She opens her eyes and looks to the shadows. They are dense as cloth and she cannot see through them. Anything could be in that darkness.

You can never leave.

Diego Peña hates the sun: it's mocking him up there above the trees, shining its white light into his eyes and cooking his throbbing brain as he drives east along Flatland Avenue. If he could draw his service weapon and shoot the thing down he thinks he might actually do it. Watch it drop like a dead bird and go out like a candle.

He burps, almost vomits, and swallows it back.

He doesn't know how many drinks he had last night at Roberta's but it was at least half a dozen too many. He should just stop going there and make O'Connell's his regular place. He's incapable of regulating himself at Roberta's.

Ever since he answered a domestic disturbance call and took a roll of barbed wire to the face from her ex-husband Jimmy Block, Roberta has given him free drinks. Ever since she got the bar in the divorce settlement six months later and changed the name from Jimmy's to Roberta's, anyway, though some few partisans refused to go along with the name change and even now call it Jimmy's. Diego burps again and swallows back what comes up. He shouldn't have eaten the leftover *rabo de toro* for breakfast. But he'd thought his time kneeling before the toilet was finished. He thought a little food might soak up what alcohol was left in him.

If the look on Cordelia's face this morning was any indication, his wife thinks over four years of free drinks has been enough. Of course he was hunched over the toilet at the time, and when he looked up with spittle on his chin she turned and walked away, so maybe he misread her expression in that brief moment before her back was to him and she was saying, '. . . *hace lo que le sale de los cojones.*'

What he needs is a red rooster: light beer, tomato juice, hot sauce, a splash of clam juice, and one raw egg. That would do him well. He glances at his watch. Seven thirty. Roberta's morning bartender won't even be in for another two and a half hours. He'll have to suffer this.

He guesses he's on duty then.

Kind of.

Pastor Warden came into Roberta's last night around eight thirty, just as the place was coming to life, and announced he'd pay ten dollars a head for each dachshund returned.

'Dead or alive?' Andy Paulson said from his stool at the bar, glancing over his shoulder, grinning through his broken china teeth, beer foam hanging from his ridiculous waxed mustaches.

'Alive,' Warden said. 'Dead'll get you a six-hour sermon on the sins of intoxication come Sunday morning.'

Then he turned and left. As soon as he was out the door half the bar burst out laughing. But now it's morning and ten bucks a head doesn't strike Diego as a bad deal, even if he is feeling under the weather. After the way Cordelia was looking at him this morning he might just need that money to buy her some flowers at Albertsons on his way home.

He makes a right on Main Street and cruises past Flatland Park, looking to see if any dogs are running around there. But he sees nothing, so he continues south, past the Bulls Mouth

Nine where Fred Paulson—Andy Paulson's brother and owner of the U-Haul rental place next to Andy's feed store over on Wallace—looks to be finishing up a round. He's cursing and hacking away at a sand trap with a pitching wedge, face pink with rage, mouth shotgunning curses like he bought a batch on sale at Wal-Mart. Finally he slams down his club and picks up the golf ball and throws it up onto the green. He snags up his club and stomps his way up to greet it, not bothering to rake the sand trap into decent condition for the next guy.

A left turn puts Diego on Underhill Avenue. He continues along, looking left to the golf course and right to woods and blackberry bushes with fat overripe berries rotting on the ground beneath them. He's about halfway to Crockett Street when he sees a dachshund digging furiously in a kidney-shaped sand trap hooking its way around the fourth green.

He pulls his car to the shoulder of the road and swings open his door. Dizziness overwhelms him as he stands and he grabs on to the car for balance and blinks several times as he swallows back bile. Soon enough the blood gets to his head and the gray dizziness retreats and he squints in the sunlight. He looks toward the golf course. The dog is still digging. He runs toward the chain-link fence surrounding the Bulls Mouth Nine—it's only waist-level—and hurls himself over it. This turns out to be a mistake.

He lands on his feet, manages two steps, then falls to his knees and vomits. It's mostly liquid, what's left of last night's fun, and what breakfast he managed to eat this morning. He spits a couple times and gets to his feet. Then, blocking each nostril with a thumb, he blows his nose into the grass. He wipes at his watery eyes. His stomach is a bit less sour. Maybe that was the last of it and this is the turning point for this hangover. Maybe he'll start to feel human again. He spits once more and dusts the grass off his knees and looks to where he saw the dachshund.

It's now squatting in the rough just north of the fourth hole. He runs toward it, then thinks better of that, and walks briskly.

'Come here, doggy,' he says.

After putting the dog into the back of the car he slips in behind the wheel. He reaches to the glove box and flips it open. He fumbles around in there, finding and discarding pens and napkins and other shit he's stored there, till his fingers find what they were feeling for. He pulls out a travel-size mouthwash he keeps for just these occasions, takes a swig, gargles, and spits out the window.

Then he's on his way. His goal for the day is fifty bucks.

As he drives past College Avenue he sees Ian Hunt's Mustang stopped at the intersection, waiting for traffic. They wave to one another, and then Diego is past and Ian's Mustang is making a right onto Crockett behind him, presumably heading toward the police station, though that's not where Diego is headed himself.

Now that most of the alcohol is out of his system he's hungry again.

Ian pushes into the police station. Chief Davis is sitting at his desk flipping through paperwork. He looks up as Ian walks in and says, 'Mornin'.'

'Yup. What's Diego working so early for?'

'He's not working.'

'No?'

Chief Davis shakes his head. 'Someone crashed into Pastor Warden's fence and all his dogs got out. Came into Roberta's last night and offered ten bucks a head for their return.'

Ian nods. 'Any news about Maggie?'

Chief Davis was smiling when talking about the dogs, but the smile's gone now. 'No. Old man at the shoe shop didn't recognize any pictures and the rendering Sizemore's boys got from him looks like a bald John Goodman. Useless old fucker. We're still waiting on prints from the phone, though. Hopefully that'll lead to something. Also, Sizemore's got Bill Finch and John Nance looking through records of any missing kids in the county, seeing if he can find a connection between them.'

'Finch?'

Chief Davis shrugs. 'Wasn't my call.'

'I know it.' Ian turns toward the dispatch office, then turns back. 'Think you could call Sizemore, see if we can't get copies of those files they're looking at? Maybe I can poke through them myself.'

Chief Davis nods. 'I'll do that. Maybe send Thompson over to pick them up. By the way, you see this?' He holds up a copy of the *Tonkawa County Democrat*. Ian walks over and grabs it. On the first page of the twenty-page broadsheet, above the fold, this:

KIDNAPPED GIRL ONCE THOUGHT DEAD DISCOVERED ALIVE

Ian begins reading the opening paragraph thinking she was discovered alive the same way a man punched in the nose discovers a fist.

He reads about Maggie being kidnapped while her parents were 'out of the house on a date', about how she was declared dead, about how there was a funeral 'despite a body never being discovered'. He reads a description of the kidnapper that could be a description of anybody of a certain age. He throws the paper onto Davis's desk.

'Did you call them?'

Chief Davis shakes his head. 'Sizemore. He made a statement to local news channels too. It got her picture out, and a description of her kidnapper. And it put his number in people's faces. "If you have any information regarding the whereabouts of Magdalene Hunt or her kidnapper please call the Tonkawa County Sheriff's Department." You know the drill. We need it out there. Improves our odds.'

'Kidnapped while both her parents were out of the house on a date.' Ian shakes his head. 'Makes it sound like we just left a seven-year-old alone to fend for herself.'

'You weren't there. It's the truth, ain't it?'

'It's the facts,' Ian says. 'It's not the truth.'

'It got her picture into the paper, anyway, and on the TV.'

Ian nods, then walks to the dispatch office. At the doorway he says, 'Don't forget to call the sheriff for those files, huh?'

'I won't.'

Ian walks to the coffee pot and gets it started, then to his desk where he falls into his chair. He exhales a heavy sigh and puts on his headset.

Doing this feels strange. Wrong. He should be out looking for Maggie. He should be out finding her. That's what he should be doing and it's what he wants to be doing. But until there are some fingerprint matches with known criminals, or until he gets those files from the sheriff's office, or until some piece of evidence reveals itself, there's really nothing to go on. Here, at least, he can accomplish something. It's a small town and often his days are slow, but in his time in Bulls Mouth he's helped save more than one life. If he can't save Maggie's yet, well, maybe he can save someone else's. It might help to expend some of this sick energy building in his gut that comes from needing to move forward while being simultaneously locked into place by circumstance. Like trying to fire a live round through a leaded barrel, he's afraid the whole thing might blow up. If he can feel useful in some way maybe he can relieve a bit of the pressure, making the wait tolerable.

'Nine-one-one,' he says. 'What is your emergency?'

'I can't find my car keys.'

'Excuse me?'

'I'm late and I can't find my car keys.'

Ian sighs. 'What do you want me to do about it, Thompson?'

'I don't know, look around.'

'They're not here or you couldn't have driven home.'

'Well, shit.'

'Did you check your pocket?'

'Did I . . .' A startled laugh. 'Well, I'll be goddamned.'

Ian pours himself a cup of coffee and drinks it in near silence, the only sound the swamp cooler rattling in the window.

'Nine-one-one. What is your emergency?'

'Hello.' A small girl's small voice.

'Hello. Are you playing with the phone?'

'No.'

'Who are you calling?'

'I'm calling emburgancy.'

'You are?'

'Uh-huh. Are you emburgancy?'

'Yes, I'm emergency. What's your name?'

'Thalia.'

'Hi, Thalia, why are you calling emergency?'

'My mommy.'

'What's wrong with your mommy?'

'She won't get up.'

'What happened, Thalia?'

'Daddy stopped her.'

'Daddy stopped her?'

'Uh-huh.'

'What did he stop her doing?'

'Packing a suitcase.'

'Was she trying to leave?'

There is silence from the other end of the line.

After a moment: 'Thalia?'

'Yes?'

'Did you just nod your head?'

'Uh-huh.'

'Mommy was trying to leave?'

'Uh-huh.'

'Mommy was packing a suitcase and Daddy stopped her?'

'Yes.'

'How did he stop her?'

'He hitted her.'

'Where is he now?'

'He went to gone.'

'He's not at home anymore?'

'No.'

'Where's Mommy, Thalia?'

'She's tired.'

'Where is she?'

'In her bedroom.'

'Is she asleep?'

'Daddy hitted her and made her take a nap.'

'When?'

'Before he went to gone. She won't wake up. I'm hungry.'

'Is Mommy bleeding?'

'Is it okay to call emburgancy to be hungry?'

'It's fine, Thalia. Is Mommy bleeding?'

'She stopped.'

'Okay. I'm going to send a policeman over to say hello, okay? I want you to stay on the phone till he arrives.'

'Police man is the good guys.'

'Will you stay on the phone with me, Thalia?'

'Okay.'

Ian is looking through the files that the sheriff's department photocopied for him when he hears Diego push into the station and mumble a greeting at Chief Davis. Ian takes off his headset, gets to his feet, and walks to the door connecting the dispatch office to the main department.

Diego falls onto the couch which sits against the front wall. An unlit hand-rolled cigarette hangs from his face. He pushes his sunglasses up onto his head, pinning back his wavy hair. He looks very tired and his eyes are red. When he sees Ian standing in the doorway he nods toward him and grunts a greeting.

'How many you get?'

'What?'

'Dogs.'

'Oh, four. Was going for five, though.'

'Warden pay up?'

Diego nods, reaches into his front pocket, and pulls out two twenties. He holds them up a moment, then slides them back into his pocket.

'She press charges?'

'Who?'

'Genevieve Paulson.'

'Oh. No. One of these days Andy's just gonna up and kill her. Shoulda seen her face.'

'Bad?'

'Looked like a plum with eyes.'

'How was Thalia?'

'Same as always. Full of smiles and hellos.'

Ian shakes his head. It makes him sick to think of what having a dad like Andy Paulson will end up doing to that beautiful little girl. It will end up ruining her, turning her into just one more trailer-park wife whose husband beats her when the foreman at the warehouse gets on him for not loading the trucks fast enough or for not changing the tank on the forklift when it ran out of propane.

'Someone should talk to Andy.'

'I went to the feed store and did just that.'

'And?'

'He was all sorrys and it'll never happen agains.'

'Same as always.'

Diego nods. 'Same as always.'

'Warnings won't ever fix him.'

'No, he's not a man responds to words,' Diego says.

'Maybe someone should do more than just talk then,' Ian says.

Maggie sits cross-legged on the mattress in the basement, her empty lunch plate on the floor near her. The light overhead is out and the sun has already passed over to the other side of the house, shadows now beginning to lay themselves out upon the ground. The light in the basement is thin and gray, and the shadows in the corners are dense. She watches them for movement. Borden has disappeared, as he does sometimes, and she doesn't want him sneaking up on her. She doesn't trust him after the things he said this morning. She hasn't seen him since, though she has said aloud that she is not going to try a second escape. 'It's too risky,' she said. 'I think I'll just stay down here.' She said it as if she were talking to herself, but Borden was, of course, her real audience. She hopes that he was listening. She suspects that he is always listening. Maybe it will prevent him from telling.

Even if it does she now knows he cannot be trusted. She thought he was on her side, but he is not on her side at all. He is on his own side and no one else's. She'll have to get out soon and she'll have to be sneaky about her plans. Even when alone down here she'll have to be sneaky. Because alone isn't really.

Tonight will mark the beginning of her escape. She won't make her move yet. She needs to think things through. But tonight will mark the beginning. She will soon escape the Nightmare World. She doesn't care if Borden can't leave. In fact, she hopes it's true. She never wants to see him again. Soon she will escape and she will stand beneath the light of the sun and she will not be afraid.

'You're going to make Beatrice sad.'

She looks left, then right.

He's across the room, in the farthest corner, next to a stack of cardboard boxes. The boxes are full of Christmas ornaments, old magazines with pictures of naked ladies in them, cowboy novels, old clothes saved to be used as rags. He is mostly hidden in shadows, but some of him is visible. He stands very still.

'I don't know what you mean.'

'I know you're still planning to leave.'

'I'm . . . I'm not.'

'You could stay.'

'I am.'

'Beatrice loves you, you know.'

'No, she doesn't.'

'Of course she does.'

'She loves someone named Sarah.'

'You could be Sarah.'

'But I'm not.'

'You could be, you've been Sarah longer than you were anybody else. You could let Beatrice love you. If you let yourself be loved, you wouldn't hate it here so much.'

'But this isn't where I belong.'

'It is where you belong. That's why you can't escape.'

'I—' This is not a discussion she wants to have. 'I'm not gonna try to escape,' she says.

'I can see your thoughts.'

'You're lying.'

'You know I'm not. I can see the darkest corners of your mind. There's nothing you can hide from me.'

Tears begin to well in her eyes. She knows what he says is true. He has responded to mere unexpressed thought before. Throughout the years he has done this: responded with echoes of her deepest fears, fears she never voiced aloud: your parents got a new daughter and don't even think of you anymore, Henry's going to put you on the punishment hook one day and never let you down, you're going to die here.

She blinks the tears away and wipes at her eyes. She stares across the room and into Borden's glistening, rolling tar-pit eyes. His nostrils flare. His big square teeth form the shape of a smile. It is an ugly thing.

'I know everything you're thinking.'

She wipes her eyes again.

'Because you're not real,' she says. 'That's how you can do it. You're not real.'

'You can never leave.'

'You don't want me to leave because if I leave I won't need you anymore.'

'You can never leave.'

'But I don't need you anymore now.'

'You can never leave.'

'You're not *real*.'

'You can never, ever leave, Sarah.'

She closes her eyes and tries to remember when she first saw Borden. It was before she ever came here. It was before she was kidnapped and brought here. She's sure of it. It was at the petting zoo. She was seven years old and she had just lost a tooth and she was with Daddy and Jeffrey and the sun was out and the world was bright and beautiful. A ten-year-old boy with Chuck Taylor basketball shoes and cuffed Levis and a red button-up shirt that he kept tucked in was there. The shirt was rolled up to his elbows and his hands were in his pockets. She fed the last of her carrots to a miniature horse and the boy pulled a hand from his pocket and in his palm was a piece of celery and he handed it to her and said his name was Danny Borden and she said thank you and fed it to the horse. Danny Borden: a normal boy with freckles on his cheeks and brown eyes and bangs cut straight. This Borden is only a Nightmare World copy of him.

Not the real thing. Not real at all.

She looks up at him. He flickers a moment, vanishing from the room like an image on a TV that's losing its signal in a storm, like a light just before it goes out. Then he returns. His eyes roll in their sockets and then lock on her.

'You can never leave,' he says.

'You can't scare me anymore,' she says. 'You're not real.'

Another flicker.

'You can never, ever leave. If you try, I'll tell on you.'

'You can't tell on me. You're just pretend.'

He takes a step toward her, a step out of the shadows. He flickers again and she can see through him. She can see the stack of boxes behind him. Then, once more, he is solid. Except he flickers now and then as he takes another step toward her. He seems to be falling apart. An arm becomes a smear before coming back together. A leg flickers out, then returns.

'You can never—'

'You're not *real*.'

She grabs the plate from the floor and lifts it over her head and throws it across the room. It arcs through the air wobbling like a poorly thrown Frisbee and if he were real it would strike him in the head, right between his eyes, but he is not real, so it flies through him, hits the cardboard boxes stacked against the wall, falls to the concrete, and shatters.

Borden is gone.

After a few minutes she gets to her feet. The concrete is cold beneath them. She walks to where the pieces of shattered plate lie, spread outward from the point of impact. She walks with great deliberation, being very careful about where she sets each foot. She doesn't want to cut herself. Once she is standing among the shards she looks down at them. She will probably get into trouble for breaking the plate.

Don't think about that. Nothing can be done about it, so don't think about it.

One two three four five six seven eight nine ten eleven twelve.

She bends down and picks up the biggest shard of plate. It's about nine inches long and forms a crescent, made mostly of the outer edge of the plate, and ends in a sharp point. It is lined with painted vines and at the tip a blue flower. If she has to she will plant it in Beatrice. But not tonight. She carries it to the back of the stairs. There is a cavity beneath the bottom step filled only with darkness. She sits on her haunches and reaches the shard toward it, to hide it there, but hesitates as she imagines a large claw emerging from the darkness and grabbing her wrist and pulling her bodily into the shadows. That's silly, of course, and impossible. There is nothing in the shadows but more shadows. She knows that. Nothing bigger than a cat could even fit beneath that first step. Even so she simply sets the shard of plate on the concrete and pushes it into the shadows, not allowing her fingers to touch the darkness. She will have to reach into it to get the shard back out, but she'll worry about that then. For now she just wants it hidden and she doesn't think anybody will find it there. Not unless Borden is watching from the shadows.

He's not *real*.

That's right: Borden is not real and she does not have to worry about him.

She is just getting to her feet when the door at the top of the stairs squeaks open and the light comes on. Feeling sick and guilty, caught, she walks around to the front of the stairs and looks up toward the door.

Beatrice stands silent looking at the shattered plate on the floor. Her hair lies flat and dull on her head, framing a sad round face. Her wide-set eyes droop on the outside, her mouth at both corners. It's like invisible hands are pressed against her cheeks and pulling down. Her shoulders are round, dresses always hanging from them lifelessly before catching on her heavy lower body and bulging outward with lumps and ripples, making her look to Maggie like a poorly stuffed toy animal.

She turns from the plate and looks at Maggie. Her mouth hangs open for a moment and she breathes heavily from it. Finally she shuts her mouth, swallows, and says, 'What happened?'

'I dropped it,' Maggie says. 'I'm . . . I'm sorry.'

'By accident?'

Maggie nods.

'It don't look dropped.'

'It was.'

'Looks like you thrown it.'

'I didn't. I promise.'

'How'd it get way over there?'

'I'll clean it up.'

'You don't have no shoes. It's not safe. I'll clean it up.'

She turns back to the stairs and walks up them, each plank

sagging beneath her weight. Her thighs brush together beneath her dress, making a swishing sound with each step. It makes Maggie think of her daddy sanding in the garage. She would help him sometimes. She liked the feel of the fine dust from sandpapered wood on her hands. Beatrice pauses at each step, inhale exhale, and goes one more. She walks through the doorway to the kitchen.

Maggie walks to her mattress, away from what she is hiding, and sits.

When Beatrice returns she is carrying a broom and a dust pan with her, and a small plastic grocery bag crumpled in her fist. She walks down the stairs the same way she walked up, one step at a time, standing on each with both feet and taking a breath, inhale exhale, before moving on to the next. She stops at the bottom of the stairs. She breathes heavily and with great effort. Her face is pale and beads of sweat stand out on her oily skin.

Maggie stares at her with great concentration. Please die please die please die.

She hates that she has those thoughts, she feels like a bad person for having them, but she can't help it. She doesn't think she could kill a person—she knows she couldn't; the very idea makes her sick—but if Beatrice were to just die, that would be different. She knows she would feel guilty for thinking it if it happened, but she feels guilty for thinking it when it doesn't happen, so it might as well. It would make her life so much easier.

Part of her feels sorry for Beatrice. Part of her feels that in her own way Beatrice is as trapped as she is. But even so if she would just die all Maggie's problems would be solved. If she died at the right time, anyway, with Henry gone for work and the door unlocked. If he was home and Beatrice died he might take it out on her. He certainly wouldn't have any reason to keep her alive.

'Oh, Lord,' Beatrice says, large chest rising and falling, rising and falling.

'Are you okay?'

After a while Beatrice nods. 'Yeah.'

Too bad, Maggie thinks, hating the thought.

Then Beatrice walks to the shattered plate and bends down and sweeps the shards of glass into the dust pan. She dumps the contents of the pan into the plastic bag she brought with her, sweeps the floor once more, dumps the pan once more, ties off the bag, and stands.

She did not notice that a large piece of the plate was missing.

'You need to be careful about walking barefooted over here.'

'Maybe I could get some shoes.'

'What for?'

'So I don't cut my foot.'

'Henry says no shoes.'

'Okay.'

Beatrice stares at her a blank moment, then frowns. 'Did he hurt you bad yesterday?'

Maggie rubs at the thin scabs that have wrapped themselves around her wrists. They're only about the width of a man's pinky finger, but the wounds are deep, and tender purple bruises surround them. She thinks of the slaps across the face and tongues the split in her lip. She remembers the punch to the gut, the air rushing out of her, the feeling of drowning. And the fear: this time she might really die.

She nods.

'I'm sorry,' Beatrice says. 'I don't like it when he does that.'

'He's never going to stop.'

'He don't mean to hurt you. He's just got a temper.'

'He might kill me.'

'He wouldn't do nothing like that.' She purses her lips a moment, thinking. 'Not on purpose.'

'He might on accident.'

Beatrice exhales through her nostrils but says nothing.

'You could . . . you could let me go.'

'Sarah, you know we can't do that.'

'He couldn't hurt me if you let me go. I wouldn't tell anyone what happened. I wouldn't tell anyone where I'd been.'

'You don't understand the world yet. It's meaner out there than Henry could ever be, I promise you that. I know it.'

'But I don't want you to keep me here.'

'Oh, Sarah. How many times do we have to have this conversation?'

Maggie looks down at her lap, at her hands clasped there, at the brown scabs wrapped around her wrists just below them.

'Sarah?'

'Not too many more, I guess,' she says without looking up.

'Good. And don't worry about the plate. I won't tell Henry you broke it. It'll be our secret.'

Beatrice makes her way up the stairs and they protest under her weight.

Fall down and die, just fall down and die.

Beatrice reaches the top of the stairs. The overhead light goes out. A moment later the door closes, cutting off the light from the kitchen, and the deadbolt slides home.

After a while Maggie's eyes adjust to the darkness. She sits doing nothing for some time.

Then she gets to her feet and walks to the back of the stairs and looks into the shadows beneath the bottom step. She wants to hold the shard of plate again. Her stomach feels tight at the thought of reaching into the shadows. She can see one corner of it. She reaches down and quickly puts her hand upon it and slides it out of the shadows. Nothing grabs her wrist or brushes against the back of her hand or nibbles at her fingertips. She picks up the shard of plate. She holds it in her fist and imagines burying it in Beatrice's arm or leg or neck. It makes her sick to think about. It makes her sick, but she'll do it. Maybe not in the neck. She knows there are important arteries there and a person can die. She doesn't want to kill Beatrice. She just wants her hurt bad enough that she can't chase after her when she runs. If Beatrice were to die on her own Maggie would not shed a tear, but she cannot kill the woman. But stabbing her in the arm or the leg, causing enough pain that she couldn't chase Maggie up the stairs and out the front door, so she couldn't get upstairs and call Henry on the telephone, Maggie could do that. If it meant getting away she could do that.

She puts her thumb against the tip of the shard. It is very sharp, as is the inside edge. Too sharp to simply hold and attack with. She would cut her own hand to pieces. And she doesn't want to have to get too close to use it. She needs to make a handle.

She scans the basement's dark corners for something to use. There's her mattress piled with blankets, the cardboard box in which she keeps her few dresses and some books that Donald snuck down here for her (she has read them all at least three times), the sink at which she washes herself, the toilet plunger on the floor beside it for when it gets clogged, the boxes of Christmas ornaments and rags and dirty magazines and cowboy novels. She has read all of the cowboy novels, she likes that the good guy always wins, and flipped through the magazines. The magazines sometimes have good things to read between the dirty pictures.

She walks to the sink and picks up the toilet plunger and tries to pull out the handle. That doesn't work, it won't budge, so she tries to unscrew it, first one way, then the other, and that does work. After four counter-clockwise turns the handle is free of the black rubber suction cup. Hopefully the sink doesn't get clogged between now and her escape. If it does Henry will notice that the handle is missing and know she's up to something. He'll suspect it, anyway, and that will be enough. He'll be mad. He'll stand looking at her as his face goes red and his hands open and close, open and close, open and close. His nostrils will flare in his diseased nose. He'll reach into his pocket and pull out a roll of those things he eats and thumb one into his mouth and chew. He'll ask her what she's up to and no matter what she says he will call her a liar. Finally, once he's worked himself up enough, he'll come after her. She'll run, but he will catch up. He'll knock her down and kick her in the gut. All the air will rush out of her. She'll look up at his red face, and then he'll kick again. Darkness will come then. When she wakes up she will be hanging from the punishment hook. Her wrists will be bleeding. He will have found her weapon and he will walk toward her with it in his hand. He'll grin as he walks toward her. There will be no humor in his grin.

One two three four five six seven eight. She used to try counting down, so she could deal with large numbers right away, numbers that filled her head, but counting down made her feel that when she was finished something terrible would happen. Five . . . four . . . three . . . two . . .

She opens a box of rags and pulls out a yellowed and torn T-shirt. It smells like Henry, a peculiar combination of garlic and sweat and beer and bleach. Just the stink of him causes her chest to go tight, makes it difficult to draw in breath. Her mouth is dry.

With some effort she manages to tear the shirt into strips. She has to use her teeth to get the strips started, and it hurts her teeth and gums, and the cloth comes away from her mouth pink with blood and saliva, but once she gets the shreds started the fabric rips easily. After she has several strips of fabric ready she uses them to tie the shard of plate to the toilet plunger handle. She has to tie several knots and wrap one of the strips tightly around the handle just beneath the blade, putting an X around its base, to keep it from sliding down, but once she's done with it the blade is in place securely and hardly wiggles at all. She's pretty sure the glass would break before it came loose from the handle.

Now: how will she do this?

She closes her eyes and tries to picture it happening. She imagines several scenarios. In all of them there is blood.

After a few minutes she opens her eyes. Tomorrow night after Henry has left for work she will wait under the stairs for Beatrice to bring down her dinner. Henry will have been gone at least an hour by then. There will be a much better chance of things going her way if he is miles and miles away. She will wait under the stairs for Beatrice with the home-made knife in her hand. If Donald comes over to eat as he sometimes does, rather than simply picking up a plate to take back to his mobile home parked behind the house, she will wait till the night after tomorrow. But if things are as they usually are, if she and Beatrice are home alone tomorrow night, she will wait under the stairs with the home-made knife in her hand and when Beatrice walks down them she will thrust the blade between the steps. She will slice Beatrice's ankles. Beatrice will fall down the stairs. She will scream but the walls are concrete: no one will hear. She will scream and fall down the stairs, and at the bottom of the stairs she will hit her head on the concrete floor. She will be knocked unconscious. Then Maggie will simply run up the stairs and out the front door. She will run through the woods to the street. She will run down the street to the phone. She will call her daddy and her daddy will come and pick her up and take her home. He will let her sleep in his arms. She will be safe.

If Donald is here she will wait till the night after tomorrow—she does not want to have to confront him if she doesn't have to—but no longer than that. She cannot stand to wait longer than that. She has to get out. She would do it tonight if she could, but can hear Donald upstairs already. She can hear him laughing at something on TV. But that means he'll almost certainly not come over tomorrow night. It is a rare night when he eats dinner here.

She can do this.

Tomorrow night she will feel her daddy's arms wrapped around her.

And she will not feel afraid.

Henry pushes his way into the second-floor ladies' room, leaving the cart in the doorway. He pulls a pair of yellow rubber gloves from the back pocket of his dirty Levis and slips his hands into them. The insides are still wet with sweat from the last time he wore them and slick, so his hands slide right in. He flexes his fingers within them, then pushes into the first toilet stall, its brown-painted metal door swinging open and hitting the inside wall.

Bracketed inside each stall is a stainless steel receptacle for tampons and sanitary napkins. He pulls this one from its bracket and walks it to his cart and turns it upside down over the trash can and shakes. He glances inside. Bloody pads stick to the stainless steel walls. He bangs it against the inside of the trash can. He hates the smell of this part of the job: a musty stink of curdled blood and pussy. He glances inside the receptacle. One blood-streaked pad still sticking to the bottom. He reaches in and pinches it between two gloved fingers, index and middle, and pulls it out and drops it into the trash can.

Then back to the toilet stall and sliding the receptacle into place.

It is strange to him to be doing this. He remembers when this college wasn't even here. When he was a boy this was just trees and weeds and mustang grapevines and blackberry bushes. He remembers climbing the vines. They grew so thick they weaved themselves into baskets and sagged between the branches of the hickory and oak trees. He would climb in those baskets of vines and lie in them like hammocks.

It is strange how a town can grow up around a person. You're standing still but all around you the world is moving, and one day you look up from your tiny piece of it and you're lost: all the landmarks you used to know are gone, replaced by new landmarks that might mean something to someone but mean nothing to you. The woods in which you played as a boy were cut down for cordwood and have been smoke in the wind for decades, replaced by a city college you're now expected to clean.

And when you look in the mirror you don't even recognize the face looking back at you. Who is that old man with his fat, fleshy face, with eyes like unpolished wood buttons, with a mouth like an angry scribble? Some stranger, surely. No one you've ever met before.

There was a story in the *Tonkawa County Democrat* this morning about a girl who was kidnapped seven years ago, about a girl who made a single phone call only to vanish once more into the ether, and in that story there was a description of her kidnapper, and that description could easily be of the man you daily see in the mirror. Maybe they're one and the same. But if they are it can't possibly be you you see. A small, innocent boy who used to climb in trees pretending he was Tarzan could not possibly grow to be a man who kidnapped a seven-year-old girl from her own bedroom in the dead of night, who did that and worse. So why does that man gaze back at you when you look in the mirror?

Why do his memories hold a place in your mind?

The answer is clear: stop lying to yourself, Henry.

Yes: he is that man. If it weren't for Beatrice he wouldn't be. But if it weren't for Beatrice he wouldn't be anything. He'd have killed himself long ago. He'd have drowned in his own vomit in the dirt parking lot outside O'Connell's or the paved one outside Roberta's. He'd have drunkenly driven himself into a tree. He'd have accidentally shot himself in the face. She is the only person who made him believe he might have something to offer someone. Despite the fact he's not the sharpest axe in the shed, despite his temper, despite occasional trips to the county jail for public drunkenness or a fight (when drinking or incredibly angry he sometimes forgets his boy-howdy smile and back-patting personality; he forgets to keep what he really is locked in a room in the back of the house). She has stood by him. Unlike his momma who always told him he was just like his daddy, a useless hunk of no good who couldn't find his ass with both hands free. Probably gonna grow up to be a drunkard whoremonger too.

Beatrice has always stood by him. Always. So how can he be a bad man for standing by her too? He just did what he had to to keep Bee happy.

Newspapers don't understand those kinds of things. They describe everything as black and white: they have to have a villain. But he just did what any loving husband would do. Newspapers don't understand that nor mirrors.

Henry sprays the toilet down and then wipes it off with a thick blue paper towel. When he's done with it he walks to the next stall and gets to work cleaning that one.

Ian does not drive straight home after work. Instead of taking Crouch Avenue down to Crockett, he cuts south at Wallace, drives past the U-Haul rental place, and pulls into the dirt parking lot in front of Paulson's Feed Store. He could lose his job for doing what he's about to do, but somehow he doesn't care. He cannot let Andy continue to hold Genevieve and Thalia hostage in that house. It isn't right. He has to do something.

He pushes open his car door and walks across the dirt to the front door, and then through it. The feed store is filled with the dusty but not unpleasant smell of feed pellets and hay. Andy is nowhere to be seen. The place seems abandoned. It is silent and still. Then the sound of movement from behind the store.

Ian walks through the place and into the shed area out back.

Andy is there with hooks in his hands, loading three bales of hay into the back of Vicki Dodd's old Chevy pickup truck. When he is done, he throws the hooks onto a stack of hay bales and slaps the back of the truck two times. 'See you next week,' he says.

Vicki's liver-spotted hand pops out the window, her truck starts, and then she's gone, leaving Ian and Andy alone.

Andy turns to him and smiles. 'Ian,' he says. 'What can I do you for?'

'We need to talk.'

'What's going on?'

'It's about Genevieve.'

'Aw, hell, Ian, I feel awful sorry about that. I swear it'll—'

But Ian doesn't let him finish. He rushes Andy and grabs him by the throat with his left hand, drawing his SIG with his right. He slams Andy against the sheet-metal wall, which sends a noise like thunder through the entire place, and puts the gun to Andy's temple.

'You're goddamn right it'll never happen again.'

'What the hell are you doing?'

'I'm telling you, you dumb son of a bitch, that if you so much as touch a hair on Genevieve's head again, I'll kill you. You got me?'

'She was trying to leave. She was gonna take Thalia. You of all people must understand that. She's all I got and she was—'

Ian slams the butt of his gun against Andy's temple. Andy lets out a grunt of pain, and his knees buckle. Ian continues to hold him up by his throat. After a few choking gasps, Andy manages to get his feet back under him.

'Hurts, doesn't it?'

'Listen, Ian—'

'Shhh. I don't care. She tries to leave again, you just let her leave. If she stays you'll ruin that little girl. She'll end up with some fuck-up like you. You love her, you let her out of your grip. You understand that?'

'I'm trying not—'

'There's no trying here, Andy. I'll kill you if you touch Genevieve again. I will kill you dead and put you where no one will ever find the body. Do you believe me?'

Andy nods.

'I want you to say it.'

'I believe you.'

'Good.' And it is good, because though Ian only came here to frighten Andy, he finds that he is telling the truth. He has it in him to do what he is threatening. He could pull the trigger and simply be done with it. But he does not. He reholsters his weapon and takes a step back.

'See you around,' he says.

When he gets home, he pulls out the phone book and sets it on his lap, flipping through it till he finds PAULSON, A. & G. He dials the number and waits. Genevieve picks up after four rings, and a tentative 'Hello?' escapes her mouth.

'Genevieve,' he says. 'It's Ian Hunt.'

'Ian . . . ? Oh, hi, did . . . did something happen to Andy?'

Ian might be mistaken, but he believes he hears hope in her voice.

'No,' Ian says. 'But I wanted you to know that if you should decide to leave, he won't try and stop you. We had us a serious talk, and he knows better now than to do again what he did this morning.'

With a saucepan in hand, he walks to the couch and sits down. He sets the pan on the table and stirs the ramen noodles inside before forking a dripping mass of them into his mouth. Then he grabs the files the sheriff's department photocopied for him and sets them in his lap. He flips one open. Jamie Donovan was kidnapped from the bedroom of her home in Mencken in 2002. She was eleven. Her body was found in a ditch four days after she went missing. It had been posthumously sodomized and mutilated. There is a picture of her in the file, a color photocopy on a letter-size sheet of paper. Brunette. Sad brown eyes. Something timid in the way she held herself.

His cell phone rings. His first thought is that it's Jeffrey. He drops the fork into the pan and picks up his phone. He glances at the number. It isn't Jeffrey.

'Hello.'

'Ian.'

'Deb.'

'How are you?'

Ian scratches his face. His beard is growing in. It itches. 'I don't have any updates on Maggie. I'm sorry.'

'I know.'

'You do?'

'Bill.'

'Right. I guess he'd know.'

'Yeah.'

'So why are you calling?'

Debbie doesn't answer for a long time, though Ian can hear her breathing.

After a while Ian says, 'Are you and Bill fighting?'

'No, it's not that. Maybe I shouldn't've called.'

'It's okay. I'm not busy.'

'You never stopped believing she was alive, did you?'

'I never stopped hoping she was alive.'

'You never doubted?'

'Of course I did.'

'But you never gave up hope.'

'No.' Ian grabs a bottle of Guinness from the coffee table and takes a swallow.

'How did you . . .' More silence. Then: 'I saw the way you looked at me yesterday.'

'How did I look at you?'

'Like you wanted to strangle me. Like you hated me.'

'I didn't mean—'

'I guess I deserved it.'

'You didn't. You have a life—a new husband, the twins—and you have every right to want to live it. I shouldn't blame you for that.'

'But how did you—'

'Because it's all I have.' He looks down at Jamie Donovan's picture, and then closes the file on it. The image is still in his mind. He takes another swallow of his Guinness. The mental image changes. Maggie. She smiles at him. Then she looks over her shoulder. A man appears behind her. He is out of focus, so Ian cannot identify him. His face a blur, as if smudged out with a wet eraser. Maggie screams and turns back to look at him. 'Help me,' she says. 'Daddy, please.'

'I don't understand,' Debbie says.

'"Now I am dead you sing to me."'

'What?'

'Nothing. What else do I have, Deb?'

'Are you drunk?'

'I don't get drunk anymore.'

'You quit drinking?'

'No. I just don't get drunk.'

Debbie is silent for a long time. Then: 'Do you think if what happened with Maggie didn't, hadn't, do you think we would have made it? You and me, I mean.'

'No.'

'Why not? We were good for a long time.'

'Because something else would have happened. That's life. One thing happens, then another thing happens, then another thing happens. Only looking back can you try to make sense

117

of it. So something would have happened and we'd still have separated, and we'd still be where we are now, or somewhere like it, wondering what the fuck happened to us. Life happened. It happens to everyone. The lucky ones, anyway.'

Not even breathing from the other end of the line: silence.

'Deb?'

'I'm glad she's alive, you know.'

'I know. You just wanted an answer and you gave yourself one. The only answer that made any sense, really. Ninety-nine times out of a hundred you would have been right. Seven days later it would have made sense to assume the worst. Seven years later it would have been insane to think anything else.'

'Really?'

'Really.'

She sniffles on the other end of the line. 'Have you told Jeffrey?' she says.

'No.'

'You should. He feels responsible, you know.'

'I know, but I don't know if he wants to hear from me.'

'I don't either,' Debbie says, 'but he needs to know and you need to tell him.'

'I still love you, you know.'

'But life happens.'

'Right.'

'Okay, Ian.'

'Okay,' he says, then hangs up the phone. He opens the next file.

THREE

Ian makes a right onto Crockett Street and heads north toward work. As he drives he passes the Skating Palace, Bulls Mouth Theater (where they play whatever was on most screens six months ago, the scratched film rolling through a projector that runs louder than the sound system), Wok House, Morton's Steakhouse, a Dairy Queen, and several other places.

He makes a left onto Crouch Avenue and drives past Interstate 10, Bulls Mouth Baptist Church, the petting zoo, and is rounding the bend that borders the north side of the Dean woods when he sees a police cruiser up ahead. It's rolling in the opposite direction, headed toward him. Its horn honks and the driver's side window comes down. The two cars stop side by side and Diego nods at him.

A dachshund barks from the back seat.

Ian nods toward it. 'What'd he do?'

'Tried to rob Sally's Gun & Rifle.'

'Then he deserved to get caught. Nobody with half a brain fucks with Sally.'

'Not if they want to keep their nuts.'

'How much you make so far?'

'Seventy.'

'How many dogs still loose?'

'Three or four, I think.'

'I hope you're reporting all this to the IRS.'

'It's not income. It's beer money.'

'You haven't bought a drink in five years.'

'Four. And that's just for myself. I still buy for my friends. If you ever stopped into Roberta's you'd know that.'

'I don't get drunk anymore.'

'You buy a six pack every day from Bill's.'

'Six doesn't get me drunk.'

'So have six at Roberta's.'

'With that markup?'

'I said I'd buy.'

'Maybe.'

'You hear about Genevieve?'

'What about her?'

'She finally left.'

'Yeah?' Ian says. 'Good for her.'

'Weird thing, though. When Andy showed up at Roberta's last night, left side of his face was cut and bruised. Refused to talk about it.'

'That is weird,' Ian says.

'It reminded me of what you said about maybe someone should do more than talk to him.'

'I don't remember saying that.'

'Are you—' Diego licks his lips—'are you all right, Ian?'

Ian looks at his watch. 'I better get to work,' he says. 'Don't wanna be late.'

'Ian—'

He rolls up his window, puts the Mustang into gear, and gets the car moving. He glances in his rearview mirror and sees Diego's car still stopped in the street, taillights glowing red.

In another seven minutes he pulls into work.

At three o'clock he steps outside for no other reason than he wants a few minutes away from his desk. He reaches into his car and pulls a plug of cigar from the ashtray and lights it with a match, exhaling a cloud of blue smoke from the corner of his mouth. He squints at the horizon. Probably should get a bite to eat. Maybe he'll see what's floating around the fridge when he heads back in. Pretty good chance he left a carton of General Tso's chicken in there on Monday, and if no one else got to it—a possibility with these barbarians—he'll have that.

While he's out here he should make a call. He should make two calls, one leading directly to the other. Personal calls it would be better not to make from the office. He reaches into his pocket and pulls out his cell phone, then scrolls through his contacts till he finds the one he's looking for.

It rings three times, then: 'Hello?'

It's a strange thing: Ian does not miss Lisa, but hearing her voice makes him miss the past, a past in which his future, now past itself, was still ahead of him and filled with possibility. He met her when he was twenty-two.

He'd already been married—and divorced—once, to a girl named Mitsuko he met on a train in Paris. They made eyes at each other while they shot through the darkness underground, and when the train stopped at rue du Sentier they both got off. Eventually it became obvious they were headed to the same place—Chartier—for dinner. They got a table on the second floor near the stairs and every time a waiter walked by he would have to tuck in his elbow to avoid getting bumped (and it happened often as against the wall opposite was the silverware cart). Ian would have been mad except every time it happened she laughed and said, 'Your face.' He didn't know what was so funny about his face, but her laugh was adorable. Two weeks later Ian's trip was over and, not wanting to separate from Mitsuko just yet, he proposed marriage. She flew to Los Angeles a week after him and they said their I dos at a quick-wedding spot in Torrance. And two months after that they were divorced. Mitsuko finally got the courage to call her parents in Japan and after twenty minutes of crying she said she was flying back home. Ian was eighteen when that happened, and in truth he was relieved. He wasn't nearly as ready for marriage as he'd thought.

But four years later, when he met Lisa on the sand in Venice Beach, he thought he was much older and wiser. He was twenty-two: no kid. She was beautiful and surfed better than half the guys in the water and had a smile that was all tomboy confidence. Looking at her beneath the Los Angeles sun he could imagine a future for himself. Before he even knew her name he could. A happy future with five kids and a house on the beach. His mom still owned Dad's surf shop then (she hadn't sold it to pay for the several cosmetic surgeries she was convinced would land her a new husband), but he ran it, and it seemed that as long as she had enough money to stay in vodka and cigarettes she was okay and happy to let him run it. He would have his house and his five kids and his father's surf shop. The old man was five years dead by then, and it didn't even hurt much to think about anymore. The future was as bright then as it had ever been. Everything seemed lined up in a row as he stood on the sand and watched her come out of the water soaking wet with a board under her arm.

But now the future is past, and in the end he couldn't see it clearly at all; it turned out so different.

'Lisa, it's Ian.'

'Ian! God. Is it 1985 again? Please tell me it's not. I've gotten rid of all my stonewashed jeans.'

'No such luck.'

'I take it from your tone this isn't a nostalgia call.'

'Afraid not. I was hoping you could tell me how to get hold of Jeffrey.'

'Yeah, do you have a pen?'

'I'll remember it.'

The phone rings five times. Ian is about to hang up when the sixth ring is cut off and replaced by a 'Hello?'

Ian licks his lips. His chest feels tight.

'Hello?'

'Jeffrey.'

'Who is this?'

'Jeffrey, it's me.'

Now it's Jeffrey's turn to go silent. Then, finally, 'Dad.'

Ian nods. 'Dad,' he says.

'How'd you get my number?'

'I called your mom.'

'What's going on?'

'I have some news.'

'What is it?'

'It's Maggie.' Jeffrey says nothing, so Ian continues: 'She's alive. I thought you should know.'

Silence from the other end of the phone but for a sound like a desert wind.

'Jeffrey?'

'Alive?'

'We still haven't got her back, but she's alive.'

'Really?'

125

'She got to a phone day before yesterday, called for help. We're working on finding her. But it was her and she's alive.'

'Jesus.'

'I know. Hard to wrap your head around.'

'Yeah.'

'It wasn't your fault, Jeffrey. I know you felt like I blamed you, and I know I've been a crummy dad. I'm sorry for that. But it wasn't your fault.'

Jeffrey does not respond.

'Jeffrey?'

'I'm here.'

'I missed your birthday last month.'

'You've missed a few.'

'I know. I'm sorry. I'd like to—'

'Listen, I'm at work. I should go.'

'You got a job?'

'Of course.'

Of course is right: his son is the same age Ian was when he met Lisa. He had an apartment and worked at his dad's surf shop and had already been married and divorced. He doesn't know why he's surprised to learn that his son is growing up. Part of him expected Jeffrey to stay frozen in time, waiting for Ian to be ready to act once more as a father. But that just isn't the way things work. It never was.

'What do you do?'

'I work on a reality TV show. One of those stupid dating shows. I'm an assistant editor. Mostly I just shuffle footage around on an AVID. But, look, I really don't have time to talk. I'm glad you called and told me about Maggie.'

'Okay,' Ian says. Then: 'Hey, remember that chess game we were playing?'

'Yeah?'

'Queen to b4. I promise to be much quicker about my next move.'

'There is no next move, Dad. I put that game away years ago.' Click.

Ian pulls the phone away from his ear and looks at it. The call's duration is on the screen: 3:53. Less than four minutes.

He should have said different things. He shouldn't have mentioned that goddamn chess game. He should have said different things.

He drops his cigar to the ground and snuffs it out with the heel of a shoe. He pockets his phone and heads back inside, straight to his desk. He's decided not to have lunch after all.

Maggie walks around to the back of the stairs. She sits on her haunches and looks at the darkness beneath the bottom step. She doesn't want to reach in there. She is afraid to reach in there. She swallows and sticks her hand into the shadows. But she does not find the hand-made weapon. Her fingers brush cold concrete, nothing more. Her first thought is that Borden must have taken it. He must have taken it and hidden it from her or destroyed it or showed it to Henry who will now punish her with it. He's going to make sure she is forever trapped in the Nightmare World, stuck here with him and the damp shadows that lay themselves over everything.

But then she remembers that Borden is not real. He is not real. He is made up, and things that are made up cannot hurt you. Not unless you let them.

But maybe Henry took it.

Maybe he knew she was up to something and came down here last night and took it. He could even now have plans to punish her. He could come down here and tie her wrists with that bloody yellow rope and hang her from the punishment hook and drag the sharp edge of that shard of plate across her softest parts, across the flesh of her stomach and throat and—

One two three four five six seven eight.

Calm down. It has to be here.

Nobody came down here last night. She would have woken

up. No one came down here last night and no one took her weapon, so it has to be here.

Her fingers brush across the wooden handle. She wraps them around it and pulls it from the shadows. She gets to her feet.

It feels good in her grip. Good and solid and dangerous.

Looking out the window she sees that the sun has already moved to the other side of the house. The shadows have begun to lay themselves out on the ground like picnic blankets. Midday has come and now it is leaving. It has begun its retreat. Before, she had always dreaded the sun passing to the other side of the world. All she knows is what she can see through the basement's sole window and she has always wanted it lighted. But now she is anticipating the night. The sinking of the sun. The sound of the front door closing with Henry on the other side. His truck's engine rumbling to life. The sound of its tires crunching on the gravel driveway and that sound fading.

She has not seen Donald's El Camino pull to a stop in front of his mobile home yet, which means it's still early, but the time has to be approaching. In another hour, maybe two or three, but surely no more than that. Then she will find out whether Donald will be eating with Beatrice or alone. Usually he eats alone in his mobile home and Beatrice eats alone here, or eats at the card table down here with Maggie, and Maggie is counting on the same tonight. She doesn't want to have to wait another day to make her escape. She wants out of here.

Now that she has tasted the air outside she cannot stand the claustrophobic prison of the Nightmare World.

She is counting on it: her escape will be tonight.

Donald will drive up to his mobile home and disappear inside. He will do whatever he does in there for several hours before coming over for a plate of food, and by then Maggie will already be gone. Beatrice will have come downstairs with a plate for her and Maggie will have been waiting beneath the stairs. By the time Donald comes over Beatrice will be lying on the concrete floor in the basement in a pool of her own blood and Maggie will be in the arms of her daddy.

She looks outside at the shadows. It's only mid-afternoon but evening is coming.

And with it, escape.

Gripping the weapon in her hand, Maggie nods to herself.

Soon.

Diego drives north on Main Street. He's on his way to the library on the corner of Wallace and Overhill. The librarian, Georgia Simpson, is having some trouble with Fred Paulson's kid. Junior's apparently passed out drunk in the children's section and Georgia doesn't want to go anywhere near him. He's got puke on his boots and down the front of his shirt. Diego doesn't blame her for wanting nothing to do with him. He's dreading having to deal with the little shit himself. He's so useless his own dad won't hire him, so Junior simply wanders around getting drunk and causing trouble.

Diego's just passing the summer-abandoned high school when a dog, one of Pastor Warden's dachshunds, runs out of the woods to his right and into the street.

'Shit.'

Diego stomps the brake and the car screeches to a stop, the rear end sweeping left a quarter turn before the whole thing rocks on its springs and stands still. Diego's heart thumps in his chest and his hands grip the wheel tightly. He swallows and looks to the street in front of him, but the dog is not there. He knows he didn't hit the thing. He'd have felt that.

He looks around for it—catching it in his periphery.

It's now in the school's football field on the west side of the street.

Diego pulls the car to the dirt shoulder of the road, kicking up a cloud of summer dust that hangs in the air a moment before thinning into nonexistence. After a truck rolls by he swings open his door and steps from the car, a greasy paper bag hanging from his fist. In the greasy paper bag, leftover fried chicken he bought from Albertsons yesterday morning. As he jogs into the football field, a sorry thing since last year's chinch-bug infestation, he pulls a piece of chicken from the bag and calls to the dog.

It's halfway across the field, but when Diego calls, it turns and looks at him, deciding whether it's interested, Diego thinks. There is something in its mouth. A bone maybe.

Diego whistles.

'Come on, boy,' he says, sitting on his haunches and holding out the piece of chicken.

The dog walks toward him.

The bone or whatever it is in its mouth is large. Too big to belong to a squirrel or a gopher or a rabbit. But every once in a while someone will hit a deer with their car, and it could be a leg bone from one of those. Not a full-grown one, but still.

Three years ago Carney Dodd, now stuck in a wheelchair as a result of a different accident, slammed his pickup truck into a monster buck must have weighed a quarter ton, and Carney, never one to wear a safety belt, was propelled through the windshield. According to his own version of the story he landed on the asphalt twenty feet away, hitting it face first, and he had the skin missing from the bridge of his nose and his forehead to prove it. As soon as he landed, though, again according to him, he got to his feet and stomped to his truck and pulled out his Remington 1100 and finished the fucking thing off with a deer slug to the face. 'Take that, y'son of a bitch.'

Maybe somebody other than Carney Dodd hit a deer that didn't die immediately, that made it out into the woods before dropping, and maybe this little floppy-eared dachshund found it and decided to take a piece.

That's what Diego thinks at first.

But as the dog approaches a seed of dread sprouts in his belly.

The bone is white and meatless. On one end, a knot. A few black strings, maybe tendons, maybe plant matter, hang there like tassels. On the other end, though, Jesus fuck, a small hand. A small human hand. The ends of the first three fingers are eaten away to the bone, and in fact part of the first finger is gone altogether, but black skin or decomposed muscle, or something, still clings in places to the rest of the hand like a driving glove.

When the dachshund reaches him he grabs it by the scruff of its neck and pulls it to him and pries the jaw open. He doesn't think; he just knows that he must get this small limb out of this dog's mouth. After a moment of prying it falls to the grass. It does not look real lying there on the ground. It cannot be real. Real arms are attached to people. This thing just lies there like a discarded beer bottle after a drunken Friday night.

He picks up the dog and gets to his feet and looks down at the arm on the ground.

It cannot be real, but it is.

The dog struggles against him and tries to nip at his face. Diego pulls his head back just in time, and then carries the dog to his cruiser. He puts it into the back with the windows cracked, and then pops the trunk. He finds a pair of gloves and a large plastic bag, puts on the gloves, and walks back into the field.

He feels strange approaching it. A bodiless arm lying on the football field behind Bulls Mouth High School. He picks it up and puts it into the plastic bag. He has to bend the fingers down to get the bag sealed.

When he returns to his car he sets the bag on the passenger's seat and grabs his radio.

Diego steps into the woods with a roll of yellow tape in his right hand. He feels sick to his stomach. He's been a cop for six years now and this will be his third body. If he can find it. The Deans own a decent chunk of land and there's no telling how deep into it the body might be. Of course, if someone killed a child and simply used the woods as a convenient place to dispose of it it's probably no more than twenty or thirty yards from Main Street, just far enough into the trees that a person could park on the shoulder of the road, carry a corpse and a shovel, and dig a shallow grave without being seen by anyone driving past. People's cars break down all the time. No one would think twice about someone's old banger sitting on the shoulder of the road. Most people probably wouldn't even notice it unless it belonged to someone they knew.

He thinks about how small that arm was. A child's arm. A five- or six- or seven-year-old. And it was just bone but for a few scraps of leathery flesh or muscle. Dead a long time.

Somewhere a mother weeps.

Diego doesn't have children of his own, but he has spent the last four years raising his nephew Elias, now nine. Elias's parents, Diego's baby sister and her husband, died in a car accident that the child survived. Diego and Cordelia are his parents now, and over the last several years Diego's gotten used to that idea. He couldn't imagine how he would feel if Elias went missing and, some time later, someone discovered his dry bones clenched in the jaws of a dog.

He can't imagine.

As he walks through the woods he rips pieces of yellow

tape from the roll in his hand and ties them to tree branches to mark his path. He remembers getting lost in the woods as a boy and being terrified. He was only lost for an hour and a half, an hour and a half of panic before he realized he could hear cars passing by and ran out to the street, but it was the longest ninety minutes of his life.

Even now, twenty yards into the woods, the street has vanished behind him and the light below the canopy is gray save a few blades that have managed to stab their way in between the branches and leaves, and the air is cooler than out on the street by several degrees.

Twigs break beneath his feet. The ground is softer here as well, feet collapsing the composted leaves that cover the earth. He tries to avoid poison oak and ivy as he makes his way deeper into the woods.

Five minutes ago he thought he was on his way to flirt with Georgia Simpson while she shelved Louis L'Amour and Zane Grey novels. Now he is hunting a corpse. It doesn't seem much of a trade off. A lot can happen in five minutes.

He swallows. His heart beats rapidly in his chest. He knows there's no reason for that, but he knows, too, that a man doesn't have much control over his heart.

He tells himself all that was left was the bone. He tells himself there's no chance the person who did the murder, if it was a murder, is still out here. No chance at all.

But still his heart beats rapidly in his chest.

Something scurries past to his left and he spins toward the sound and draws his SIG.

A squirrel disappears behind a tree.

Diego laughs at himself and reholsters his weapon. He continues walking.

But fifty yards or so from the street he stops again.

Something on the ground makes him stop. He looks at it and swallows. A thatch of hair lying amongst the dead leaves. The hair is very dirty, small pieces of leaf and dirt ground into it, and there is a blue barrette clipped onto it, holding it together. A blue barrette with a small piece of cut glass like a jewel glued to its center. The barrette is somehow worse, more affecting, than anything else. The hair is just hair, but the barrette—Diego can imagine a small girl standing before a mirror and clipping it into her hair and smiling at herself and how pretty she looks. The hair is blond. Might once have been, anyway.

He ties a piece of yellow tape around a fallen twig and stabs the twig into the ground near the thatch of hair. Then continues on.

In another fifteen or twenty yards he comes across a black shoe with a silver buckle. Poking from the black shoe is a white sock with a small pink bow sewn to it. The white sock has a hole eaten through it, and at the edges of the hole what might be black blood. Perhaps some insect ate the bloody part of the sock away. Diego picks up the shoe. Within it is a foot. The remains of a foot: nothing but dry bone, the rest long ago eaten by flies and beetles and such. He can easily hold the shoe in the palm of his hand without either end of it touching air. The girl it belonged to could not have been older than two. The girl it belonged to was smaller than the girl or boy whose arm is even now lying bodiless in Diego's police cruiser.

There is more than one body out here. He is sure of it.

He sets the shoe back down and ties yellow tape around a nearby rock.

And continues walking.

A hundred yards into the woods he comes across a piece of tattered, rotting fabric.

And twenty yards beyond that, disturbed ground. The floor of the woods has been uniformly covered in a blanket of decomposing leaves from which small plants are growing—weeds, and mushrooms like boils, and young trees—but here the ground is disturbed, the leaves clawed aside, and it is here that he—

'Oh, fuck.'

It is impossible to tell how many bodies are here, as only parts of them have been uncovered. An arm jutting from the soil here. A foot there. A scrap of yellow fabric. One human eye socket staring out of a white skull, all the soft parts long destroyed by time.

He walks to a tree and leans against it. He stares down at the ground. The ground spins.

After a moment he begins to cordon off the area. It takes him only a minute or two, and when he's done he starts making his way back out to the street, following the yellow flags he left on his way to this bone-scattered nightmare. The boys from the sheriff's department will be arriving soon, and he'll have to lead them to the crime scene.

As he walks he pulls his cell phone from his pocket and dials Ian.

Ian pulls the headset off and gets to his feet. He picks up his cup of cold coffee and takes a swallow, just to wet his suddenly dry mouth. He walks out to the police station proper.

Chief Davis is sitting with the phone to his ear, saying, 'Well, goddamn it, just let her do it then. I don't know why you call and ask if you don't care. All right. Goddamn it. All *right*. I love you too.' He hangs up.

'Chief.'

'Uh?'

'We got a situation, maybe related to my daughter.'

Chief Davis takes off his glasses, cleans them with a Kleenex, and sets them back onto his narrow nose, blinking at Ian.

'What's the situation?'

'Couple corpses in the woods.'

'No shit?'

'None.'

'So Diego found the owner of the arm?'

'Looks like. Plus more.'

'And it might be related to your daughter?'

'Little girls.'

'Diego didn't say one of them might be,' he licks his lips, 'might, uh, be your . . .' Chief Davis lets it trail off and finds a thread on his shirtsleeve that needs to be pulled.

'He doesn't think so.'

'He say why?'

'There's nothing left but bones and a little bit of hair and fabric.'

'But little girls?'

Ian nods.

'Sheriff's boys on the way, yeah?'

'They are. Might even be there. Nance was in town to go over the case with Finch.'

'I should be heading down too. And you wanna go?'

'There might be something there to lead us to Maggie.'

'All right,' Davis says, getting to his feet. 'We'll get Thompson on the phones. You wanna ride with me or take your own car?'

Ian pulls his Mustang to a stop on the side of the road. All he can think is that this might bring him one step closer to finding his daughter. He knows that girls' bodies were found, two at least, and he knows that's sad. But he doesn't feel anything like sadness right now. He doesn't even feel anything that might live on the same street as sadness. Each body was once someone's daughter but none of them is his daughter. His daughter is alive while they are dead. His daughter is alive and he will find her and bring her home safe. If these bodies help to make that happen, then—well, he denies the fleeting thought that these deaths were then worth it. He tries to deny that thought. But even as he shoves it into the darkest corner of his mind, out of the light of conscious thought where he might be shamed by its ugliness, his heart believes it. Every beat speaks the truth of it.

A hundred bodies sacrificed would be worth it, a thousand, if in the end he got his daughter back.

As he and Chief Davis step from their vehicles Ian looks at the line of cars. There are two from the sheriff's department here already. They're parked behind Diego's car, and behind them is Chief Davis's car, behind which Ian's car is parked. Deputy Kurt Oliver, who works out of the Bulls Mouth office, sits on the hood of one of the county vehicles. His eyes are closed and his head is tilted toward the afternoon sun.

Chief Davis says, 'Detective already here?'

Oliver opens his eyes and turns to look at them lazily. 'Yeah,' he says, 'John Nance, down from Mencken—and Bill Finch is here too.'

'Anyone else?'

He shakes his head. 'Sheriff's on his way.'

'Coroner?'

'Not here yet.'

Chief Davis nods. 'Where they all at?'

Oliver nods toward the line of trees. 'Follow the trail of yellow tape. It'll lead to the bodies.'

A dog barks from the back seat of Diego's cruiser.

Chief Davis puts a hand on Ian's shoulder. 'Let's see what we got,' he says, guiding Ian toward the woods.

'Hey, Oliver,' Ian says, 'why don't you drive that dog up to Pastor Warden's place before this heat kills it?'

'What for?'

'I just said, so this fucking heat don't kill it.'

'Why don't you do it?'

'Because I'm going to the crime scene. You're sitting here useless. For fuck's sake, Oliver, get your head out of your ass and drive the goddamn dog up—'

'Pastor Warden'll give you ten bucks if you take that dog to him.'

Deputy Oliver slides off the hood of his car. 'No shit?'

Davis nods.

'Well why the fuck didn't you say so?'

A few minutes later Ian and Chief Davis arrive on the scene. One of the sheriff's detectives, John Nance, has cleared out a large hole, or a few small ones, in which the bones from three bodies are piled. Three female bodies, if the rags hanging on them is any indication. And young. The one that still has hair, just a snatch of it hanging from the bone, has blond hair. They are all in decomposing dresses.

'Not waiting for the coroner or forensics?' Chief Davis says.

'I'm not disturbing nothing. The insects took care of most of this a long time ago. Forensics guys can play with hair and teeth and bloodstains . . . if they ain't too badly degraded.'

'Were they buried all at the same time?' Ian says.

Nance looks over to him. 'That's outside my expertise, but I'd say no.'

Ian nods.

Nance is in his late forties or early fifties, with gray hair and a face like melted wax. When he's standing he looks like pulled taffy sagging under its own weight, shoulders slumped, arms hanging down, cheeks droopy. But he is not standing. He's sitting on his haunches over a row of skeletons and piles of seemingly random belongings: shoes, clothes, toys. The belongings were once in bags, but two of the bags have disintegrated, leaving behind unrecognizable fragments. Nance pulls a dirt-covered hair brush from a pile beside the oldest corpse and lays it down on a sheet of plastic he or Finch spread across the ground to his left. He sets it next to other items he's already pulled from the earth: a bracelet, a pair of empty shoes, a bunch of small dresses, a one-eyed doll.

Bill Finch stands over Nance with a small mini-DV camera and records the process. 'Want me to get some still pictures too?'

'No need yet.'

'Right.'

Diego, who's been standing several feet away rolling a cigarette, tucks the cigarette behind his ear and walks over to Ian.

'They're all too young,' Diego says.

Ian nods. 'I know.'

'But look at them. Maggie was only seven when—'

'But they're not her.'

'No,' Diego agrees. 'They're not. You should come look at the clothes. Some of the stuff that was buried looks the wrong size for any of these three. I think maybe the killer came back out here and buried some of her stuff.'

'Yeah?'

Diego nods.

'Why would he do that?'

'I dunno. People do weird things.'

'You think some of it might have been Maggie's?'

'Maybe.'

Ian walks around to where the plastic's been laid out, to where various dirt-covered items lie, looking like the results of an archeological dig: this is what the late twentieth and early twenty-first century will look like to the aliens when they finally arrive and find human civilization beneath a pile of ash. Ian silently scans the items, looking from one to the next. A strange numbness at his core as if his middle had been hollowed out and replaced by stone.

'That's my daughter's.'

He points to a pink nightgown folded into quarters and covered in dirt and leaves. There are a few drops of what looks like blood near the collar. She was hurt.

Nance looks up from the hole. 'Your daughter's?'

Bill Finch says, 'That's Ian Hunt.'

'We met once a couple years ago,' Ian says.

'And that's your daughter's?' Nance says, nodding at the nightgown.

'It is.'

'You sure?'

Just after dinner the night Maggie was kidnapped and Ian was sitting at the table going over their taxes. Debbie was in the back getting dressed and Maggie was in the bathroom. She called to him. He walked to the bathroom and pushed open the door and she was standing in the middle of the room, skinny little-girl body dripping water onto the tiles while behind her the bathtub drain made gurgling noises.

'What?'

'I forgot a towel.'

'And?'

'And can you get me one?'

'Can I get you one what?'

'A *towel*.'

'That's not what I meant.'

'Can you get me one, *please*?'

'Can I get you one what, please?'

'*Dad*.'

'Okay.'

He walked to the linen closet and pulled out a towel for her. He tossed it to her.

'And a nightgown.'

'Did you forget to wash, too?'

'*No*. Well.'

'Well?'

'I didn't wash behind one of my ears.'

'Why?'

'Experiment.' She grinned a wide, gap-toothed grin.

'What kind of experiment?'

'Mom said if I didn't wash behind my ears I'd grow broccoli there.'

'She did?'

Maggie nodded.

'But you didn't believe her?'

'I don't know. It's an experiment.'

'But you washed everywhere else?'

'Duh. I'm not gross.'

'Okay. Let me get your nightgown.'

'The pink one!'

Three drops of blood next to the collar like an ellipsis. Covered in dirt and dead leaves. Lying on a sheet of plastic beside things he's never seen before. Things that belonged to other little girls, now dead.

'Yeah,' Ian says. 'I'm sure it's hers.'

'All right,' Nance says. 'If we got someone alive, the daughter of one of our own, your daughter, then I say let's kick this with both feet.'

Chief Davis blinks several times. 'What do you have in mind, detective?'

'Well, I think we should move on the most obvious suspect before he has time to prepare. Ask questions, imply we got more than we do, see how he reacts.'

'The most obvious suspect?'

'Whoever owns this land.'

'Henry Dean,' Ian says.

'We should get Sizemore to approve it, and—'

'I don't work for Sizemore,' Chief Davis says.

'But the sheriff's department handles murder cases because we got the murder police,' Bill Finch says. 'Nance is murder police. This ain't Fred Paulson crashed his car into a tree. It's a multiple homicide.'

Davis squints silently at Finch for a moment, then says, 'Fair enough.'

'So we get the okay from Sizemore,' Nance says, 'and we bring Henry Dean in for questioning, intimidate him as much as we can, see if he cracks.'

'It's close to Main Street, though,' Diego says. 'Anybody could have dumped the bodies.'

'But you don't get nowhere until you pick a destination,' Chief Davis says. 'Can't drive to every place at once.'

'Exactly right,' Nance says.

'I think both departments should be in on this,' Chief Davis says. 'I know Henry Dean, known him since first grade, and I know what buttons to push.'

'First grade?' Nance says.

'Yup.'

'You think he's our guy?'

'Could be.'

'I mean based on his personality.'

'Who knows? In my experience you never know who's capable of what till they gone and done it and you're catching flies in your open mouth.'

Nance nods at that, then turns to Bill Finch. 'Where was the sheriff at last time you—'

'My ears are burning.'

Sheriff Sizemore moves toward them, his big belly swinging in front of him like a wrecking ball.

'Sheriff,' Nance says.

'I want to go to the Dean house,' Ian says as he, Chief Davis, and Bill Finch walk toward the street. Diego stayed behind so he could tell the coroner exactly how he came upon the bodies and give him the legal time of death.

Chief Davis shakes his head. 'No chance, Ian. You're too close to this.'

'It's my daughter.'

'Now, Ian—'

'I'm going,' Ian says.

'There's nothing you can do,' Finch says. 'Sizemore just wants us to bring him to the station so he or Nance can question him.'

'Things might get hairy,' Ian says.

'I'll bring Deputy Oliver.'

'Deputy Oliver couldn't blow his nose with a stick of dynamite. My daughter might be in that house, Finch. You might've got your fingers in every part of my life, but it's still my life. My fucking family.'

'Now hold up,' Finch says. 'I know Maggie might be in there. I know you love her. But look at you, man. You're already worked up and we don't know if he's done a damn thing. You're not going. You'll just cause trouble.'

'You got no authority over my officers, Finch,' Chief Davis says.

'He's an officer on a technicality. He sits at a desk all day. And you said yourself he was too close to this.'

'I did,' Chief Davis says, 'but I can. He works for me. That don't mean I like the guy who weaseled his way into his wife's bed trying to—'

'I didn't weasel my way—'

'Look,' Ian says. 'This isn't up for debate. I'm going.'

They walk out onto the street and into the sunlight.

'Fine,' Chief Davis says, 'but I don't even want you to get out of your car unless we need you. I mean it.'

'Okay,' Ian says, walking toward his Mustang. 'Fair enough.'

His mouth is very dry.

Maggie paces the floor and looks at the ceiling. Strange noises come from above: banging and talking, footsteps back and forth, and things sliding and shifting. The sounds are making her nervous. Usually the only noise from upstairs is the drone of the television—daytime dreaming with eyes wide open. But this is different. She does not like different. She does not want different. It is worrying her.

What's going on up there? Maybe they know her plans and are building some terrible torture device with which to punish her. Maybe they're—

One two three four five six seven eight.

They don't know anything. It is true that they're making strange noises, and it is true that they're talking about something, something that's causing Henry to raise his voice at Beatrice, but she doesn't think it has anything to do with her. When Henry is mad at her she knows it right away. Still: it makes her nervous.

Today is her day for escape and, except for that escape, she wants today to be like every other day. She wants today to be more like every other day than any day has been yet. She wants it to be perfectly normal. Normal is predictable and predictable is what she needs if she's to escape, and she needs to escape: fresh air in her lungs and sunshine on her skin and Daddy's arms wrapped around her.

If strange things are happening upstairs, and they are, that might ruin her plan.

No. It will work out. It has to work out, so it will. That's all there is to it. There's no point in thinking about it not working out.

She walks to the back of the stairs and pulls the weapon from the shadows for the third or fourth time today. She does not hesitate. The thought of staying here even one more day is much worse than anything she can imagine lurking in darkness.

It makes her sick when she thinks of what she plans to do with this weapon in her hand, it makes her stomach feel like rotten milk, but she also wants it done. She wants to be through it and up the stairs and through the front door and standing outside beneath the yellow sun.

She closes her eyes and imagines the sharp edge of the weapon hacking into the flesh of Beatrice's ankle. She imagines seeing beneath the skin, seeing the opening in the skin like a slit in a piece of thick leather, seeing all the organic levers and pulleys that make up the moving parts of a human being, seeing blood pour from within and splash in great red drops on the dirty wooden step before the woman tilts like a great tree felled.

She can do this. She just has to be patient. In another two hours Beatrice will come down here and she will—

A metal thwack as, from the other side of the door, the lock is turned and the deadbolt retracts.

She looks out the window. It is too early for this to be happening. Donald's El Camino has not yet even rolled down the driveway. It is far too early for this to be happening.

Should she do it now, anyway? Should she make her move now or should she wait? Something is happening, something she doesn't understand, and if she waits she might never have another chance. This isn't the way it's supposed to be. This is all wrong. Everything about this is wrong and wrong and wrong.

Borden told. He is real after all and he told. He wants her stuck here in the Nightmare World forever and ever. He wants her to suffer and—

Borden is imaginary. He's not real. He's never been real.

The door at the top of the stairs creaks open and a bulging silhouette fills the doorway. Beatrice. It's Beatrice and she's coming down. She's not carrying a plate. She's not bringing dinner down. Maggie knew she wouldn't be. It's too early for dinner. Henry is still home and the shadows are not yet long, so it's too early for dinner. She can hear his deep voice vibrating through the wood floor and into the basement. There are other voices up there, too. She can feel them but she cannot hear them. But they're there and they vibrate differently than Henry's voice. Something is wrong.

She ducks once more behind the stairs, hiding in the shadows there with the weapon gripped in her now sweating hands. She can't decide what to do. She can't decide whether to put the weapon away or use it. If she doesn't do this now she might not have another chance. There are strange voices upstairs, there was banging earlier, and Henry yelling.

But the plan was to wait for Henry to leave. Another couple hours, no more.

Except Henry may not leave. She has no idea what's going on and she cannot count on things happening like they normally do.

This might be her only chance.

She's not going to wait. When she attacks Beatrice the woman will scream. She'll scream and that will draw Henry. When Henry comes running down to see what happened she'll slice his ankles too. He probably won't be down for good, but that doesn't matter. As long as she has time enough to get upstairs and out the front door that doesn't matter at all.

She can do this.

It can all still be okay.

The stairs creak as Beatrice makes her way down. Her breathing is heavy and somehow thick. Her feet drag across the wooden steps, and the steps sag beneath her weight.

'Sarah?' she says.

Maggie does not answer. She stands in the shadows beneath the stairs gripping the weapon. Her breath is still in her throat: dead air: waiting for what happens next.

Another step down from Beatrice and her right ankle is now in front of Maggie's eyes, visible between two planks of wood. White and soft and easy to reach—easy to cut.

She can do this.

Her heart pounds in her chest.

Her face feels numb.

She can do this. She knows she can. She has to do it, so she *can* do it. That's how it works. She is not too weak for what must be done. She is strong. She is strong and brave. Her daddy said so. Her daddy once told her she was the bravest person he ever met.

Beatrice lifts her left leg to bring it down next to the right.

Maggie lifts the weapon with both hands and hacks at the flesh between the boards, drawing a red line where before was unblemished white skin.

Blood splashes on Maggie's hands and arms. It is hot. Much hotter than she expected it would be.

Beatrice screams.

Back up. Watch the sun rise from the western horizon. See clouds in the bleached denim sky once blown apart by the wind pull themselves together again. Cars reverse down streets. A shattered drinking glass reconstructs itself and flies up from a tile floor and into Roberta Block's right hand and she sets it into a sink full of soapy water and unwashes it. A turkey vulture flies backwards through the sky. Genevieve Paulson sits in bed in her parents' guest bedroom and tears roll up her cheeks and vanish into the corners of her eyes. Her daughter Thalia unsays something that unbreaks her heart and walks backwards out of the bedroom door and down the hallway to where her grandma is unbaking cookies. The hour hands on all the time pieces spin counter-clockwise, pulling their ticks and their tocks back out of the time stream to be spent once more. Now stop.

The same turkey vulture hangs motionless in the sky above the Deans' house just south of Crouch Avenue like it was nailed into the blue.

For a moment everything is very still. Then—after a beat: exhale—time moves forward once more. The turkey vulture flies over the house and toward the woods, trying to catch a scent of death in its nostrils.

And Henry Dean steps through the front door of his house, keys dangling from his index finger. He's out of beer and wants a couple-three more before heading to work. And for work. A good buzz helps the night pass. He walks down the steps and across the gravel driveway to his truck. He yanks open the door and slides the seat of his Levis across the seat of the truck, stopping behind the wheel. He starts the engine and shoves the transmission into first, releases the clutch, and gasses the thing with a booted foot. The tires spit gravel and the truck gets moving.

When he hits the street he makes a left, and then cracks the window to get a breeze in the cab of this Ford-brand oven. But he doesn't turn on the air conditioner. Henry refuses to use an air conditioner. People managed for thousands of years without them and he'll be damned if he's gonna prove frail and womanish by using one hisself.

Sweat trickles down his forehead, catches on a thick gray eyebrow, and holds there a moment before rolling along the arc of hair and running down the side of his face. He smears it away with his palm, pushing it into his retreating hairline.

Then he turns left on Main Street and heads toward Bill's Liquor.

Some ways down, through heat fumes rising from the cracked asphalt, he sees several cars parked on the shoulder of the road up ahead and pulls his foot off the gas.

'What the hell?'

He downshifts to third, then second, then first as he approaches. Two cars from the Tonkawa County Sheriff's Department and one from the Bulls Mouth Police Department. A sheriff's deputy is sitting on the hood of one of the county cars, staring at nothing in particular and smoking a cigarette.

Henry brings his truck to a stop and rolls down his window.

'Hey, dep,' he says, 'how the hell are you?'

153

'All right, Henry. How you doing?'

'Can't complain.' He smiles. 'Hot, though, ain't it?'

'Shit yeah, man. Hotter'n a pussycat in a pepper patch.'

'What's with all the police?'

The deputy glances over his shoulder, sees nothing of concern, and leans toward Henry conspiratorially.

'You really wanna know?'

'No, I ast 'cause I wanted you to lie to me.'

'Bodies.'

Henry's face goes numb. He tries not to show it.

'Bodies?'

'Little girls. Two or three of 'em buried in the woods.'

'No shit?'

'None.'

Henry forces a surprised whistle and the shake of a head. 'Well, I'll be goddamned.'

'Indeed.'

'What kind of bastard would go and kill little girls?'

'The sick kind. Probably raped 'em first.'

Henry feels his face go hot, feels anger clamp down on his chest like a pair of channel-lock pliers. He's no rapist. He's a family man. He loves his wife and would never cheat on her. Especially not with a rape to no little girls. He feels an urge to reach out his window and grab the deputy by the collar and slam his face against the metal door of the truck. Instead he nods and says, 'Probably did. It's a sick world. I hope you catch the son of a bitch.'

'I'm sure we will,' the deputy says.

'Well, good luck to you,' Henry says, tossing off a sharp salute.

He puts the truck into gear and lets off the clutch and presses the gas and continues south on Main Street. As soon as he knows the deputy can no longer see him the life drains from his face and his friendly expression sags into a dead scowl. The light leaves his eyes and his mouth curls down at the corners.

His mind is a gray fog which no thought can penetrate, which nothing can penetrate but an uncomprehending animal dread. But as he approaches Hackberry Street he sees Chief Davis's car heading toward him, and behind it a red 1965 Mustang, and that clears the fog in a hurry.

They found the bodies. It won't be long before the police figure that two plus two equals four. Even if there's no evidence on the bodies themselves—and his guess is that with all the science they got these days the police will find him all over them—they're on his property. He'll be the first person they question. They may even get a search warrant. Sheriff Sizemore is friendly with some judges that might make it happen in a hurry. If they get a search warrant they'll find Sarah. If they find Sarah it's over.

The little bitch said she'd called her daddy. He hadn't wanted to believe it. It meant his life would shortly be falling apart. Which meant it couldn't be true. Except it was true. It was true and it still is. He doesn't know how she knew about the bodies, but she did, she must have known about them, and—

After the two cars pass by, he makes a u-turn.

The beer is canceled. Work is canceled. His life is canceled.

It's time for a new plan. He drives toward home, toward what has been home for over forty years, and thinks about what he should do. His brother Ron has a place in California, in a practically deserted mining town called Kaiser just other side of the Arizona state line. He and Beatrice and Sarah can go there. They'll hide out there till the heat dies down. He has no doubt that there will be heat. People care about dead little girls. He'll be tried and convicted on the news shows within days. The media need a villain. But they can hide out in Kaiser till the heat dies down, and once it does . . . well, that's where things break down a little bit in his mind.

If the police don't have enough to arrest him he might be able to come back home. His running will be suspicious, but suspicious behavior ain't evidence. It seems more likely, though, that Bulls Mouth is about to become a part of his past. In which case they'll head down to Mexico. It won't be safe to try for Mexico till things quiet down, but once they do quiet down they should be able to make it across the border without too much trouble. Most eyes are usually focused on those trying to enter the United States, not on those trying to leave it. He's not sure how exactly they'll get by in Mexico, but he's sure they will get by. Maybe they can even get a house on the ocean. He's always wanted to see the ocean. Or maybe Canada instead. They speak English there. He can work that out later.

Up ahead Chief Davis's car and the Mustang pull to the shoulder of the road. Henry drives by them a moment later. He maintains his speed despite a great urge to put the gas pedal to the floorboard. He can't act suspicious.

At Crouch Avenue he turns right, and again into his driveway two minutes later. Gravel kicks out from the tires and shotguns against the side of the house as he brings the truck to a stop.

He storms up the wood stairs to the porch, takes two steps across the porch, and pushes his way through the door and into the house.

'Bee!'

'What?'

He walks into the kitchen.

Beatrice stands at the sink, a soapy plate in her hands. She looks at him, her eyes searching his face. 'What is it?'

'Put that down. We gotta get out of here.'

'Get out of here? What are you talking about?'

'I'm talking about we gotta get out of here. Pack some shit. Whatever you want to take with you. Whatever you can get into boxes in the next twenty minutes or so. We're leaving town and my gut says we gotta make it snappy.'

'Leaving town? Why would we leave town?'

'There's some trouble.'

'What kind of trouble? Did we do something wrong?'

'We didn't do nothing wrong, but people will say we did. Pack some shit. We gotta go.'

'Well, how long we going for?'

'Probably forever. Goddamn it, Bee, we don't have time for questions.'

'How are we supposed to pack everything in twenty m—'

'We're not packing everything. Only things we have to take. Now, goddamn it, get your fat ass moving. We don't have time to fuck around. I got no idea when the police will be here, but I fucking know they *will* be. So move.'

Beatrice's chin begins to tremble and her eyes get glossy with tears. A strange, sad squeak escapes her throat.

'I'm sorry. I'm sorry I yelled at you, Bee, but we need to leave. I don't have time to answer a lotta questions. What I need is for you to go to the garage, find some cardboard boxes, and start packing whatever you can think to pack. Can you do that?' He strokes her round smooth cheek with a callused hand. 'Can you do that, Bee?'

She nods.

'Good girl. Now get to it.'

He gives her a quick kiss on the mouth, then turns to the bedroom.

'Bill's Liquor.'

'Donald.'

'Henry. What's up?'

'Me and Bee are leaving town. You might want to do the same, though I don't know for sure if it's necessary for you.'

'What's going on?'

Seventeen minutes later there's a knock at the front door. It came faster than he'd expected. He was hoping to be out of town before this could happen. They shouldn't have tried to pack anything. They should have simply got in the truck and gone. But the idea of leaving behind all those years of life without taking even—

'Henry?'

'I'll get it, Bee!'

'Okay.'

He closes his eyes and exhales and opens his eyes. Then slips a hand between his mattress and box spring and wraps it around a Lupara and pulls it out. He breaks it open and checks both barrels are loaded. They are. He tucks the gun into the back of his Levis, then grabs a few more shells and stuffs them into his pockets. He doesn't think it will come to gunfire, but he's not counting it out only to find hisself with his face in the gravel while some cocksucker from the sheriff's department is slapping cuffs on his wrists and ramming a knee up into his balls. His hope is that it's just Chief Davis come by to let him know what's going on. Sorry to bother you, Henry, how you been? Good to hear it. Just stopping by because, well, have you ever seen anything suspicious out in your woods? Any trespassers or anything? He hopes that will be the beginning and the end of it, but he's not counting on it. As he heads out of the bedroom, he stops at the closet and grabs a .22 rifle from the shelf.

No one ever went into battle with too many weapons.

He walks into the kitchen where Beatrice is packing dishes. He grabs her by the arm and spins her around. A plate slips from her hands. It drops to the floor and shatters.

'Not dishes, Bee. Goddamn it, we don't need to take no fucking dishes.'

'But—'

'Look, just head downstairs till I say so.'

'Oh. Okay.'

'Go.'

'Okay.' She nods at him, looking like she's fighting back tears.

There's another knock at the front door. Buckshot barks at the people on the other side.

'On my way.'

He glances over his shoulder to see Beatrice pulling open the basement door and disappearing behind it.

He nods to himself. Good, she'll be safe down there. He heads to the front door. Buckshot sits staring at it. He barks once. Two human shapes behind the yellow pebbled glass. He leans the .22 against the wall where they won't be able to see it with the door open.

He reaches into his shirt pocket and pulls out a pack of Rolaids and thumbs one of them into his mouth and chews it with his eyes closed. Nothing going on here. Everything is finer than frog hairs. No, sir, I didn't see nothing out of the

159

ordinary, but truth is, I don't really keep too close an eye on that land. Trees don't tend to cause much trouble unless they get a few drinks in 'em, you know, and these ones are twelve-stepping it. Ha-ha.

He tongues chalky powder from a molar.

'It's okay, boy,' he says, petting the dog's head.

A fist rises into the air on the other side of the glass, ready to knock a third time.

He grabs the door handle, thumbs the paddle, and yanks open the door before it can.

Ian sits in his car watching Chief Davis and Bill Finch walk across the gravel driveway to the front door. He wants to be there with them. He wants to look into the man's eyes. If he could look into the man's eyes he would know. Instead he is here in his car. The window's rolled down and a convection-oven wind is blowing against his face. His stomach feels sour and his mouth is dry and his eyes are burning. He pulls a plug of cigar from his ashtray and stabs his mouth with it and chews on it but does not light it.

Chief Davis raises his hand and knocks on the yellow pebbled glass that fills the top half of the front door. The muffled sound of a dog barking.

Ian leans forward, waiting. The door does not move. For a long time it does not move.

'Knock again,' Ian says under his breath.

After a moment Chief Davis raises his hand to do so, but Bill Finch grabs his wrist before the fist can make contact.

'I'm in charge here,' he says.

Chief Davis shrugs and blinks. 'If it makes you feel manly.'

Finch stares at him a long moment. Then turns to the door and knocks himself.

The dog on the other side of the door barks again. Then the sound of a voice from within, though Ian cannot hear the words from this distance. And still the door does not move.

Chief Davis and Bill Finch stand side by side before it, motionless, and wait. And wait.

'Fuck this,' Ian says under his breath. He pulls the wet cigar from his mouth and drops it into the ashtray, then pushes open the car door and steps out onto the driveway. Stones grind beneath his feet and Chief Davis throws him a look that stops him. He remains outside the car, but only stands there with his hand holding his car's open door, neither shutting it and heading toward the front door nor getting back into the vehicle.

Bill Finch is raising his hand to knock again when the door is pulled open.

The dog barks.

'Hush now,' Henry Dean says, petting him.

And there he is. Is he the man who kidnapped Maggie, the man who stole Ian's daughter? Sagging face, bald head, dead eyes like unpolished stones pressed into sucking mud, veined nose bursting forth. Ian can think of at least a dozen times he's seen him around town. They've nodded to one another, maybe even exchanged howdys. It makes him sick to think about. All those times he could have grabbed the man and choked him till he was dead. All those times he was but one violent move from his daughter. Seven years and only this fat old man has stood between them. If he's the one.

As Henry Dean looks at the cops a light enters his eyes and a smile broadens across his face. 'Hey, fellas,' he says. 'What's going on?'

'We need to talk,' Chief Davis says.

Bill Finch glares at Davis a moment, then turns back to Henry Dean. 'It's a serious matter,' he says.

Henry Dean licks his lips. 'Shit.'

'Shit?'

'You know why we're here?'

''Course I know,' Henry says. 'It can only be one thing.'

'And what's that?'

'Someone saw my truck and put two and two together.'

'Your truck?'

'All them scratches.'

'What about them?'

Henry thumbs something into his mouth, a mint or an antacid, and looks at them perplexedly. 'You ain't here 'cause I run into Pastor Warden's fence?'

Chief Davis shakes his head.

Bill Finch says, 'It's a more serious matter than that.'

'Oh. Shit. Forget I said anything, then. What's going on?'

Sweat runs down Ian's face. His hand clenches his car door till the bones ache with the pressure of it.

'Just arrest the motherfucker already,' he says under his breath.

Henry Dean couldn't possibly have heard him, but his eyes dart toward him for a fraction of a second before moving back to the men standing nearest.

'Maybe it would be best if you stepped outside,' Bill Finch says.

'Stepped outside?' Henry says, and laughs. 'What the hell for?'

Chief Davis puts his hand on his service weapon. 'Is there anyone else in the house, Henry?'

'Chief. Todd. We grown up together. What are you doing with your hand on a gun?'

'Answer the question,' Bill Finch says.

'My wife,' Henry says.

'We need you to come down to the station and answer some questions.'

'What about?'

'Step outside.'

The faint sound of a woman screaming.

Both Chief Davis and Bill Finch look past Henry toward the sound of the scream. In that moment Henry Dean produces a weapon from behind him, a sawed-off shotgun, and Bill Finch's chest explodes.

The dog at Henry's side starts barking wildly.

A mist of blood hangs in the air even as the man drops to the weathered porch and rolls down the three steps to the gravel driveway. He lies face up, staring at the wild blue sky.

Chief Davis jumps left, but still catches one from the second barrel. Catches it in the face. There isn't even a scream. There isn't time for one. One second his face is fine, the next it's a mask of blood and musculature, and white teeth and pieces of bone splatter on the driveway behind him in a thick and widening triangle of red liquid like his head is a ketchup packet that's been stomped on.

By the time Ian is once again looking to the doorway Henry Dean has dropped his sawed-off shotgun to the ground and is pulling a rifle from behind the door.

Ian dives behind his car, unlatching his holster and drawing his SIG in one smooth motion. He pokes his head up briefly to get an idea of where he is in relation to Henry Dean and hears a shot explode on the air. It carries death though it sounds no more harmful than someone popping a paper lunch bag. The bullet grazes the trunk lid and chips of gray metal cut into his head and cheek.

The dog continues to bark wildly.

Ian drops to the ground again, gravel digging into his arm and his side, and tries to catch a glimpse of the man from under the car, but the angle is wrong. He can't see anything but more gravel and the base of the house.

'Go get 'im, Buckshot! *Get* 'im!'

Running across gravel. Barking. A brown blur seen from under the car.

Ian turns around in time to see the dog coming around the back of the vehicle with teeth bared, its eyes black, foam hanging from its jaw in frothy strings. It leaps at Ian and Ian has just enough time to pull the gun around toward it and pull the trigger.

There is a brief yelp and then silence.

The dog continues through the air, lifeless, and drops on top of him, its dead open mouth on his throat. Hot spittle runs down his neck. Hot blood soaks into his uniform. He pushes the dog off and it falls to the gravel with a meat-sack thump, wet and viscous, and lies there, still.

'You son of a bitch,' Henry says, and there is another shot. It only kicks up gravel.

Ian pulls himself up into a crouching position, making sure his head is below the level of the trunk. Inhale. Exhale. He'll be on the porch waiting for him. He'll have to get his own shot off quick and drop again if he doesn't want to take one in the face like Chief Davis did. The man is fast. Inhale. Exhale.

He catches his breath in his throat and jumps to his feet, ready to take a shot. But he never has the chance.

Before he even catches sight of the man—standing at the bottom of the steps now, feet distanced, rifle pressed into the crook of his shoulder, left eye closed, aiming at where he rightly reckons Ian will pop up—there is a dull thwack in his chest just to the right of his sternum, like someone thumped him with a rubber mallet. It doesn't even hurt. Not at first. But suddenly he can't breathe. He inhales and hears a strange sucking sound from beneath his shirt. He looks down at himself, confused. A small dot of blood appears on the fabric. He looks up at Henry Dean to ask him just what the hell happened, but the man is heading up the steps and into his house. Ian drops to his knees, both of them popping on impact. Gravel digs into the flesh, and though he is aware of it he hardly feels it at all. He looks down again and sees drops of blood splashing to the gravel.

This isn't how it was supposed to happen.

Then he's face down, sucking in chalky white dust. He spits. Whenever he tries to breathe his chest makes that wheezing noise: a low whistle, like a punctured tire.

Sounds of feet on gravel stepping quick.

Ian rolls onto his side to see what's happening.

Henry Dean is helping his wife Beatrice into a green Ford Ranger pickup truck. That seems like it should be impossible. Henry was just standing on the gravel aiming a gun at him and a curl of white smoke was slipping from its barrel. It doesn't seem like he should have had time to go inside and get his wife and bring her outside and put her into their truck. She is crying and her right foot is covered in blood and a skin flap hangs from her ankle.

Ian blinks.

In the next moment Beatrice is sitting in the truck and the door is shut and Henry Dean is halfway up the steps leading to the house.

What's happened to time? Someone broke time.

I need my gun. I can get him if I can get to my gun.

He rolls in the other direction. It hurts and the sharp points of stones dig into his back. He looks for his gun. There it is, just over three feet away; within reach, if he's lucky. He puts his arm out toward it, fingers stretched. His fingers touch it. He pulls it toward him. Then wraps his hand around it. He rolls back toward the house.

Henry Dean is now dragging Maggie out the front door of the house. She is pale and thin and her nose is bleeding, but it is Maggie. His daughter. She's so grown up. Practically a woman. And that man with his hand clutching her wrist stole her from him and stole her childhood.

Ian raises the gun in his hand.

But Henry Dean sees him and pulls Maggie to him and lifts her and uses her as a shield. She tries to pry his hands away, but cannot manage it. Blood drips from her nose and onto the man's large arms.

'You gonna shoot your own daughter, Hunt?'

Ian tries to aim at the man's legs, to shoot them out from under him, but his hand is too shaky, and he is afraid of hitting Maggie. He would never forgive himself for that.

The man walks toward him, using Maggie as a shield, and once he's close enough, he kicks the gun away.

'Help me, Daddy! Daddy!'

She reaches for him and a bloody snot bubble grows in her left nostril and pops. Tears stream down her face. Her teeth have blood on them.

Ian reaches for her.

'Baby,' he says. 'My Maggie.'

But then a boot swings toward him at great speed, a blur of motion, and kicks him in the face. Hello, darkness.

He comes to to the sound of that punctured-tire wheeze. That strange sound of air leaking from his chest. The pain is greater now, overwhelming. Something in his chest feels closed off. Like a door slammed shut. He cannot seem to breathe.

His eyes are open and staring at the back tire of his car. Rust and splattered mud. And beyond his car is Chief Davis's

167

car. And in Chief Davis's car is a radio. He turns over on all fours. He grabs the rear bumper of his car and pushes himself to his feet. Chief Davis's car is only twenty feet away. If he can get to it everything will be fine. Thompson is working the phones and if he can get to the radio everything will be fine. He takes a step and his knees buckle and he falls. First to his knees, then to his side.

Thompson is working the phones.

He has a phone.

He reaches into his pocket for his cell phone. He can feel it. He doesn't need to get to the car. He can just call nine-one-one. He's never been on this end of an emergency call. If he can get Thompson on the line everything will be okay.

Everything will be fine.

Henry throws Maggie into the truck and gets in after her. She looks through the back window at her daddy. She hasn't seen him in forever and there he is. He's lying on the gravel. He's on his right side and his chest is bleeding and his head is tilted down to the gravel and red blood is flowing from his nose and down his face and his eyes are closed. He isn't moving at all. His right arm is stretched out before him. It's flat on the gravel, palm up. Several feet from it is a gun. Maggie wishes he would pick it up and shoot out one of the truck tires. He could still stop Henry. Unless he's dead. He isn't moving.

'Sit down, you little bitch,' Henry says. He grabs her by the shoulder and shoves her down into a sitting position.

The truck roars around in a half circle, spitting gravel, and heads out of the driveway. Past a man with no face. A policeman with no face. She can tell by the uniform that he's a policeman, but he has no face. And past another policeman whose chest is a red bowl filled with a thick black liquid that can only be blood.

'Henry, I'm bleeding,' Beatrice says.

'I know it, Bee.'

'Why am I bleeding? What happened?'

'Not now.'

'But why am I—'

'Not now. Just hush up. I need to think.'

The truck screeches out to Crouch Avenue, burning black rubber onto the ancient gray asphalt as it hooks right.

'But why am I bleeding?'

'Would you shut the ever-loving fuck up?'

'Oh,' Beatrice says. 'Okay. Sorry.'

She looks out the window.

Maggie looks down at Beatrice's right ankle. It is sliced open and pouring blood. The blood is pooling on the floor-board. It makes Maggie sick to look at, but she can't look away. She almost escaped.

'Fuck,' Henry says.

Maggie looks at him, but he's staring straight ahead.

In another five minutes they're headed west on Interstate 10.

Diego rolls down the driveway, dread heavy upon him. Based on the call Ian made, things went bad, very bad, and he's anticipating some ugliness. But a moment later, as he rounds the last turn in the driveway and is facing it, he knows he wasn't ready for it. He was not at all ready for this kind of ugliness. There's an ambulance on the way, but he radios for a second before he steps from the car.

Chief Davis lies on the blood-soaked gravel with a missing face. The fingers on his left hand twitch spasmodically, but Diego cannot tell whether the man is conscious and trying to accomplish some goal or if the movement is merely the result of his dying brain emitting a last few electric impulses before going silent as stone.

A few feet beyond him lies Bill Finch. He is flat on his back. His chest is concaved and filled with blood, air bubbles rising from within him and popping on the dark surface. His open eyes stare at the blue sky. The wide open blue sky, lighted by a white sun.

He does not move at all.

Nor does Ian, further down the driveway, lying on his back with a cell phone in his hand and a bullet hole in his chest. His eyes are open, red-rimmed slits in a pale face translucent with exhaustion and clenched into a grimace. He is looking at Diego. Beside him, in a pool of blood, lies a dead dog.

'Ian, what the hell happened here?'

'I think they're dead.' Barely a whisper.

'How are you?'

'Not . . . dead.'

Diego nods, then walks toward Chief Davis and looks down at the man. His face ends just below his upper lip in a line of shattered teeth like the serrated edge of a bread knife. Diego could toe the roof of the man's mouth if he wanted to. He does not want to. The skin on the upper part of Chief Davis's face has been wiped off completely, and one eye is gone, replaced by a steak-red hollow, half-filled with black liquid. The other eye, brown and alive with fear and pain, shifts toward Diego, and Diego has to fight the urge to step back from him.

'Ambulance is on the way, Chief.'

A gurgle from the hole at the back of his throat. A slow ooze of blood runs down onto his neck and is soaked up by the collar of his shirt.

'You're not gonna die.'

Another gurgle.

Chief Davis's eye twitches left, toward his hand. His ring finger twitches.

'Betty knows you love her, Chief. I've got to check on the others.'

Diego steps away from him. He walks to Bill Finch, and though he's never liked the man—he stole a friend's wife—he likes the blank stare he's throwing at the sky even less.

Diego leans down.

'Bill?'

Silence. His chest neither rises nor falls. There is no movement in his extremities. No sound escapes his throat. What now lies before Diego is nothing more than a wax replica of a man he once knew.

'Dead?'

Diego nods.

Ian closes his eyes and lets his head rest on the gravel.

'You okay, Ian?'

No response.

Diego turns in a circle, feeling helpless and overwhelmed, and falls to a sitting position in the middle of the driveway as in the distance sirens wail.

Paramedics load Ian and Chief Davis into ambulances and declare William Francis Finch Jr, age forty-two, survived by wife and two children, dead. Diego wonders if he should call Debbie. It might be better to hear it from a friendly voice than from Sheriff Sizemore. The thought of having to put those words into the air makes him sick. Your husband is dead. With four words a world destroyed. And she's already been through so much. He reaches for his cell phone. He has to call her. She'll need a sympathetic ear.

But before he can dial, Henry's brother Donald is coming down the driveway in a primer-gray El Camino with an expressionless expression on his face: blank as unmarked paper. He passes the ambulances as they wail their way out to Crouch Avenue and then the Mencken Regional Medical Center. The car comes to a stop behind Diego's and Donald steps out.

'What the hell—'

Diego walks up to him, grabs him by the arm, and leads him to his car. He yanks open the back door. He shoves Donald toward it. 'Get in.'

'What for?'

'Get in the fucking car.'

'Am I under arrest?'

'Do you want to be?'

Donald looks at him over his shoulder for a moment, tonguing the inside of his cheek. And he must see the scene behind Diego as well: blood and bone splattered across the driveway, several police cars, a covered dead body, a dead dog. And the absences: Henry's truck and the man himself. He must be able to piece at least some of it together. After a moment he nods and steps into the back of the car.

Diego waits till he pulls in his left leg and slams the door shut on him.

'I don't know anything about it.'

'You're lying.'

'I'm not.'

'Are you and your brother close?'

'He's twenty years older than me. Old enough to be my father.'

'That's not an answer.'

'No, we've never been close.'

'But you eat dinner at his house.'

'Sometimes.'

'You eat a lot of dinners with people you don't like?'

'I didn't say I didn't like him. I said we weren't close. And except on weekends he ain't there anyway.'

'But you eat dinner at his house.'

'Yeah, sometimes. I already said I do.'

'Ever notice anything unusual?'

'Unusual like what?'

'Unusual like unusual. Use your brain.'

'Henry and Bee have always been unusual.'

'Like how?'

'I don't know.' Donald scratches at his beard stubble. 'Look, if you're asking if I ever noticed anything criminal, the answer is no. I haven't.'

'Nothing?'

'No.'

'You never suspected they had a third person in their house?'

'I don't know. I guess not.'

'Don't guess.'

'I never thought about it.'

'Well, think about it now.'

'No. I mean, I seen kid stuff around now and then, but I guess I thought it was from their own kid.'

'They had a kid?'

'Died over twelve years ago.'

Diego scratches his cheek. He remembers hearing this story before, maybe at Roberta's, but he's only spoken to Henry half a dozen times over the years, so it didn't mean much to him—till now. 'Boy or girl?'

'Girl.'

'How old was she?'

'Not even one.'

'How'd she die?'

'Drowned in the tub.'

'You only saw kid stuff that could belong to an infant?'

'I don't know.'

'We're searching the house.'

'I know.'

'And if we find stuff all over the house for a teenager we'll know you're lying.'

'I know it. I'm not lying. I never thought about it.'

'You don't do much thinking, do you?'

'I don't know.'

'You don't seem to know much either.'

Donald shrugs and exhales through his nostrils.

'You never heard any noise?'

'Not that I noticed.'

'You really expect me to believe you lived in a trailer not twenty yards from Henry and Beatrice, that you ate dinner there sometimes, and you never had any idea that for seven years they were holding someone captive? That's what you want me to believe?'

'It's the truth.'

'And you don't know where he might be headed?'

'I already told you like an hour ago.'

'And if you told the truth you should be able to remember what you said.'

'I said I didn't know but if I had to guess, Juarez by way of El Paso.'

'Is your brother that fucking stupid?'

'Well, he ain't a Mensa member.'

'But you think he's dumb enough to try to cross a border with every cop in the state looking for him?'

'I don't know. It was just a guess.'

'A pretty shit one. Your brother's not that stupid and you know it.'

A knock at the door, and then it squeaks open.

Diego looks over his shoulder. Sheriff Sizemore pokes his Stetson-topped head into the room. He wipes at his mouth with his palm.

'Officer Diego.'

'It's Officer Peña.'

'Let's talk.'

Diego nods, then gets to his feet and follows the sheriff out into the empty front room of the police station, making sure the door is locked on the younger Dean brother.

'What is it, sheriff?'

'You've been going in circles for over an hour.'

'I know, but he'll slip. I'm wearing him down.'

'Look, this is our case. A county case. You don't have the resources. I agreed to the hour outta courtesy for what happened to Officer Hunt's daughter. For what happened to the chief. I know it means something to you guys. And, yeah, I thought maybe you'd be able to get something we could use. But one of ours got shot too, died, and the fucking hour is up, Officer Diego.'

'Officer Peña. And I just need another thirty minutes.'

'You can't have it.'

'I can't have it?'

'Nope.'

'Well, what the fuck?'

The sheriff shrugs, seeming suddenly bored by the conversation. 'That's just the way it is,' he says. 'I got a manhunt going on and I'm done letting you dance in circles with our only possible source of information.'

Diego watches Sheriff Sizemore lead the younger Dean to the back of his car and put him into it. Then Sizemore looks back at Diego and nods. Diego does not nod back. Sizemore gets into his vehicle and drives way, taking Donald to the sheriff's office down the street.

Diego tries to roll a cigarette, but his hands are shaky. He cannot seem to keep the tobacco in his paper. It shakes from the paper and falls to the asphalt. Finally, after his third try, he balls the rolling paper in his fist and throws it to the ground. He turns around and heads inside.

Didn't really want a cigarette, anyway.

Picture a calm sea of oily black. Horizon to horizon: only this sea, flat and featureless. An entire planet covered in liquid midnight. A moon overhead like a silver dollar, and a few stars, but nothing more. There are no islands or trees. No fish or whales. Just a dead calm. Nothing other than one man floating on his back in the middle of it: Ian. Ian, floating in darkness. Arms and legs spread like the Vitruvian Man. Eyes open. He looks toward the heavens expecting God, but all he gets is the voice of the darkness between the stars: a hollow call like a desert wind.

Then something touches his left hand. Some*one* touches his left hand. It is human. He is not alone. He tries to turn his head to the left but he cannot. Someone is stroking the web between thumb and index finger.

He doesn't understand why he can't turn his head to the left.

Open your eyes.

They are open: the moon like a silver dollar and the points of stars.

Open your eyes.

He does and the night sky gives way to a white ceiling, first out of focus and soft, then gaining sharpness. He blinks several times and turns his head to the left.

Debbie looks up from her lap. Her face is thin. She looks

old, somehow, and tired. He has never thought that of her before, but he thinks it now. She is not wearing makeup and her eyes are red and the skin beneath them is blotchy and dark gray and the corners of her mouth are turned down.

'Hi,' he says, but it is little more than a whisper.

She says nothing at first, just looks at him. She wipes her nose, her red-rimmed nostrils, with the back of her wrist. Finally: 'Bill's dead.'

'I'm sorry.'

Then he coughs, and there is that strange feeling like trying to breathe underwater. He coughs and coughs, and feels like phlegm or something should come up, but nothing does. His muscles tighten as he coughs and pain ripples through his body from the dropped-pebble point where the bullet said hello. He hears a strange liquid sucking sound from beneath a thin blanket which covers his torso. He lifts the blanket. A clear tube, a catheter about as big around as a woman's pinky finger, sutured into his chest just under his armpit. Thread stitched through his flesh and then wrapped around the catheter to hold it into place. The skin pursed around it like lips around a straw, like some strange alien tulip. In the tube, blood and pus combined to form a thick pink liquid. A knot of it flows down the catheter to a small box on the floor with PLEUR-EVAC written on it.

He coughs again, and more liquid flows from his chest and into the tube. It hurts to cough. It hurts even to breathe.

'Jesus,' he says when he gets his breath back.

'You were shot.'

After a moment, after he manages to get his breath back, he says, 'I know.'

'You had a collapsed lung.'

Ian nods.

Debbie frowns and looks down at her lap once more.

'The twins are too young to remember Bill. They'll grow up without any memories of their father to look back on.'

Ian is silent for a long time, lost on a strange raft of wooziness. Then what Deb said registers and he says, 'Maybe— maybe that's for the best. If it had to happen. Maybe you can't miss something you don't remember.'

Debbie shakes her head. 'I don't think it works that way.'

He squeezes Debbie's hand. 'I'm sorry about Bill. He made you happy. You deserve happiness.'

Debbie nods but says nothing. Instead she turns to look at an empty chair in the corner. She looks at it for a long time.

'Did they get him at least? Is Maggie safe?'

Debbie shakes her head.

'Bill's dead, Chief Davis is in critical condition, he has no face, he'll have to eat through a tube for the rest of his life, if he lives, and you're here—yet that son of a bitch still has Maggie. It's not right. It's not fucking—' Her voice chokes off and she looks down at her lap, and her shoulders shake.

'We'll get her back, Deb.'

'How?'

'I don't know, but we will. I'll think of something.'

He squeezes her hand again, but then another coughing fit overwhelms him, sending pain through his body like poison, and more blood and pus drain from his lung and into the catheter flowing from his chest.

'Oh, fuck,' he says. Then, once he's caught his breath, 'I'll think of something. I'll think of something and I'll get her back.'

'Do you really believe that?'

'Yes.'

Debbie nods. 'Then I'll believe it too.'

The sun, partially hidden behind the western horizon (looking to Maggie like a grapefruit-half laid face-down on a table), spills pink light into the evening sky. The Ford Ranger rolls along the road toward it though Maggie knows if that's their destination they'll never make it. This thought reminds her of a conversation she once had with her daddy. She asked him why moths like light bulbs so much and Daddy said they thought light bulbs were the moon, that moths at night used the moon for guidance and flew toward it constantly, though they never reached it, and that they did the same with light bulbs, but once they'd reached the light they had no idea what to do with it. The moon had taught them that they would never have to worry about actually reaching their destination.

'That's kind of sad,' Maggie said.

But Daddy just shrugged and bit the end off a cigar.

Henry glances over her head to Beatrice. 'How you feeling?'

'I'm still bleeding. I feel dizzy. I don't even know how I cut myself. Did you see, Sarah?'

Maggie shakes her head and looks down at the pool of blood on the floorboard. Then she looks to Beatrice's pale and sweaty face. She almost escaped. Beatrice collapsed as Maggie'd imagined she would, dropped like a felled tree, screamed and went down, but Maggie forgot her plan to wait for Henry and tried to run by the woman to get upstairs, and Beatrice reached out and grabbed for her. She grabbed her ankle and said, 'Sarah, what happened?' and Maggie went sprawling forward and hit her face on the third step and felt a strange bending in her nose, and blood flowing down her face. Everything went gray, a gray fog swept in, and by the time it cleared Henry was downstairs, helping Beatrice up the stairs and locking the door behind them as they left the basement. A moment later he came down for her, picked her up, and brought her outside where her daddy lay bloody in the gravel with a hole in his chest.

'Look up yonder,' Henry says.

He points to a small brick house about a quarter mile from the road. A few horses graze on brown grass in the pink evening. The house looks quiet, a single window illuminated. A gray Dodge Ram pickup parked by the side of the house, under a carport made of weather-grayed four-by-fours and plywood. A tire swing dangles still and lonesome from a big oak tree in the front yard.

'We'll stop there,' he says, 'get you fixed up and get rid of this truck. We ain't safe driving it.'

'I still don't understand what happened, Henry.'

'I know it.'

'I don't know why we had to leave the dishes.'

'We're in some trouble with the law, Bee. I explained that already. Hell, you seen—'

'I didn't see anything.'

'You seen the cops in the—'

'I didn't see nothing. I was in a lot of pain, Henry.'

He looks at Beatrice for a long time, an unreadable expression on his face. Maggie has no idea what to make of it. Nor of the conversation itself. Beatrice must have seen the blood, she must have seen the policemen lying motionless in the driveway. You can't not see something like that. Yet she says otherwise.

'How you feeling, Sarah?'

Maggie turns and looks at Beatrice. 'Okay,' she says.

'You know we'll get through this, right? You know we love you?'

Maggie does not respond. She looks up ahead to the house they are quickly approaching. She looks at the light in the window and wonders what kind of people live within it. She imagines a cowboy hat with salt-white sweat stains on it hanging from a rack by the door. A man in dirty coveralls sitting on a couch. A woman mending socks. A baby playing in the middle of the floor wearing nothing but a cloth diaper. She wonders if they'll be able to help her. If Henry stops there maybe she can get help. She can move her mouth silently when Henry's looking the other direction. Help. Me. If she could just get help she would get away.

'You better mind your behavior, too, Sarah, you hear?'

Her face goes hot. She feels as if she has been somehow caught. As if he has read her mind. As if he has shuffled through her thoughts like index cards and spied everything that was written there. As Borden so often did.

But Borden wasn't real and Henry is.

Real enough to shoot her daddy, to leave him bleeding to death in a gravel driveway.

It's her fault. If she hadn't called him none of this would have happened. He wouldn't have come and he wouldn't have gotten shot. None of the policemen she saw would have gotten shot. They'd be eating dinner with their families instead of in the hospital or dead.

'Sarah?'

She looks up at Henry.

'You hear me?'

She nods.

'If we go in there and take care of business and nothing goes wrong, whoever lives in that house will still be alive when we leave. But if you try any funny business, they're dead, and you're not any better off than when they was alive. You hear?'

She nods again.

'Good.'

'You're not really gonna kill nobody, are you, Henry?'

'Quiet, Bee.'

'But Henry.'

'I mean it. Hush up.'

Beatrice looks out her window.

Henry reaches into his pocket and comes out with a kerchief. He spits on it and thrusts it toward Maggie. She takes it hesitantly, not knowing what to do with it. She can smell his spit and it makes her stomach turn.

'Clean your face up,' he says. 'We can't roll in looking like something from a horror movie.'

Henry pulls off Interstate 10 and rolls down a single-lane stretch of gray asphalt. The window is cracked and though evening is coming on quick the air is still unpleasantly hot.

He pulls to a stop in front of the brick house. A gate blocks the driveway. He steps from the truck to swing it open, so he can drive on in, but the gate is padlocked. He walks back to the truck, reaches into the open door, and honks the horn. It sounds very loud in the still evening air. He's unsure about what he will say to whoever's on the other side of that door, especially about what happened to Beatrice, but he'll think of something. He usually does.

He briefly considers tucking the Lupara into the back of his pants, but decides against it. He won't need it. It can stay on the floor of the truck, beneath his seat, for now.

The front door swings open and a man of about thirty-five, fellow looks like a scarecrow in Levis and a T-shirt, comes out to the front porch in his stocking feet. He squints at the drive-way. Henry raises a hand in greeting and smiles. The skinny guy waves back, then grabs his boots from the porch by the door and slips into them, hopping around on one foot then the other as he slides each heel down into place. That done, he walks out to greet his visitors. As he approaches a dart of brown tobacco juice shoots out from between his lips with a sound like a wet fart. The spit hits the dirt in a stream and the dirt absorbs it, forming a hard bead around the liquid.

Henry smiles and holds out his hand above the gate.

'Howdy,' he says.

'Howdy,' the man says and shakes the proffered hand. 'You lost?'

'Not hardly. Just run into a little trouble.'

The skinny guy takes a wary step back and squints at him. 'What kinda trouble?'

'Wife got herself hurt.'

'Yeah?'

'Yeah. We stopped at the side of the road so she could, well, so she could do her business, and she done fell over backwards. I laughed my ass off when I seen it—I know it ain't nice to laugh at a fallen lady, but I done it—but turns out she cut her ankle pretty awful. Don't even know on what. Didn't stay to find out.'

'Cut bad?'

'Uh-huh.'

'All right, come on in.'

He unlocks the gate and lets it swing open on its own. It slides into a well-worn groove in the driveway and stops when it hits the edge of the driveway and the grass grown tall there. Then he walks away from them and toward the house, sparing but a single look at the sun sinking behind the horizon.

Henry wants to tell him to enjoy it; it'll likely be his last.

The skinny man, whose name turns out to be Flint, helps Beatrice inside and kicks a wooden chair out from the dining table and gets her sitting in it. His wife Naomi, a pretty woman in her early- or mid-twenties, paces back and forth wringing her hands and then stops and says, 'What can I do, Flint?'

'Call Doc Peterson.'

'No,' Henry says, maybe a bit too forcefully.

Flint squints at him. 'No?'

'I . . . I'd rather we just take care of it ourselves. Ain't so bad it requires a doctor.'

Flint continues to squint at him for a moment, tongues the wad of tobacco tucked under his lip. He picks up a Coke can from the dining-room table and squirts a stream of brown spit into it. Then wipes at the bit that dribbled onto his chin and sets down the can.

'How'd she really hurt her ankle, friend?'

'Just like I said she did. You calling me a liar?'

'I ain't calling you anything.'

'Sounds like you are.'

'What d'you got against doctors?'

'Can't afford 'em.'

'Peterson's just a vet. Prolly won't cost fifty bucks.'

'If you got some needle and thread I'll just stitch her up myself. Or even a fishhook and some line. Clip the barb off and it'll work fine.'

'I don't know,' Flint says.

'Can you move your ankle, Bee?'

'I think so.'

'Try.'

Beatrice straightens her leg and tries to turn her ankle. She cringes, but she manages some movement as well. 'Yeah,' she says.

'I still think she should see a doctor,' Flint says.

'I appreciate your help and all, Flint, but this ain't a debate.'

Flint scratches his cheek. 'Get my tackle box, Nam.'

Ian puts the off-white telephone into its cradle, letting it simply slip off his fingertips and rattle to a resting position. He feels numb.

'What's wrong?' Debbie says.

He swallows. It hurts to swallow.

'Help me up,' he says. 'I don't have time to lie around.'

'What did Diego say?'

'He said Sheriff Sizemore released Henry Dean's little brother. Didn't find anything incriminated him at Henry's house or the mobile home—at least not till lab results come back—and he didn't slip under questioning so they let him go. Told him to stay in town in case anything came up, but that's all.' Ian pushes the blankets off himself and puts his legs over the edge of the bed. His feet feel very cold and look very white.

He looks around the room. 'Do you know where my clothes are?'

'Ian, you've been shot.'

'Donald is lying. He as much as said it was his brother when I talked to him at the liquor store the day Maggie called. I should have realized it at the time. He knows something. I can't just lie around waiting for someone to find Maggie's mutilated body on the side of the road somewhere between here and—'

The words are cut off by coughing. It's a deep lung-cough

that brings up blood which splatters into his palm and runs down his chin. He looks at his palm, then wipes it off on the bedding. He wipes at his chin with the back of a wrist. The pain, though constant and worsened by the coughing, is tolerable. He must still be full of painkillers. His swimming mind is evidence of that. He closes his eyes to try to center himself.

'Jesus,' he says.

'You should lie back down.'

He opens his eyes and looks to Debbie. 'That's not gonna happen.'

'Ian.'

'Do you know where my clothes are?'

'They threw your clothes out. They cut your shirt off of you, and your pants were covered in blood.'

'Shoes?'

'Ian.'

'Shoes?'

'I don't know.'

'Wallet? Phone?'

She reaches into her purse and removes a clear plastic bag with a wallet, a cell phone, some loose change, a book of matches, and a watch inside. He must have left his keys in his car's ignition.

'Good,' he says.

He looks at the IV bag hanging from a pole by the head of the bed. The tube twisting off it, the needle stabbed into the back of his hand and taped in place. He has no idea what it is. Fuck it. He yanks the needle from his hand and scratches at the hole. A small bead of blood grows there. He smears it into the skin, then pushes himself off the bed and onto his feet. The floor is cold. His head swims. Everything goes gray and small black specks float before his eyes. For a moment he thinks he's going to lose consciousness, but he doesn't. He manages to hold on to it. Just.

Once he's sure of himself he looks at Debbie and smiles.

'Your car's in the lot, right?'

'I'm not doing it.'

'Do you want to get Maggie back or don't you?'

'Don't do that. You know I do.'

'Then let me get her back.'

'This isn't about that. Don't make it about—'

'That's all this is about.'

The car is quiet as they drive from Mencken down to Bulls Mouth. Ian looks out the window at the sun sinking into the earth. Just the top of it is visible above the horizon. He is cold and hot simultaneously. He believes he has a fever. The Pleur-evac chest drainage system sits on the floor between his feet. He can feel Debbie glancing at him as she drives but refuses to look back. If they make eye contact she might see how sick he really is. If that happens she'll try to stop him. He will not be stopped.

'You can drop me off at the police station,' he says. 'I reckon that's where they moved my car to.'

'What are you going to do?'

'Whatever I have to do,' he says.

'What the hell does that mean?'

Ian doesn't respond. Instead he cracks the window and says, 'Still hot out, isn't it?'

She pulls the car into the police station parking lot and drives around to the back where Ian's Mustang is parked. She brings her Toyota to a stop beside it and puts the transmission into park and simply sits there. She stares straight ahead at the brick wall that is the back of the station, both hands gripping the wheel.

'I'll get her back,' Ian says.

Debbie says nothing. She does not even nod. She simply continues to stare ahead.

'Deb?'

After a long moment: 'Just go, Ian.'

He nods and pushes the door open and steps barefoot onto the asphalt. He grabs the Pleur-evac drainage system by the handle at the top with his left hand and painfully uses his right to push himself to his feet.

'My stuff.'

She pulls the plastic bag with his things in it from her purse and hands it to him.

'Thank you.'

He's about to slam the door home when the sound of Debbie's voice stops him.

'Ian,' she says.

He looks at her.

She tilts her head up and sideways to look at him. Her eyes sparkle in the fading light.

'Be safe,' she says.

He stares at her for a long time, but does not say anything. He doesn't really think there's anything *to* say. Instead he simply nods and pushes the door shut. He stands there and looks at her through the glass. After a moment she reaches down, slides the transmission into reverse, and backs her car out of its spot. Then she is out in the street.

He watches the red taillights shrink as she recedes.

Armando Gonzales is sitting at the dispatch desk and clicking through a game of computer backgammon, saying, 'You *would* roll a fucking six, you cocksucker,' when Ian glances in on him. Ian walks unnoticed past the door. He walks to Chief Davis's desk and pulls open the top right drawer. There he finds his keys as he knew he would. Car key, apartment key, police station key, and a small fob with a mechanic's logo and phone number printed on it. He pulls them from the drawer and pushes the drawer closed.

Then he walks to the back of the station, past the interrogation room and the small kitchen, and into a storage room. The room is about fifteen feet wide and twelve feet deep and filled with rows of metal-framed shelves. On the shelves are boxes stacked upon boxes, loose file folders with last names scrawled upon them, stacks of photographs, orange cones, hand signs suggesting people YIELD or SLOW or STOP, yellow vests adorned with reflective tape, yellow tape for cordoning off crime scenes, Sam Browne belts, loose bottles of pepper spray, loose speed loaders for service revolvers they no longer use, old clips, handcuffs, and PR-24s. And against the wall to Ian's left sits a locker about the size of a grandfather clock. Inside is a clutter of guns the Bulls Mouth PD has confiscated over the years.

He walks to it and unlocks it and pulls it open to take a look at what's available: not much, as it turns out. But he does find a pump-action Remington shotgun with a six-inch barrel and the stock cut down. He grabs that and continues to look through the stockpile. He'd like something for long-distance shooting, but there's nothing here for that purpose. He'll just have to stop by Sally's Gun & Rifle.

He walks back down the hallway, shotgun in one hand, Pleur-evac system in the other. He glances in at Armando before heading out, but Armando doesn't notice him.

Once outside he allows himself to lean against a wall and cough. Just doing this has worn him out, and he still has a long night ahead of him.

He pushes himself off the wall and walks to his car.

At home, he changes into a pair of Levis and a button-up shirt, letting the catheter in his chest feed out the bottom. Then he straps a satchel over his shoulder. He extends the strap to hang as low as possible so there will be no backflow to his lung. Then he puts the Pleur-evac system into the satchel. He's going to need both his hands free.

Twenty minutes after arriving he leaves his apartment.

Sally's stays open till eight, and it's seven forty-five when Ian pulls his Mustang into the lot on the corner of Crouch and Reservoir.

She's standing behind the counter, the most anomalous thing you ever saw, like a tiger sipping tea. Look at her: five feet eight inches of Italian sucker punch ready to send you into the fourth dimension, wearing a Versace dress and fuck-me pumps, lips smeared red, breasts spilling out, hips cocked to the right and waiting for someone to pull the trigger. It's unbelievable that she owns a gun shop in Noplace, Texas, and though Ian's asked she's never told him how it happened.

'Ian Hunt,' she says as he walks through the door. 'I am surprised to see you.'

'The rumors of my death,' he says, 'are greatly exaggerated.'

193

He coughs into his hand, then wipes it off on his Levis. 'Slightly exaggerated, anyway.'

'How are you, honey?'

'Like two hundred and twenty pounds of offal.'

'Come here.'

She walks around the counter and holds out her arms.

'Be careful,' he says as he walks to her, 'I'm delicate right now.'

They hug, painfully for Ian, and Sally plants a wet kiss full on his mouth.

'You look good for a dead man.'

'You look good, period.'

'Then how come we never hooked up?'

'You'd kill me, Sally. It'd be like a teddy bear trying to cuddle dynamite.'

She laughs long and loud. 'Then what can I do for you?'

'Two things. First, I need a rifled shotgun that'll shoot deer slugs accurate up to a hundred and fifty yards.'

'Done.'

'And second, I need a long-distance rifle.'

'How long-distance?'

'I dunno, thousand yards. Fifteen hundred.'

'Oh.'

'You got something like that?'

Sally purses her red lips and a smile glimmers behind her eyes. 'What kind do you want?'

After a few minutes of discussion she decides she'll lose a DPMS Panther .308. She sets it on the counter, beside a Remington 11-87 with a rifled barrel, and then gets out three boxes of ammunition and stacks them one on top of the other.

'Are you shooting tonight?'

Ian shakes his head. 'No, I don't think so,' he says. 'Tonight will require more intimacy than that.'

Sally smiles. 'Well, then, I wish I could be there.'

'No,' Ian says, thinking of his plans for the evening. 'I don't think you do.'

Maggie sits at the foot of the dinner table. Across from her, at the head of the table, Henry sits hunched over his plate, fork gripped in his fist. Flint and Naomi sit side by side to her left. Beatrice to her right. They all have pieces of chicken on their plates and mounds of mashed potatoes from which slices of roasted garlic jut and piles of buttery peas. Maggie pokes at the peas with her fork, trying to only get them onto the left-most prong. One by one she gets them onto the fork, lined up like a string of pearls. Once she has six of them skewered she sucks them off the fork one at a time.

With a mouthful of mashed potatoes Henry says, 'I gotta tell you guys, we sure do appreciate your hospitality, don't we, Bee?'

Beatrice nods, but keeps her head down and her eyes on her plate.

'Not a problem,' Flint says.

'Well, it's damn neighborly of you.'

Flint nods.

'And this is a real fine meal. Fine meal, ma'am.'

'Thank you,' Naomi says, smiling slightly before picking up a glass of Coke with cubes of ice floating in it and taking a drink. The ice clinks against the glass.

'No,' Henry says, 'thank *you*.' He picks up a chicken leg and sucks the skin off it. It flaps against his chin, smearing grease on it, before it vanishes into his mouth. Then he takes off a piece of meat and chews.

'Flint made the rub for the chicken.'

'Damn fine, Flint,' Henry says through a mouthful.

'I saw your tire swing,' Maggie says.

'Hush up, Sarah.'

'Kids are allowed to talk at my dinner table, Henry,' Flint says.

The two men stare at one another for a long moment, but when Henry says nothing, Flint turns to her and smiles. 'What was that, Sarah?'

'I saw your tire swing.'

'Yeah?'

She nods. 'Did you . . .' she licks her lips, 'did it come with the house?'

'No, we have a six-year-old.'

'Is he in bed?'

'Spending the week at his grandparents'.'

'Oh.' She goes back to poking at her peas for a moment, and then looks up again. 'What's his name?'

'Samuel.'

'That's a nice name.'

'Thanks,' Flint says. 'It's Naomi's dad's name.'

'Six years old?' Henry says.

'Yeah,' Flint says coldly.

'Naomi's a little young to have a six-year-old, ain't she?'

'Naomi's twenty-eight, Henry, not that it's any of your business.' He sets his fork down beside his plate. 'You reckon you guys'll be leaving right after dinner?'

Henry takes another bite from his chicken leg, chews slowly, swallows. Then he sets it down on his plate and picks up a napkin from his lap and wipes his face off with it and then his hands. He sets the napkin down on his plate.

'Well, no,' he says finally. 'I don't guess we will be leaving right after dinner.'

'Pardon?'

'Why, you fart or something?'

Maggie looks from Henry to Flint, and though neither man has said anything precisely confrontational, and though neither of them has used a tone that suggests anything but pleasantness, she can feel that something is happening: the temperature in the room has changed: the weather's gone bad. It makes her stomach feel tight and her appetite has vanished. She looks at the two men to see what will happen next while simultaneously dreading it.

Flint sucks at an eye tooth. 'You know,' he says, 'I been awful generous with you and your family, Henry.'

'I know it.'

'Let me finish.'

Henry extends an arm and bows his head slightly. 'You may.'

'I know I may. It's my goddamn house.'

'I don't know what you're getting your panties in a bunch about, Flint. I know it's your house. Go ahead and say what you gotta say.'

Flints hits the table with the flat of his hand and while Maggie, Beatrice, and Naomi all jump at the sound Henry does not. Flint exhales heavily through his nostrils, closes his eyes for the length of a breath, and then opens them again. He looks at Henry.

'I been generous with you and your family, Henry,' he says, 'but truth is, I just ain't comfortable with you guys staying the night. You get on the interstate and drive west another fifteen, twenty miles you'll come across a perfectly nice motel where I'm sure they'll be happy to put you up. If you leave after dinner you can get there before bedtime, no problem.'

'Well, if it was just a matter of sleeping quarters that might be okay, but it ain't just a matter of sleeping quarters. There's more to it than that.'

'We've been plenty hospitable. Whatever more there is to it ain't my problem.'

'Unfortunately, Flint, it is your problem.' Henry reaches into his shirt pocket, pulls out a roll, thumbs a round tablet into his mouth, and chews. 'I'm making it your problem.' He tongues at a molar.

'You're making it my problem?'

'I'm afraid so.'

'You know what,' Flint says, taking his napkin from his lap and throwing it to the table, 'I don't think I'm gonna wait for y'all to finish up. I'm asking you to leave right now.'

'Now, honey,' Naomi says.

Flint doesn't even glance toward Naomi. His eyes stay locked on Henry. 'I'm asking you to leave,' he says again.

'Well, shit,' Henry says, smiling, 'you're feisty.'

When for a moment Henry does nothing Maggie hopes, despite what she knows of him and his temper like a loaded gun, that he will remain calm. He won't do anything crazy. He'll stand and walk to the door and call for Maggie and Beatrice. He'll open the door and they'll walk through it. They'll all head out and Flint will slam and lock the door behind them. They'll get in Henry's truck and drive away. That could happen. There's no reason for it to go any other direction.

But as Henry gets to his feet it does go another direction. He grabs a steak knife from the tablecloth where a moment before it lay beside his plate and lunges at Flint.

Maggie slides down her chair and hides beneath the table. She puts her hands over her ears, but that does not block the sound of Naomi's scream. She closes her eyes, but not before she sees blood splatter to the floor.

'Well, shit,' Henry says, smiling, 'you're feisty.'

His stomach is a tight knot of hatred, and despite the antacid he just ate he can feel bile burning the back of his throat. He tried to play the smiling fool for this son of a bitch, but the man saw through him, same as the cops did earlier. The cops had already seen past the facade—some doors can't be closed—but Flint, well, maybe he didn't try very hard with Flint. There was no reason to, really, not when he knew he'd have to kill him. He thought he'd kill Flint and Naomi while they was sleeping, but it's come to it a little sooner than that. He needs their vehicle and he's not leaving without it, and if they're dead they can't report it missing.

He grabs the steak knife from the tablecloth and lunges at Flint. The man's eyes go wide and his mouth becomes a black zero—and that is what comes out of it: nothing and nothing and nothing—but he still manages to get an arm out in front of him to block the attack. Arms and flattened palms, however, aren't much protection against a stainless steel blade. Henry sticks the knife into the palm once, the serrated blade sawing at the bone of the ring finger's knuckle, twice, into the meat of the thumb, and a third time, severing a pinky finger that just dangles from a single piece of flesh like a macabre keychain fob. Then he pushes in close and stabs the man in the arm and the shoulder.

But Flint grabs him by the wrist with one hand—Henry can feel the loose pinky brushing against his skin like a ghost—and punches him in the neck with the other, and suddenly Henry can't breathe.

He staggers backwards, gasping for air, and Flint rushes him. This is a mistake. He overestimates the damage his blow has caused Henry. As Flint rushes him Henry simply turns the knife out and ducks his head to the left as a fist swings past it. Flint rushes onto the blade. Henry jams it into his belly further, till his fist is buried in stomach and the tip of the blade grinds against spine at the back of him, and then yanks upwards as if trying to lift the man by the blade's handle, and in fact he does momentarily lift him off the ground, until his weight causes him to slide back down it, splitting him open.

When Henry was ten or eleven his family had a cow. One of his chores was to feed her every morning, and it was a chore he took very seriously. Over the course of a year he began to feel that she was his friend. He named her Moo and sometimes after school, if he'd had a particularly bad day, he'd sit on the fence and tell her about it. She would sometimes lick his hand with her fat, coarse tongue. Then one day, as Henry walked up his long and winding dirt driveway, books under his arm, he saw his dad cutting off Moo's head with a meat saw while Uncle Fred cut slits in the Achilles tendons and slid in a gambrel. They used a winch to hoist Moo into the air. Blood thick and dark and full of bubbles drained from her neck and into the dirt. It ran down the driveway in a stream. As Henry walked up the driveway his dad stuck a blade into the cow's stomach and dragged it down toward the neck. He had never seen so much blood before in his life. It was frothy and rich as crude oil.

As Flint falls to the floor and blood pours out of him Henry is reminded of that day.

He reaches down and pulls the knife out of the man.

He looks toward Beatrice. She is staring down at her lap and rocking herself gently and saying, 'This isn't happening, this isn't happening, this isn't happening.'

But it is happening, of course, and it's happening for Bee.

He looks toward Naomi.

Her face is white and her eyes are wide. She is very pretty, especially when frightened. Dishwater-blond hair, lips full, fine wide hips. It's a shame, really, what he has to do. But he does have to do it.

She is, apparently, frozen with shock. She has not made a sound since that first scream, nor has she moved. Her mouth is open slightly, and there is a strange twitch at the side of her left eye, but otherwise she is motionless.

'I guess you know what's next,' Henry says. 'I don't suppose it's no consolation, but we're Christians and we'll bury you with a prayer.'

A small groan escapes Naomi's throat.

Then he rushes her.

But something strange happens: halfway there his feet lose contact with the floor. His feet stop while the top half of his body continues forward. He flies through the air, turning mid-air from a vertical position to a horizontal one. And then he hits, chin first. His teeth clack and he bites the side of his tongue. The steak knife is knocked from his hand.

He glances back over his shoulder with watery eyes and sees Sarah hunched beneath the table, one of her legs still extended.

'Run,' she shouts at Naomi. 'Run and get help! Run before he gets you!'

The words seem to snap the woman out of her paralysis.

'Oh,' she says.

And then she turns and runs toward the back door, grabs the knob and pulls. The door doesn't budge. She looks over her shoulder, eyes alive with fear, unlocks the door, pulls it open, and rushes through it, disappearing into the night.

Henry pushes himself up and backhands Sarah.

'What the fuck do you think you're doing?'

The slap opens a split in her lip, and blood trickles down her chin, but she does not make a sound, nor does she look away. She simply stares at him and bleeds.

He gets to his feet and drags her out from under the table. He raises a booted foot, fully intent on stomping her fucking face into mush. Stomping till she's unrecognizable. That'll teach her to pull shit like this. It'll teach her to fuck with—

'Henry!'

Beatrice limps around the table and wraps her arms around Sarah and strokes her hair and says, 'He didn't mean it, Sarah.' She looks up at him. 'Tell her you didn't mean it, Henry. Tell her you didn't mean it.'

'Don't let her leave the house.'

He turns around, grabs the bloody knife from the floor, and runs out the door after Naomi. If she makes it to a neighbor's house they won't be able to use Flint's pickup truck, and he really doesn't want to have to go through this shit again with someone else.

He scans the horizon. In the distance a yellow light in a window. And running toward it, Naomi. She falls as she runs, then pulls herself to her feet, and continues on.

Henry runs after her.

Ian sits in darkness. A hatchet rests on his knees. His car is parked behind Donald's trailer so that, when the man finally arrives in his El Camino, he will not be alerted to Ian's presence. Ian now simply sits and waits. There was a time, and not long ago, when he would not have been capable of doing what he plans on doing here tonight, if he has to, but that time has gone, a small moment in his past that gets smaller as he moves further from it and into the future.

He thinks of Andy Paulson, of realizing that he was capable of following through on his threat. Capable, yes, but he did not do it. This, he may follow through on. But even knowing what it will make him, he believes the price will be worth paying. He can't be certain until he has actually paid the price, and held what he purchased in his hand, but he believes it will be.

Car tires crunch on gravel outside. An engine goes silent. A door swings open and then slams shut. Footsteps come nearer, first on gravel and then on the steps outside the door. The doorknob rattles. The front door of the mobile home swings open and a shadow enters.

Ian grabs the hatchet by the handle and gets to his feet. He turns the blunt edge of the hatchet forward and swings it down. It hits the shadow on the side of the head. A soft thunk, like someone tapping a melon to check ripeness.

The shadow collapses to the floor with a dumb grunt.

Ian reaches out to the wall and finds the light switch and flips it. An overhead light comes on. The light is in a ceiling fan. The fan's blades spin lazily. Ian looks down at Donald. He's lying unconscious on dirty green carpet, bleeding from a split in the skin just inside the hairline behind the left temple. He smells of cheap beer. Several flattened cardboard boxes he carried in are lying beneath him. Apparently he was planning on packing when he got home, packing and leaving town, most likely. That won't be happening now.

Ian sets the hatchet down on an end table and gets to work.

He's sitting in an easy chair watching TV when, thirty minutes later, the first groans escape Donald's throat. He picks up the remote from the arm of the chair and hits the power button. The sound of a sitcom laugh track is cut off and the screen goes blank as tomorrow. He looks over at Donald. He is naked, hands and feet taped to a wooden chair. His head hangs down, chin resting on his chest. A bit of drool hangs from his mouth and drips upon his hairy belly. His greasy hair hangs down from his head. Blood has dripped from his hairline, run down the side of his face, and begun to dry to brown. He groans a second time, lifts a head he momentarily can't seem to hold steady, finally does manage to hold it upright, and looks around. His face is twisted with pain and confusion. After a moment, his eyes meet Ian's.

'Donald.'

'What the fuck are you doing h—'

But the last word catches in his throat, the question apparently no longer of concern now that he realizes he can move neither his arms nor his legs. He looks down at his wrists. They are held in place by duct tape. As are his legs. He is still a moment. Then he shakes violently in the chair, trying to pull himself loose. His face purples in concentration and exertion, his hands form fists, his toes curl. He cannot get loose. His body relaxes again and his chest heaves. He swallows and looks at Ian.

'So what do you want?' After that display of violence his voice is surprisingly calm.

'A man after my own heart,' Ian says. 'Skip the chit-chat. How about that weather, did you hear what Cora did to an eggplant at Albertsons, John Roberts has been arrested again. I want information.'

'What?'

'Information. You know what that means?'

'Go to hell.'

'If there is one, I suspect you'll get there first.'

'Fuck you.'

'Where's your brother headed?'

'What?'

'Your brother. Henry Dean.'

Ian pushes himself up to his feet, feeling lightheaded but trying not to show it. The pain is tremendous, the pain-killers pumped into him at the hospital finally wearing off. He stands motionless a moment, thinking he may be sick. He isn't.

Once he's sure of himself he picks up the hatchet from the end table on which he set it and walks toward Donald. He simply lets it hang from his fist.

Donald looks from the hatchet to Ian.

'You can't do anything with that.'

'No?'

Donald smiles, shaking his head.

'And why is that?'

'You're the police.'

'I'm just a dispatcher these days.'

'You still can't—'

'There may be consequences, but I can do whatever I want, Donald, because those come later, and right here, right now, tonight, it's just you and me alone with an axe.'

Donald swallows, the smile gone. 'I don't know anything.'

'I don't believe you.'

'But I don't know—'

Ian sets the hatchet blade down on Donald's bare leg. Donald flinches. It must be cold. Ian drags it gently across the pale skin from the inside of his thigh to his knee. It's not quite sharp enough to draw blood from pressure of its own weight, but it draws a thin pink line across the flesh.

'Thing is,' Ian says, 'what you know and what you don't know—that's less important than what I think you know. Less important for you, I mean. You may be telling the truth right now, Donald. It's possible. But I don't believe it. And what I believe is what matters. Again, it's what matters for you. Because I'm going to take you apart one piece at a time until I get the information I want. The information I believe you're hiding from me in that thick fucking noggin of yours. Do we understand each other?'

Donald licks his lips. They're dry and chapped. He looks from the hatchet to Ian's eyes. Ian looks back. He can tell Donald is sizing up the situation, deciding what he will say, and Ian hopes, for Donald's sake and his own, that the man says the right thing.

Instead what he says is, 'Maybe I don't believe you either. Maybe I think all you got is talk, and maybe talk don't intimidate me.'

'Questioning my sincerity right now would be a mistake, Donald.'

'You're lying. You don't have the sack to—'

Ian slams the hatchet down into the floor, and lets go of it. It stays there at an angle, held by the wood into which it's been imbedded.

Ian watches Donald's face. For a moment he does not seem to realize what's happened. Then he looks down at the floor. The hatchet's blade is stuck between Donald's right foot and his two small toes. The small toes lie on the green carpet looking like grapes that have been hiding under the couch for the last six months, shriveled and ancient, practically yellow raisins. Then the blood begins to flow.

Donald's breathing gets strange and heavy. He does not scream, but his breathing gets labored and a series of groans escapes him, and he looks at his foot unbelievingly.

'You can't do that!'

'Do what?'

'You just cut off my fucking toes!'

'I was just trying for the pinky toe. Hatchet isn't exactly a precision tool.'

'Put them back. You can't fucking do that. You're the *police*.'

'That's the kind of thinking that's going to get you into trouble tonight, Donald. You need to understand that I can do whatever I want, and you need to understand that I will.'

'I don't . . .'

He closes his eyes. He breathes in and out.

Ian watches him, feeling strangely detached from everything that is happening. There have been times when merely seeing an old man struggle down the sidewalk while pushing a walker in front of him has broken his heart: thoughts of the man sitting alone at some cockroach-infested diner eating a three-dollar bowl of soup, the only dinner he can afford on his pension; the pictures of his dead wife that surely litter the small house in which he lives; the house itself in disrepair; the lonesome bed; the going to sleep without knowing if tomorrow will come; the hope that it does not. Nothing more than a liver-spotted hand gripping a walker has broken his heart, but here he is staring down at fear welling in a man's eyes and he feels nothing but contempt. Contempt and hatred. This man knows where his daughter is and he's not talking.

Soon he will be.

He leans down, picks up the toes, wraps them individually in torn pieces of paper towel, and sets them in a glass bowl into which he's broken several ice cube trays. Then he pulls the hatchet from the floor. Blood drips from the blade.

Very soon he will be.

'Sooner you talk,' Ian says, 'sooner you help me get back what I lost, sooner I stop chopping—and you get to the hospital and have a chance of getting back what you lost.'

'Go fuck yourself,' Donald says.

'Have it your way,' Ian says.

He swings the hatchet.

Ian stands in the bathroom staring at his own reflection in the toothpaste-spotted mirror above the sink. He looks very tired. He looks very sick. He's having a hard time breathing. He turns around and looks over his shoulder at his back in the mirror. There is a red spot about the size of a dime on his orange button-up shirt. The place where the bullet came out. He tore the stitches while swinging the hatchet. It hurts like hell, especially since whatever they gave him for pain at the hospital is wearing off, but mostly he's glad he did not tear the catheter from his chest.

He sits on the toilet lid and puts his elbows on his legs and his face in his hands.

He has taken all of Donald's toes and the man has still not talked. He has to start on the fingers next. But first a moment of peace.

He sits silently and thinks about nothing.

Somewhere a tumbleweed rolls through desert sands.

'Okay,' he says after a few minutes, and gets to his feet. He opens the medicine cabinet and looks through the bottles there, knocking several into the sink below before finding some 50-milligram tramadol tablets in an orange prescription bottle. 'Take one tablet by mouth every four hours, as needed, for pain.' He thumbs the cap off and pours three or four pills into his mouth. Then turns on the water, brings a palmful to his lips, and swallows. He pockets the bottle and wipes at his chin before heading back out to the living room where Donald waits and bleeds.

'For all I know he went down to Florida to try to catch a fishing boat to Cuba.'

That's the sentence that loses Donald the pinky finger on his right hand—the hatchet also cutting halfway through his ring finger. He swings the hatchet down into the arm of the chair, taking off a small chunk of wood along with the finger. The finger drops to the carpet like a dead bird.

Donald groans and clenches his teeth and grimaces with cracked, bloody lips. The groan stretches out, becoming a sob. Tears stream down his face.

Ian picks up the finger, rolls it in paper towel, and sets it among the other digits. The ice is beginning to melt, making a bloody soup in which pieces of Donald float. Ian thinks of going to the fair when he was a kid, of bobbing for apples. His stomach clenches.

Turning back around to Donald he says, 'Did you try that one on the police, too?'

Donald doesn't respond. He simply glares at Ian through bloodshot eyes.

'Do you want to try again?' Ian says.

'You're no better than he is,' Donald says between labored breaths as tears stream down his face from bloodshot eyes. 'You're no better than he is.'

'Then you know what he is.'

'He's my brother.'

'He's a piece of shit.'

'What are you?'

'I'm a man trying to get his daughter back.'

Donald actually laughs. Taped to a chair, toes hacked off, fingers on his right hand now gone too, naked in a pool of his own blood—he laughs. 'You think Henry doesn't have justifications for what he's done? You're everything he is.'

'And you?'

'I've done nothing. I'm just a man protecting his brother.'

'Then you made your choice too.'

Ian brings the hatchet down on the left arm of the chair, taking off the two middle fingers on Donald's left hand. Donald clenches his teeth. Blood merely oozes from the wounds. When Ian began this thing there was much more bleeding, but now most of the blood is already on the outside, and what little Donald has left is hesitant to leave him. Each new wound bleeds less than the one before. Donald is pale. Weak and pale. He's already momentarily lost consciousness once. Ian doesn't know how much longer the man can hold up. But he'll find out.

Donald glares up at him, defiant.

211

'Tell me where he is and I'll call an ambulance.'

'Don't try to lay what you are on me.'

'What?'

'You motherfucker,' Donald says. 'You relentless, heartless motherfucker. Don't you try to lay on me what you are. Saying I made my choice. I didn't choose for you to come in here with a hatchet. I didn't choose to be bound to a chair. I didn't even choose to have Henry for a brother. At least admit what you are. You're . . .' he stops talking, breathing hard, and his chin drops briefly to his chest before snapping up again, 'you're no better than he is. You're just as willing to . . . just as willing to hurt . . . I hate . . . Fuck you both.'

Donald's chin drops to his chest again, but just as it drops his head snaps up once more. For a moment his eyes are lost. Then they find focus, and Ian, and Donald glares at him.

'I'm not the same as your brother,' Ian says.

'You're no different.'

'My daughter is an innocent. All those little girls were innocents. You're no innocent. You might try to tell yourself you are, that you never did anything, but we both know different. You know what he is. You probably have always known. But you never stopped him. You could've stopped him but you never did. That makes you an accomplice. He stole my daughter, my life, and you knew. You knew and you did nothing. Every day I saw you and you said nothing—for years.'

'That doesn't make you right.'

'I don't care if I'm right,' Ian says. 'I want my daughter back.'

Donald's eyes flutter and start to roll back in his head, but he manages to hold on to consciousness. Just barely, by all appearances.

'I gave her books. I even gave her lessons when I could. History, math. I checked on her. To make sure she was okay.'

'But you didn't do what you should have.'

'I did what I could without betraying my brother.'

'I want her back.'

Silence for a long time, then: 'Fine.'

'Fine what?'

'I'll tell you. He doesn't . . . he doesn't deserve to be protected from the consequences of what he . . . I'll tell you where he's headed, but you have to tell me some—' He stops here a moment, closing his eyes and swallowing. 'You have to tell me something.'

'What?'

'You were gonna kill me no matter what I said, weren't you?'

Ian is silent for a long time, in part because he is not certain of the answer. He knows he told himself he would only go this far if he absolutely had to, but he doesn't know whether or not he was lying.

You were gonna kill me no matter what I said, weren't you?

He licks his lips, and after a while he nods. 'Yes,' he says.

FOUR

Ian is on the road before first light. He lay down last night after he was finished with Donald, after he had gotten what he needed from the man; he was exhausted and in pain and did not have any choice in the matter, it was lie down or fall down, but he set the alarm for four o'clock and is after Henry before the morning sun breaches the horizon.

After the first five minutes on the interstate, during which Bulls Mouth lies to his left like a pile of tangled Christmas lights, most of which are broken, the town is history and he sees little more than the gray strip of asphalt that is the road rolling out before him. The lights of the small town are replaced by a vast flat nowhere decorated occasionally by scatterings of trees that can barely be seen in the darkness. Fireflies dot the air here and there, and Ian drives through them. They splatter on his windshield, and his wipers leave glowing streaks smeared across the glass. He cannot see much of anything beyond the road. It is pleasant to drive that way. It shrinks your world to nothing but the road in front of you: everything there is is what your headlights splash across. Everything before you is comprehensible. The drone of the tires is pleasant: a song to send you to sleep. There are no other cars on the road.

He drives this way for some time, time itself nonexistent. Time means nothing when every moment is like the one that just passed. He stops for gas at a Citgo in Schulenburg at some point, but as soon as he's back on the road, it's as if it didn't happen, like a dream after waking. Then, around six thirty, with the sunrise on the flat line of the horizon behind him splashing into his rearview mirror, something to signify that minutes and hours have gone by, he arrives in San Antonio, passing the Shady Acre Tavern, Lone Star Truck Equipment, Southern Tire Mart, and a couple dozen other businesses that skirt the city. He finds a Denny's on Frederickburg and eats a Grand Slam Breakfast and drinks five cups of coffee. When he is done he tips his waitress, Doris, twenty percent.

By just past seven he is back on the road.

Maggie sits on the ground behind the house, Beatrice beside her. They silently watch Henry cover Flint and Naomi with dirt. It took him a long time to dig the hole into which he dumped them, grunting and levering out hard chunks of earth, but the filling of it goes quickly. His shirt is off and tucked into the back pocket of his Levis, and he's covered with an oily layer of sweat and dripping with it. His face is red. He digs the shovel into his pile of dirt and dumps it over the bodies, one load of dirt after another.

Maggie feels sad. She could not bear to watch Henry dragging Flint and Naomi to the hole; to see how Flint's arm flopped lifelessly as Henry rolled him into it; to see Naomi stare blankly with one eye, the other covered in blood from a knife wound in her forehead; to hear the potato-sack thud-thud of the bodies hitting the bottom of the hole. She has seen so much death lately. She never wants to see it again. And she liked Flint and Naomi. They helped when they didn't have to. You don't repay someone who helped you by killing them.

Henry told her if she kept her mouth shut they would not be killed, but she did keep her mouth shut and they were killed anyway. Henry lied.

He finishes covering the hole and pounds the dirt down with the flat of the shovel, and then throws his shovel into the bed of his Ford Ranger, which he drove around back of the house earlier this morning.

After that, but before digging the hole that would become Flint and Naomi's grave, he removed the license plates from the Ford and threw them out into the field. Now he pulls open the door and takes out a pair of guns, and puts them into Flint's Dodge Ram. He puts the long rifle behind the seats and tucks another smaller gun under the driver's seat. Then he takes the boxes from the bed of his truck and puts them into the bed of the other.

When he's done he takes his T-shirt from the back pocket of his Levis and wipes his sweaty face on it, and then slips back into it. It is covered with moisture and smeared with dirt.

Maggie wants to run—if she could just get away everything would be okay—but she feels certain Henry would catch her.

He caught Naomi. He caught Naomi and she was a grown up. He caught her and he stabbed her in the face and the neck and the chest, and he dragged her to the back of the house by her hair and dropped her and kicked her even though she was dead, and covered her with a blue tarp that he pulled from a stack of cordwood and dropped pieces of that wood onto the corners of the tarp to keep the wind from blowing it off the body. She watched him through a window, working in the circle of the back-porch light. There was blood on his hands when he was finished and he reached down and scooped up a handful of dirt and rolled his hands around in it before dusting himself off and coming inside. He pulled the steak knife from his back pocket and dropped it into the sink as if nothing had happened. As if the blood on it did not belong to a man and a woman who had never done anything but help them. As if nothing terrible had just happened at all.

It didn't take him five minutes to return with Naomi after

he ran out the back door. Not five minutes. When he left she was alive, when he returned she was dead. Maggie had tried to help save her. She had tried. Not for herself. It only occurred to her later, after Naomi was out the door and running, that if Naomi could get to help maybe that help would come here and rescue her. But when she did it, when she tripped Henry and yelled at her to go, it didn't even cross her mind. She just wanted to help save the woman from Henry. But she did not save her.

Maggie wants to run, but she's afraid of meeting the same fate.

She knew that if she tried to escape the Nightmare World Henry might kill her, but yesterday morning the idea of death was just that: an idea. She has seen death since, though, and she is not okay with it. She wants to live. She does not want the light inside her to go out.

And Henry is scared. She can see it in his face. He is scared of getting caught, and that makes him more likely to kill her if she causes too much trouble. Cornered animals lash out. Her daddy told her that once and she has never seen a reason to disbelieve it. Cornered animals are the most dangerous kind.

If she's to run again she must pick her moment carefully; she must be certain of getting away. As certain as possible.

She nods to herself.

She'll wait for her moment, then run.

Henry trudges over to them, wiping sweat from his brow. He blows his nose with his fingers, then shakes snot off his hand and wipes his hand off on his Levis. He squints at her and Beatrice sitting beside one another.

'Well,' he says, 'let's get the fuck out of here.'

Diego knocks on Ian's front door. There's a smear of burgundy on the white-painted wood by the brass doorknob and a bloody thumbprint on the knob itself. From Diego's perspective the bloody thumbprint on the knob appears to have been smashed into the left cheek of his distorted reflection.

When Ian does not answer his door Diego knocks again.

'Ian?'

Still only silence from the other side.

'Ian?'

Diego grabs the knob and jiggles it. It is locked but not dead-bolted, and the door is loosely fitted. He turns the knob as far as the lock allows and jerks toward the hinges and presses his shoulder against the door. The first time it does not give, but the second time, with some minor cracking of the doorjamb, it swings open.

'Ian?'

And still nothing, no response: a response in itself.

Earlier this morning when he called her Debbie would not tell him where Ian was. She said she didn't know, but Diego did not believe her, nor does he now. And he is worried. Ian left the hospital last night, and Donald Dean did not show up at Bill's Liquor this morning. Diego thinks Debbie knows something about the connection between those two events, but she isn't talking, and he is unwilling to push it. The woman just lost her husband (wife-stealing asshole though Bill Finch was, may he rest in peace), and Maggie is as much her daughter as she is Ian's. And Maggie's reappearance may be harder on her in a way: she believed her daughter dead.

He steps into the apartment and closes the door behind him. He looks around.

Just to his left is a hat rack with a never-worn Stetson hanging upon it, as well as an Anaheim Angels cap that, as far as Diego knows, Ian wore only during the 2002 World Series (and for which he would have been taunted, except nobody in town really gave much of a shit about the Giants either). To his right, the kitchen: tile counter top, stainless-steel sink, small white refrigerator with a couple pictures of Maggie stuck to its door with magnets. Straight ahead, the living room: blue couch, coffee table on which a chess board and a few empty Guinness bottles sit, a television set.

There is a smear of blood on the arm of the couch.

'Ian?'

Silence.

He walks down the bookshelf-lined hallway to the bedroom. The bed is made but looks as though it has been lain upon. The blankets are wrinkled and there is a dent in its middle. Within the dent is more blood. And on the floor between the bed and Diego a hospital gown in a pile.

A dresser drawer has been left open. A shirt hangs from it.

Blood. Signs that Ian was here but left in a hurry, and no sign of Ian himself.

And Donald is missing.

He has to go to the Dean place.

On his way he tries to call Ian's cell phone for the third or fourth time this morning and, as happened before, the call goes to voicemail after five rings. He thumbs the button to end the call without bothering to leave a message, and then pockets his phone.

Rolling down the driveway is a surreal experience. All around are traces of what happened yesterday. Gravel stained red. Yellow tape cordoning off the house. A .22 casing missed by the county boys at the foot of the stairs, catching a glint of sunlight.

Diego drives past this to the single-wide mobile home behind the main house. It's sitting on blocks, the axles and wheels long ago rusted, the tires rotted away and lying on the dead grass beneath like prehistoric serpents. Steps made of plywood and two-by-fours weathered to a pale gray, the dull copper of rusted nail heads dotting them.

The mobile home itself is a powder green, the metal siding dented in several places, tattered and torn window screens hanging from their frames like the flags of those who lost the war. An antenna juts above the asphalt shingles that line the roof.

He parks next to Donald's El Camino and steps from his car.

'All right, Diego,' he says to himself, and unsnaps his holster with the twitch of a thumb. He walks up the steps—heel-toe, clunk-clunk—stopping at the narrow metal front door. He looks down. He is standing upon a welcome mat with Yosemite Sam on it, aiming a gun up at him from the ground. Hasn't even announced himself yet and already there's a gun pointed at his face.

'Pow,' he says, then presses the doorbell to the left of the door.

It ding-dongs inside. He waits. When, after several beats, he does not get an answer, he bangs on the hollow metal door. It rattles in its frame.

'Donald, it's Diego. Officer Peña. Open up.'

Donald does not open up.

Diego draws his SIG with his right hand and with his left grabs the doorknob. He turns it gently to see if it will give and it does. He pushes a bit. Waits, exhales, and shoves the door open with his back to the wall just left of it.

He looks in quickly, not long enough for someone to take aim, and pulls out again. The place is dark and hot. The curtains are drawn. Only one light is on, a dim lamp in the lazily spinning fan in the ceiling. The wood-paneled room feels sick and claustrophobic. Flies dot the ceiling.

'Donald, it's the police.'

No response.

After another breath he steps into the living room. At first he sees nothing out of the ordinary, but this is only because he does not see what's on the other side of the open door. All he can see is what's to the left of him and what's to the left of him is a single man's living quarters. A sagging chair, a sagging couch, a dinner tray, empty beer cans littering the floor, a nudie-magazine centerfold thumb-tacked to the wall.

But then he takes another step into the place, clearing the front door, and can see into the dining room. The first thing he sees is a dining table stacked with papers, a few loose socks, pens and pencils, a set of keys, a yellow legal pad smeared with bloody fingerprints. A single white candle made flaccid in the summer heat sits upon it, and a glass bowl filled with a soup of brown water and clumps of something wrapped in pieces of paper towel. Then he sees what is between him and the table, a wooden chair tipped on its side and a man within it. The man is Donald. He has no fingers or toes. It is strange how inhuman a hand looks with no fingers, just red stumps with bone-white cores. Flies crawl on his face. They crawl on his blank staring eyes. They crawl on the stumps where his digits once were, laying their eggs.

Diego swallows back sick. His friend did this. A man who has eaten dinner with him and his family. A man who has slept on his couch. A man who has played video games with Elias. It seems somehow unbelievable.

He walks to the glass bowl on the table and looks down into it. He swallows. After a brief hesitation he reaches into the brown soup and pulls out a wad of paper towel. It is heavier than he expected. He unwraps it and is soon looking at a grown man's pinky finger. A white core surrounded by red meat and cased in wrinkled skin that reminds Diego of pickled pigs' feet.

He drops the finger back into the brown soup.

His friend did this. Ian did this.

Ian came to get information that neither Diego nor the sheriff could manage to pry from Donald, and he worked hard for that information. He killed for it. What Diego can't tell, what the room will not reveal to him, is whether Ian managed to get it. He worked for it, but that doesn't prove anything. People work for things they don't attain every day, and attain things they didn't work for with equal frequency.

Diego arms sweat from his forehead.

He looks at the legal pad on the table smeared with bloody finger prints. Shouldn't the bloody prints mean it was used during or after what happened here last night? He picks up a pencil and holds it sideways and brushes it gently across the page. As he does this he finds an address revealed in relief.

372 Conway St
Kaiser, CA 92241

He tears the top sheet from the legal pad, folds it into quarters, and pockets it. Then he glances at the glass bowl of brown soup just to his right, and then the body on the floor. He can't help but feel this is partly his fault. If he had held on to Donald the man would be safe in a cell right now. Diego might even have managed to get the information out of him himself without resorting to . . . what happened here. What happened here.

Diego is a fairly intelligent man, graduated high school with a good GPA and got his AA from the community college in Mencken without any trouble at all, spending most of his time falling madly into and out of love with various coeds, and what happened here would be obvious even to a very dumb man. What happened here was murder, plain and simple.

And after he was done killing Donald, Ian went home for a while, changed clothes, grabbed a gun maybe, and got into his car and headed west. Headed toward Kaiser, California, with a catheter threaded into his lung meat and a bullet hole punched clean through him. Headed toward, based on Henry's shooting, what will almost certainly be his own death.

If Diego had just managed to get that information out of the son of a bitch Ian wouldn't—

If Sheriff Sizemore hadn't let him—

He needs to think this thing through. He's got an address now. He knows where both Henry and Ian are headed. He could get the federal law involved. They're almost certainly involved as it is. A kidnapped girl in the possession of a murderer on the run. Feds are probably at the Tonkawa County

Sheriff's Office in Mencken right now, getting whatever information Sizemore has and collecting his files to take back to the Houston field office. He could simply call them. That might be the smart thing to do. Except that Ian killed a man. Ian tortured a man for information and killed him, and though this is something that Diego could never have done himself, he knows that Ian did it out of desperation, and out of love, and he understands these things. The horror before him reveals just how ugly even the purest of emotions can be—but he understands them. Besides which, Ian is his friend. The man has slept on his couch, shared his meals, played videogames with Elias. He let Diego see him cry when Debbie kicked him out. He was drunk and probably doesn't even remember it, and Diego would never mention it to him, never embarrass him with it, but it happened all the same. If he gets the FBI involved they'll come poking around, and they will uncover what happened here last night.

But if he stays silent the FBI might not even come in here. Their focus will be on finding Henry. Field agents will be everywhere but here. Here is where they know he isn't.

But what if he covered the scene up here and called them? Or made up a story and got them involved?

Goddamn it, Ian, why did you have to leave such a fucking mess behind?

But Diego knows why. Ian wasn't, and isn't, concerned about anything but getting his daughter back. Everything else is peripheral.

He can't cover the scene up enough to ensure he doesn't leave evidence behind—evidence that might incriminate him. And he doesn't want the FBI questioning him about how he came upon the address in California. He understands why Ian did what he did, even if he could not do such a thing himself, and he's not going to throw him to the wolves for doing it. Maybe he should, but he won't.

He can't cover up the scene and contact the FBI, but he can't just leave it as it is either, can he? There's a chance no one will come by for a long time, but there's also a chance someone will come by tomorrow, and that someone would find what Diego found.

'Goddamn it, Ian,' he says.

He closes his eyes to think. Then opens them and gets to work.

He puts on gloves and untapes Donald from the chair. He drags him to his couch and lays him across it. He unwraps the digits cut from Donald, and lays them out so the corpse discovered will look whole (having to rush to the bathroom to be sick once). He washes the murder weapon and sets it by the door. He picks up the chair and puts it back into place. He walks through the mobile home, making sure all the windows are closed and locked.

Then he walks to the kitchen and puts oatmeal and water into a sauce pan, puts the pan on the stove, and turns on the gas. It is an old stove that does not self-light, but Diego does not light it either. The stove hisses, telling him to shhh.

He can hardly believe he is doing this, but doing it he is.

He walks back out to the living room. He thumbs a match to life and lights the flaccid candle sitting on the dining-room table. So long as no one digs through the ash too carefully this should do the job. He hopes so, anyway. It will look like Donald got up, put on some oatmeal and lay on the couch to wait for it to be ready when something happened. Something.

Diego blows out the candle and walks to the body. He moves it to a sitting position, puts a cigarette between its lips, and a lighter into its palm. Then he walks back to the candle and lights it once more. The smell of gas is strong now. He has to get out. He's done what he could.

He thinks there might be hatchet marks on the bones that forensics people will eventually find, but this should buy Ian a few days. And with any luck there will be no evidence that Diego was here at all.

Diego heads out the front door, grabbing the hatchet on his way out, and closing and locking it behind him.

He walks to his car and gets into it, throwing the hatchet on the floor. He starts the engine and turns the car around. The tires crunch over gravel. As he drives away he glances into his rearview mirror, but the mobile home simply sits there, silent.

When he reaches Crouch Avenue, he turns left.

The explosion is loud and sudden and its force blows a wind through the surrounding trees and birds take flight. Diego's heart pounds in his chest and his face feels hot. He looks out his window as he drives and sees smoke billowing behind the trees, a thick pillar of smoke holding up the sky.

When he reaches his house six minutes later the fire engines have still not left the station. Diego is glad. He wants the place to have a chance to burn.

Now to talk to Cordelia.

'I wish you wouldn't.'

'He's my friend, Cord.'

'You have lots of friends.'

'Ian doesn't. I'll be back in a few days.'

'Shit.'

'Don't be like that, Cord.'

'What if I told you don't go?'

'I wouldn't go. Are you telling me that?'

Cordelia looks away for a long moment and then looks back. 'Be safe.'

'I will.'

Diego stops his car on the dirt shoulder of the road to allow two screaming fire engines to pass, and then he pulls back onto the asphalt and continues toward Interstate 10.

He looks at the smoke filling the sky and hopes he has made the right decision.

By the time he gets the fifth call from Diego, the one he decides to answer, Ian is about thirty minutes out of Comfort, Texas. The land on either side of him now is lined only with occasional feeder roads, private roads, lonesome-looking houses, and summer trees. But he likes the emptiness. He grew up in Los Angeles where his only escape from civilization was the sea, and he finds this unpeopled land beautiful.

He answers the phone. 'I've decided you're not gonna quit calling,' he says.

'You've decided right.'

'Do I win a prize?'

'Only if you guess where I am. You get one chance.'

'Roberta's.'

'She don't even open for another half hour.'

'I bet she would for you. If you said please real nice and made puppy-dog eyes.'

'I'm at a Shell station in Columbus,' Diego says.

'What the hell are you doing in Ohio?'

Despite the tone of their conversation, a cold feeling slides into Ian's stomach like a blade. Diego knows where Ian is headed. He knows and he's going to try to stop him before he can make Henry pay for what he's done, before he can get Maggie back. He knows and he's going to arrest him, have him arrested, for killing Donald Dean.

The FBI is probably already awaiting his arrival at a road-block somewhere to the west.

He knew he should have cleaned Donald's place up—he knew that—but by the time he was finished with him, he was simply finished. He had neither the mental nor the physical energy to dispose of Donald's body. He did not know what to do with it, and even if he had, he'd just been shot: he barely managed to do what he'd gone there to do. And when he woke in the dark of morning he felt only a great urge to get on the road.

But that was a mistake. That Diego is calling him makes it obvious it was a mistake.

'I've been to your apartment. And to Donald's place.'

'I know.'

He coughs into his open hand and tastes blood. He looks down at the catheter winding its way out from under his shirt and to the passenger-side floorboard where he put the satchel, and sees a knot of white liquid working its way down. He wonders what it means, this liquid in his lungs. He should have brought antibiotics with him. Grabbed some from his medicine cabinet. He had some left over from something or other. At least he got some pain meds stronger than Tylenol. They make him feel strange and drowsy, but he can function.

'It's not too late to straighten this out, Ian.'

'I know,' he says. 'That's what I'm trying to do. Straighten this out.'

'I don't think you're going about this—'

'Who else knows about Donald?'

A long pause, then: 'No one.'

'You didn't report it?'

'I'd be lying if I said that didn't hurt my feelings. You're my friend.'

'I am, but—'

'I'm loyal to my friends.'

'Then turn around and go back to Bulls Mouth and let me finish this thing.'

'I'm even loyal to my suicidal friends.'

'What the hell does that mean?'

'Henry will kill you.'

'You don't know that.'

'I do know that, and so do you.'

'He has my daughter, Diego. He stole my life.'

'Your life is what you made it.'

Ian doesn't respond for a long time. He knows what Diego says is true. He is what he is and has done what he's done and it produced the life he lives. These are just facts and there is no point in pretending otherwise.

'Ian?'

'I know,' he says. 'You're right. That's why I'm doing this.'

'I don't understand.'

'You don't need to.'

'It doesn't have to happen like this. I burned Donald's trailer. They'll think he had an accident with the stove. We'll get the FBI or somebody involved, tell them what's going on, and then we—'

'You did what?'

'Come home. The FBI has resources. They can—'

'The sheriff had resources too. I appreciate what you're doing, Diego, you don't know how much, I know you put yourself on the line here, but I'm not stopping.'

'Ian, goddamn it, would you just listen to—'

'Go home to Cordelia, Diego, and leave me alone.'

'If you—'

'I'm throwing this phone out the window now. Give my best to Cord.'

'You selfish son of a bitch, would you fucking—'

He rolls the window down, the summer heat blowing into the car at sixty-eight miles per hour. He turns his face to it a brief moment, then throws his phone out the window. It seems to hang in the air a second, and then flies backwards, flipping end over end. In the rearview mirror he watches it hit asphalt and disintegrate, twisting and throwing off pieces of itself until there are no more pieces to throw off and it is gone. He rolls the window back up and turns on the radio.

He knows Diego. The man will keep coming after him. Ian just hopes he'll be able to stay ahead of him and take care of what needs taking care of before Diego catches up. He doesn't want to put anyone else in danger. He doesn't want what happened to Bill Finch and Chief Davis to happen to anyone else.

Nor does he want what happened to him to happen to anyone else.

Diego is a good man with a loving wife and a beautiful boy he is raising as his son. He should remain a good man with a loving wife and a beautiful boy he is raising as his son. For that to happen he needs to keep his distance. Which means Ian has to stay ahead of him and take care of Henry on his own.

When he decided how far he was willing to go with Donald— all the way—he knew it was a negation of things he had believed all his life, of things he still believes, but he did not care, nor does he now. His only want was for the information he knew Donald had and he was willing to do everything to get it. He knew the cost going in and he was willing to pay it. He knows there will be greater costs ahead. He will pay those too. He is getting Maggie back. He knows he won't get his life back with her, but that doesn't matter: it will make his life mean something again. And that does matter.

He looks out at the unpeopled land to his left and his right.

He imagines his daughter in a yellow dress with the wind blowing through her golden hair. Just her and the landscape. She is beautiful. She is everything that ever meant anything in this entire fucked-up world, all of it within those green eyes. Everything his heart ever needed in four words from her lips: I love you, Daddy.

And that does matter.

Maggie sits between Henry and Beatrice in a gray Dodge Ram pickup truck, sweat trickling down her face. The cab smells of their sweat, a dense odor that makes Maggie's eyes water. Henry will not turn on the air conditioner. He refuses to do so, saying it'll ruin their gas mileage and he doesn't want to be stopping to fill up every hundred miles.

They're about an hour out of San Antonio now. Maggie thinks it's been about an hour, anyway. She counted to four-thousand-two, four-thousand-three, four-thousand-four, and there are only three thousand six hundred seconds in an hour, so unless she was counting far too fast, it should have been just over an hour.

She thought that she might have a chance to escape while there, but she did not. They stopped and got fast-food sandwiches for breakfast, and ate them in the truck, Maggie the entire time squeezed between Henry and Beatrice.

Every time she took a bite she would think of the people Henry buried earlier this morning. They would never eat again. She doesn't understand why Henry had to do that. He didn't have to do that. He said he had to because he needed their truck, he said he didn't have a choice, but Maggie thinks that is a lie. Maybe a lie he believes himself, but a lie nonetheless. There had to have been ways of getting a new vehicle without killing anybody. Maggie thinks that maybe Henry likes to—

'I'll be goddamned,' Henry says.

'What?' Beatrice says.

'Look.' He points through the bug-spattered windshield.

'A Volkswagen?'

'No, just in front of it.'

Now Maggie sees it too: a 1965 Mustang. It could be Daddy's. It almost has to be Daddy's. It's red except for the trunk, which is primer gray.

She remembers riding with Daddy in his Mustang. Sometimes he would let her shift the car if they were alone and no one else was on the road. He'd push down on the crutch—clutch, Mags, with an L—and she would move the shifter, jamming it into gear. It was fun and exciting: she could feel the whole car's power in the black knob at the end of the shifter, and it vibrated into her body through the palm of her hand. That made it scary, too, but that was part of why she liked it, part of why it was fun. Sometimes he let her sit in his lap and steer. She would swerve all over the road, laughing and honking the horn, and when it was over Daddy would be covered in sweat and saying she was the bravest person he ever met or the craziest. And she would stick out her tongue and shake her head and make crazy noises and laugh.

'Well,' Daddy would say, 'that answers that.'

Henry closes the distance between the Dodge pickup and the Mustang. He has to change lanes and pass the Volkswagen and then swing in front of it to do so, and the driver of the Volkswagen honks and Henry waves his middle finger at him through the truck's rear window.

Maggie looks at the Mustang in front of them. It is Daddy. She can tell by the back of his head, the shape of it, the thin blond hair. It is him. She was afraid it might not be, she was afraid that he was dead and it couldn't be him, but he isn't dead and it is him. After yesterday, with all that blood, with the way he just lay on the gravel after Henry kicked him in the head, with the way his head fell limp and he just lay there, she was so afraid he was dead. She told herself he wasn't, but she was afraid he was.

No: she knew he wasn't dead.

'That's my dad.'

A slap across the back of the head.

'Shut the fuck up.'

She looks at Henry and sees that he means it.

He looks from her to the windshield.

'Fuck.'

She thought Daddy was dead but he is not dead. It makes her chest feel warm in its center. As if she had her own personal sun. A sun on the inside. She thinks maybe she does.

'Daddy,' she says, waving her arms, hoping he looks in his rearview mirror.

Another slap to the back of the head.

'I fucking mean it, Sarah.'

'I told you he was coming for me,' she says. 'I *told* you.'

Mouthy little bitch. Where does she get off talking to him like that? If it weren't for Bee, he'd just get rid of her. Put her in the ground. She's nothing but trouble at this point. All of this is because of her: his having to kill Chief Davis and that county boy Bill Finch, his having to kill Flint and Naomi, their being on the run, all of it. She brought this upon them. She brought this upon them and she deserves to pay for that betrayal.

If it weren't for Bee, she would pay for it.

Unless a man wants to find hisself with a bloody feeding-hand some day, his daddy had told him once before getting out his .22 and putting it into Henry's hands, it's best to kill a bad pup before it gets to be a big dog. Now let's take care of this. I'll get the shovel.

If it weren't for Bee, he'd take care of Sarah. She's a bad pup if ever there was one. But women don't understand facts. They just see something cute and want to cuddle it. They don't understand that cute has nothing to do with whether something needs to be put down.

He can't believe that son of a bitch Ian Hunt found them. Found out where they were heading, anyway. And must have managed to get in front of them while Henry was busy burying the previous owners of the truck he's now driving. It occurs to him that there was only one person from whom Ian could have gotten that information. But Donald would never give him up. Henry practically raised him. After Dad had the stroke when Donald was seven Henry did raise him. Donald would never give him up. He would sit through any and all threats of imprisonment giving nothing but a dead pan to the cops and answering nothing.

Unless someone did something much worse than merely threaten him.

But Hunt is a cop.

Except he ain't exactly acting like a cop right now, is he? Out here in his own car and no other cops in sight.

If the police knew where he and Bee were heading they'd be all over this stretch of road. He'd have seen them. Seen them and holed up someplace. Or else he wouldn't have seen them but they'd have seen him. They'd have seen him and flashed their lights and he'd be in a high-speed chase or captured or escaped. Or there'd be roadblocks. Something would have happened. But nothing has. Which means the police don't know where he's heading, even if Ian Hunt does.

And there's only one way Donald would have given Henry up.

And there's only one reason Ian Hunt wouldn't get the real police involved.

'Motherfucker.'

'Henry.'

'Shut up, Bee.'

She looks at him a moment, then looks down at her lap. She flattens the fabric of her dress, rubs out the wrinkles, and stares down at the backs of her hands with an expression that suggests she doesn't recognize them. Ever since last night she has not been acting herself. He's never hidden what he is from her, but even so she has never seen the worst of what is in him. Not until last night. She has always loved him unconditionally, through drunken arrests and even through the times he lost his temper and maybe got too rough, but last night he thinks may have been too much for her. It happened right in front of her and she could not pretend she did not see it or did not understand it—and it might have been too much for her.

He sensed her troubled mind in the silent darkness last night after they went to bed, while they lay side by side, and he feels it now. He does not like the silence. It makes him nervous. Beatrice is not one to keep her thoughts to herself. But today she is almost without voice. What is she thinking? What's going on in that head of hers? He's going to have to make her understand that what he did last night was necessary. That he didn't like it any better than she did, but it was necessary. Sometimes bloodletting is the only choice. All survivors know this.

The world is a hard place with lots of sharp corners, and sometimes to survive you have to put someone else between you and the worst of it. He doesn't like it any more than she does. But he accepts it as the way things are.

He needed their truck. He needed their truck and Flint suspected something. From the very beginning Flint was suspicious of them. They simply couldn't leave him alive. He would have called the police. With him dead, with him and his wife dead, they have a clean vehicle for the next two or three days. Long enough to get them to his older brother's place in California.

Of course he'll have to get rid of Ian Hunt at some point before they get there. He can do that. Maybe he can even do that today. He'll just follow Hunt from a distance, hang back and follow. If he's careful he can go unnoticed. The man doesn't know he got in front of them. It might be difficult to remain unnoticed once traffic thins out and the land becomes more barren in West Texas, but even there it should be possible. He'll follow Hunt, wait for the man to settle down for the night. Then he'll make the fucker bleed.

He'll make him sorry he didn't die the first time.

And that'll be the end of his troubles. After that they can lie low in California for a few months. Even if the police decide to nose around Ron's house, there are places to hide. Ron has lots of places in which to wait out trouble. An underground bomb shelter with canned food and five hundred gallons of drinking water and a two-hundred-gallon gray-water tank. Abandoned buildings where he has stored supplies. According to his letters, once the iron mine dried up the town blew away with the dust and he's one of only twenty or thirty residents left. And that was years ago. It could be he's the last person in town. There will be plenty of shadows to hide in, even beneath the California sun. They'll wait it out, wait till things cool off, and then head down to Mexico. Or maybe up to Canada. But probably Mexico.

It'll be safer to cross the border in California than in Texas. And he'll have a chance to get some money before they head down. He doesn't want to be flat broke in Mexico. A different country will take some getting used to, but it's better than the alternative. The important thing is staying out of prison, staying out of prison and staying together.

But first Ian Hunt has to die.

In the two hundred miles between Junction and Fort Stockton, Texas, the landscape changes. The trees give way to shrubbery and low yellow flowers. The yellow flowers stretch from dry earth or dead grass. Desert hills erupt from the flat earth like goiters, and Interstate 10 cuts through many of them, leaving dynamited and scraped cliffs butting up to the asphalt and stacked up beside you in multi-colored layers descending into the past. The moisture leaves the air, and cacti soak up the sun, their fat pads like the flippers of some lost exotic underwater creature waving at you from the side of the road. Ancient stripper-well pumpjacks like prehistoric birds peck at the ground in the Permian Basin oil fields, moving in slow, sleepy, repetitious motion. The traffic thins to nothing but the occasional Mack truck hauling a load from coast to coast, driver red eyed and tweaked out, or some other lonesome traveler. Occasional desert rabbits splatter the shoulders of the road, revealing their hearts to you. Past the halfway point between these two towns, somewhere around Bakersfield, great fields of windmills turn slowly in the distance like ceiling fans on a mild day. Everything seems to move slowly in this mean desert heat, even your vehicle with the needle past eighty. You drive and drive but never seem to get anywhere. Then you arrive in Fort Stockton and are greeted by a large statue of a roadrunner, the world's largest, they say (every town needs a point of pride), standing behind a short brick wall faced with a sign welcoming you to town.

It's two thirty when Hunt pulls off Interstate 10. Henry follows, glad to have a chance to step out of this hot fucking truck and stretch a bit. They've been on the road for hours, his back is killing him, and Bee's complained of a leak in the canoe at least a half dozen times. Also, gas needle is south of the E, and he's spent the last twenty minutes worrying about puttering to a stop on the side of the road, miles from a gas station.

Hunt pulls into a Chevron station on the corner of Front Street and US 285, and Henry pulls into a competing station across the street from it.

He watches the man step from his Mustang and stretch his arms. His left arm, anyway. His right arm doesn't get above his shoulder. Arms stretched, he twists his neck around. There's a satchel in his right hand and after he stretches he straps it over his shoulder.

Henry wonders what's inside. Probably guns.

The man does not look like he was shot in the chest yesterday. He should be bedridden.

Well, it don't matter. He'll be dead by the time the sun kisses the horizon. By the time the sun shines on tomorrow at the latest.

Henry reaches for his pocket and finds it empty. He swallows back the sharp taste of stomach acid.

'Can I pee now?'

'Yeah, go ahead,' he says. 'Take Sarah with you, and don't let her talk to nobody. You know what? Never mind. I'll take her when you get back. She can sit with me for now. But get me some Rolaids or Tums or something like that.' He pulls a sweaty five spot from the pocket of his Levis and hands it to Bee.

'Okay,' she says, taking the damp money in her fist and stepping from the truck. 'Can I get something to drink?'

'Sure.'

She limp-waddles toward the convenience store.

He watches her go. She isn't the same since last night. She isn't the same at all. He really needs to talk to her, but he doesn't want to do it in front of Sarah. He doesn't know why, but her presence makes him feel vulnerable, and he does not like to feel vulnerable. He does not like to talk about what he's feeling or thinking under even the best of circumstances, and this ain't the best of circumstances. He can ramble on about any nonsense you like, grinning and boozing and patting backs, but he cannot open his mouth and let out what he is really feeling without great effort. It wants to catch in his throat and stay there, hidden in darkness. But he needs to talk to Bee. He's afraid he might lose her if he does not.

He glances past the traffic to Ian Hunt across the street. The man is sticking a gas nozzle into his car and squinting at the horizon. For a moment Henry thinks Hunt is staring directly at him, but he's not. Just squinting at the horizon, that's all.

Ian squints over the hood of his car at a gray Dodge Ram pickup truck across the intersection. A work truck, from the looks of it. Covered in dirt. Big white toolbox in the back. Tailgate down and hanging a little low, like someone put too much weight on it and bent it out of shape. It's been behind him for a few hours now. Every once in a while he catches sight of it, white-hot sun reflecting a shiny-nickel-on-the-sidewalk star of light on the hood. The intersection is wide and Ian's vision isn't quite what it once was (there was a time he boasted twenty-fifteen eyesight, better than perfect, he told people), and he can't see the face of the man sitting behind the wheel, but as he stands there pumping gas a part of him believes it must be Henry Dean.

Ian feels a terrible urge to grab the rifled shotgun from the back seat of his car, rest it in the crook of his shoulder, and fire a deer slug into the head of the man behind the wheel. He can envision the clear glass turning instantly white as the slug hits and sends millions of cracks through it. He can envision the glass falling away from the frame seconds later, revealing a man with a hole in his temple. Big enough to stick the fat end of a pool cue into. The blood and brains splattered inside the truck like a cherry bomb was planted in a wad of raw hamburger. The man falling forward, head on the steering wheel, weighing against the horn as it blares its single idiot note.

He can picture it so clearly.

But even if he knew it was Henry, now would not be the time, here would not be the place. Here he would have but one chance, and if he missed some cowboy would tackle him to the ground, and Henry would be able to drive away to freedom with Maggie still in his possession. If he missed Henry he might hit Maggie. Even if he didn't miss, shotgun slugs have a lot of push and it might go clean through Henry and hit Maggie.

Or some other innocent.

He hasn't given much thought to what he's become, to how far he is willing to go down this road of degradation, but he knows he is unwilling to shoot innocents in order to achieve his ends. For now he is unwilling to do that. Unless he has to.

And anyway, he is not certain it's Henry. He believes it is, he believes it might be, but he is old enough and has been wrong often enough to know that reality and what he believes don't always align with one another.

The gas nozzle clicks in his hand and stops pumping, tank full. He tops it off, getting the price to an even thirty-five bucks, then puts the nozzle back into its cradle on the pump. He screws on his gas cap. He squints once more across the intersection, then heads toward the convenience store. Halfway there he starts coughing and staggers left, into a woman and her husband leaving the store.

'Whoa there, fella,' the man says, catching him.

Ian puts a hand on the man's shoulder, trying to hold himself up, and the gunshot wound cored through him screams. He grunts in pain, then closes his eyes as sweat runs down his cheeks. He swallows back the urge to cough again. He stands upright, then wipes at his cheeks with the backs of his hands, left then right.

'You all right, hon?' the woman says.

'Yeah,' Ian says. 'Thank you. Sorry about crashing into you.'

'Sure you're all right?' the man says.

'Yeah,' Ian says. 'Cough just ran away with me is all.'

'You don't look so good,' the man says. 'Maybe you should sit down.'

'Do you want some water?' the woman asks, proffering a bottle. 'I ain't drunk from it yet.'

'No, thank you,' Ian says. 'I'm okay now.'

He sits on the toilet in the bathroom a moment, face in his palms, trying to breathe like normal humans breathe. Every exhalation creates a high-pitched wheeze bordering on a whistle. He looks down at his shirt and sees a brown spot about the size of a quarter and spreading. But not quickly. He feels hot and cold simultaneously, and though he's covered in sweat a shiver snakes up his spine.

He gets to his feet and walks to the sink. He pours two or three tramadol into his mouth, palms water in after them, and swallows.

He grabs a bottle of water, a pre-packaged tuna fish and cheddar sandwich, a bag of barbecue-flavored corn chips, and a box of caffeine tablets. The pain medication makes him drowsy and he's afraid he might fall asleep at the wrong moment. He walks to the counter. His knees feel wobbly. When he gets to the front of the line he sets his purchases on the counter and the woman behind it asks if that'll be all, dear, and he asks for a cigar. All they have are dollar shits, but he says that's fine. He doesn't plan on smoking it, anyway, just wants something to gnaw on while he drives, another way to keep himself awake. She rings him up and bags his purchases and he heads back into the mean Texas heat.

The Dodge Ram across the street is still there. He's not a hundred percent it's Henry, but the damned thing has been behind him for hours. Still, it could be a coincidence. Sometimes when driving long distances you find yourself next to someone, or behind someone, or in front of someone, and you just happen to pace one another for hours, popping into and out of sight of one another as you progress on your respective journeys, and then as the sun sets you find yourself in the same diner with them, grabbing a quick bite before bed, and when you make eye contact it's like running into an old friend. Howdy, fellow traveler.

Sometimes that happens. There's no reason it has to be Henry. But a feeling in his gut tells him it probably is.

Ian falls back into his car and pulls a sheet of caffeine tablets from its box. He pops four pills through the sheet's foil back and puts them into his mouth, dry swallowing one after the other. They are very bitter. Once the pills are down he tears the plastic off his sandwich and takes a bite. It's dry and flavorless, as he knew it would be—gas-station sandwiches are never otherwise—but his stomach grumbles all the same, anticipating its descent. He chews and swallows. A piece of cheese sticks to the roof of his mouth and he scrapes it off with a finger, chews, and swallows that as well.

He starts the car, shoves it into gear, and pulls out into the street, looking for a sign that will guide him onto Interstate 10.

———

He shifts into fourth and looks at his speedometer. Eighty-two miles per. His old car rattles loudly at this speed, and a loud wind whirs even with the windows rolled up, the rubber seals long ago rotted away.

He glances into his rearview mirror. Sunlight stars off the hood of a gray pickup truck about a quarter mile back.

He imagines letting it come up on him. He imagines slamming on his brakes and letting it rear-end him. He imagines stepping from his vehicle and—

He cannot do it like that. Maggie is in the truck. If it is Henry, then Maggie is in the truck. And he has already been shot. If he is going to kill Henry and get his Maggie back he will have to be much more subtle than that. Much more careful than that.

He sighs, curses under his breath, and rotates his left shoulder. He figures he's got another three or four hours of driving left in him today, and then he's done. He's tired and in pain and having trouble breathing. The heat is tremendous. Cold chills run through him, giving him goose-flesh. He is covered in a sickly sweat.

'Shit,' he says about everything and nothing at all.

Then turns on the radio to block out his thoughts.

From Fort Stockton to Sierra Blanca the land empties further. Traffic is sparse. Rock formations litter the horizon, and the scrublands spread out before you like a sheet.

Looking at this while he drives and eats barbecue-flavored corn chips and the second half of his dry tuna fish sandwich Ian thinks, not for the first time, about how ancient this land is. After he finished high school his mother—still mourning her husband's suicide—sent him traveling through Europe, visiting London and Paris (where he met his first wife) and Rome, and the history there made him feel very strange about coming from such a young country. It made him feel like an orphan somehow, without any real history to call his own. The curse of the American mutt: you come from nowhere, son. In America you build yourself from scratch, from the ground up, making your own bootstraps to pull yourself up with, or you don't exist. Don't expect to stand on the shoulders of those who came before: this is a land for which there is no before. But Burroughs was right: America is *not* a young land. It is old and dirty and evil. It lay here for millions of years in silence, waiting; it lay here home only to beasts with no language but the hunt, waiting; it lay here ancient and scabrous, waiting. And finally twenty thousand years ago, thirty thousand years ago, people arrived, but still the evil of the land remained trapped in the soil. Then the Europeans came to the eastern shores, and they pierced the soil with their flags, and released it. And it spread across the land and polluted the waters and the vegetables and grains whose roots the waters fed. And through the food it got into the people.

Ian pops the last of the sandwich into his mouth and washes it down with a swig of water.

As he nears Sierra Blanca he decides, because he wants to see if the gray Dodge Ram follows him, to stop someplace and buy a Coke. The town is less populated than the last one he went through, and if it is Henry behind him, perhaps he can end it here. He pulls off the interstate and onto El Paso Street, glancing in his rearview mirror. The gray Dodge Ram is just in view, a glint on the horizon. Which means his car should be just in view too.

He drives past a dirt lot, then the firehouse, a red fire engine parked inside and a sign on the garage door that says DO NOT BLOCK. Beyond the firehouse, an empty parking lot. He stops at a stop sign. There are no other cars around. Brown hills float in the distance. He takes his foot off the brake. On his right he passes a white Spanish-style building and on his left a brown structure advertising ICE and COCA-COLA. Sweat trickles down the side of his face. The ICE is very tempting.

He glances at his rearview mirror. The road behind him is empty.

If the truck was going to follow him into town it should have done so by now. Maybe it was just a coincidence. Henry Dean did not own a gray Dodge Ram pickup truck. But of course even a dumb man would know to get rid of his own vehicle while on the run, and while Henry probably isn't well-read—ain't book-smart, as they say—Ian does not think he's dumb. He thinks he's sharp as a blade and merciless in exactly the same way.

He passes a grocery store and then a place called Best Cafe with a wood shingled roof and tables draped in red checkered cloth set out on a concrete slab. He passes a motel and a Southern Pacific train car sitting on a plot of dirt. He passes the Historic Sierra Lodge and a turquoise-painted gift shop with a Dr Pepper machine out front and an American flag hanging limp in the dead heat. He glances into the rearview mirror once more.

Nothing.

He pulls to the dirt lot in front of a place called the Branding Iron Steakhouse and steps from his car. The white hot sun beats down on him.

He squints at the road behind him and sees nothing.

'Fuck,' he says.

He no longer wants a Coke.

He's shifting into third when he sees the gray truck on the side of the interstate, a Hudspeth County Sheriff's Department car parked behind it and a sheriff's deputy standing at the driver's side window.

As Ian drives by he tries to catch a glimpse of the man behind the wheel but the deputy is blocking his view. Then as he passes he glances over his shoulder thinking maybe he can see through the windshield, but it's late afternoon now and the sun is in the west, and its light glints off the glass making it impossible to see anything.

He shifts into fourth and looks behind him once more. He simply can't tell. It could be Henry. It could be anyone. It could be Jesus behind the wheel with a couple apostles piled onto the seat beside him.

'Is there wine in that jug, sir?'

'It was water when we left. I swear it, officer.'

As he continues on he can see eastbound cars pulling off the interstate and into a lane leading through a border checkpoint.

He wonders again if that was Henry back there. If his daughter was in that truck.

He doesn't know if he hopes it was—or if he hopes it wasn't.

Maggie is looking through the cab's rear window, watching the road fly out from under the truck like a gray ribbon, when she sees the police car flash its lights.

'Shit,' Henry says.

He slows the truck, downshifting, and the police car comes nearer. The man behind the wheel is big, with a round pink face and a mustache. Maggie smiles and waves at him and he waves back without smiling. His hand looks very big.

'It's the police,' Maggie says.

'Shut up.'

Henry flips his turn signal on and pulls the truck to the shoulder of the road.

'Turn around in your seat,' he says, grabbing Maggie by the shoulder. 'Buckle up.'

'He already saw me.'

'Just buckle the fuck up.'

She sits down and fastens her seatbelt. She looks up into the rearview mirror to see where the policeman is, but cannot see him. The angle is wrong. She listens to traffic. A car flies by. A moment later another one. She hears footsteps on asphalt. She leans forward, past Henry, and sees a policeman appear in the window. He is broad and has black hair and for some reason his mustache looks kind of fake up close. Maggie remembers a friend having a mustache like that. He wore it when he dressed up as a pirate for Halloween.

'Afternoon,' the policeman says.

'Howdy, sir,' Henry says. 'Hot out, ain't it?'

'Do you know why I pulled you over?'

'Can't say that I do.'

Maggie wants to mouth two words to him. She wants to but he will not look at her. He only looks at Henry.

'You were going ninety-two miles an hour.'

'Was I really?' Henry laughs. 'I'll be goddamned, I sure am sorry about—'

'There's no need to take the Lord's name in vain, sir.'

'Aw, shit, I'm sorry. My mouth runs about five steps ahead of my brain sometimes.' He flaps his right hand like a talking puppet.

'I'm gonna need to see your license and registration.'

Look my way, look my way, look my way. Maggie thinks this with great concentration while staring at the policeman's sweaty pink face.

And for a wonder he does look at her. The policeman looks right at her and their eyes meet and he has green eyes like her daddy has green eyes, like she has green eyes, and he nods his head slightly.

Help. Me.

He blinks at her, not seeming to understand.

'You mean a sorry don't cut in this county?'

'License and registration, sir.' Then he glances back toward her.

Help me. Please.

Another blink. And then, as if suddenly poked in the back by a sharp stick, his whole body stiffens and a light flashes behind his eyes. He licks his lips and his right hand drops toward his weapon. He takes a step back. His Adam's apple bobs in his throat.

'Step out of the car, sir.'

'Hold on, now,' Henry says, reaching under his seat. 'I think I got the registration down here under the—'

The policeman draws his gun and aims it at Henry. 'Put your hands where I can see them,' he says. 'No, freeze. Freeze.'

'All right.'

The policeman licks his lips. He looks confused. He takes a step back and then a step forward. He licks his lips again.

Henry is leaning forward with his right arm underneath his seat. He moves slowly, pulling away from there. Maggie thinks he has a gun under the seat.

'I said freeze!' the policeman says. 'That means don't move.'

'I'm froze, sir,' Henry says. 'I'm a fucking popsicle.'

'Shut your mouth.'

'You're making a mistake, officer.'

'I said shut up.'

The policeman reaches to the truck door and pulls it open. He licks his lips again. He looks very scared and Maggie feels kind of sorry for him. She's afraid that he won't be able to stop Henry. She's afraid that Henry will kill him. Should she open her mouth and tell the policeman that Henry has a gun? Will that make him panic? Will it make Henry panic? Maybe Henry will just pull his empty hand from under the seat. But she thought in hopeful maybes last night and two people got killed.

'Okay,' he says to Henry. 'Pull your hand out from under that seat. Slow.'

'Okay.'

'Your hand better be empty.'

'Okay.' Henry pulls his hand out from under the seat. Slowly.

Sweat trickles down the policeman's face. Keeping both hands gripped around his service pistol, he wipes his face off on his shoulder, shrugging the sweat away.

Maggie opens her mouth to speak, but too late.

Henry pulls out a gun.

Henry can feel the wooden grip of the Lupara in his sweaty palm. It feels grimy there and foreign. His face is hot. He looks to his left and can see the deputy aiming his service weapon at him. He can't be more than thirty-five, and he's scared, which makes Henry nervous. Scared people are jumpy and jumpy people are dangerous.

Henry's eyes feel hot in their sockets. They sting. Sweat trickles down the bridge of his nose and drips from the end of it. He can feel the rhythm of his heart in his temples. He swallows back bile and wishes he could chew an antacid.

Did the cop recognize him? One second the guy was cool and the next he was pointing a gun in Henry's face. Something happened. Did he recognize him? Did Sarah signal him in some way? Did Beatrice?

He wants to believe that Bee would never do anything like that, but he does not. She might. She has not been herself. If she has become scared of him she might do something like that. He doesn't want it to be the case, but he knows it's a possibility.

Stop. Focus.

It is silent now but for the sound of his heart beating. Slowly he pulls the weapon from under the seat. Waiting for his moment. Waiting for his—

The deputy shrugs a trickle of sweat off the side of his face. Now.

Henry whips the Lupara from under the seat of the truck. It almost catches on something, he feels it bang against a metal bar, but it does not catch. He brings it around quickly without raising it, just turns it in his fist, and pulls the trigger with his thumb.

The first shot hits the deputy in the hip and spins him around. Maggie screams and the smell of gun smoke fills the cab. He pulls the Lupara up and gives the deputy the second barrel. It takes away the left side of his chest, simply wipes it off like the skin from a rotten peach, revealing the meat beneath. He staggers backwards and then falls to the asphalt.

A screeching of brakes.

Henry looks left and sees a red Chevy sedan coming to a stop, turning sidewise on its locked tires and leaving a trail of burned rubber behind it. It comes to a stop only inches from the stricken deputy who even now is exhaling his last two or three breaths from colorless lips.

Henry opens the break and pulls out the spent shells, dropping them to the asphalt (there's no point in pretending he needs to be careful now), and reloads the Lupara with shells from his Levis. He aims the shotgun at the blond woman behind the wheel of the Chevy and says, 'Get the fuck out the car right now or I'll shoot you dead.'

He looks to see how many cars are around and finds the road mercifully empty. For the moment, anyway.

The woman behind the wheel is frozen in place, staring at him with wide cow's eyes.

'Get the fuck out now! Do you wanna die?'

Still she does not move.

Henry walks to the car and yanks open the door and pulls the woman out. He throws her to the ground, and is taking aim when he hears Beatrice's voice.

'Sarah, get back here!'

He looks toward the truck. It is empty.

Beatrice is limping pathetically after Sarah as she runs across the flat, dry West Texas landscape toward the low, weathered buildings of Sierra Blanca.

'Sarah, no!' Bee says. 'Come back!'

Henry runs after them, saying, 'Sarah, stop, goddamn you!'

Beatrice trips and falls and lets out a wounded-animal yelp.

Henry runs, feeling heavy and uncoordinated, and as he does the Lupara slips from the grip of his sweaty hand and drops to the ground. He stops for it, looking around. It is lost in tall dead grass. He cannot see the goddamn thing anywhere and—

'Henry! Henry, get Sarah!'

He looks toward Beatrice. She is still sitting where she fell. If he lets Sarah go, Bee will never forgive him. He can see it in her face.

He nods, leaves the Lupara—he can get it on the way back to the truck—and runs after the small girl frantically fleeing across the scrublands toward the white and brown buildings of Sierra Blanca, which are scattered across the ground like a child's forgotten toy blocks.

Two and a half hours after passing through Sierra Blanca Ian reaches his limit. He has driven through the seemingly alien landscape of far West Texas, reaching Sparks and Southview and other suburbs of El Paso, then plowed through the city itself, Mexico visible on his left as Interstate 10 scooped down near the border, passing Holy Family Church America-side and Doniphan Park in Juarez. He left the city behind, tempted to stop only once, as he passed a place called Rudy's Country Store & BarBQ near a hotel, the thought of a hot meal and a soft bed in a cool room briefly causing him to pull his foot from the gas pedal. But he was tired of Texas—it seemed to stretch on forever, and after fourteen hours on the road just getting across the state line became a goal—so he continued on, into New Mexico, and through Las Cruces and a closed border checkpoint. And now, after having passed through it, with airplanes flying overhead, landing at and taking off from Las Cruces International Airport just to his north (he can't see it, but he knows it's there to his right because he saw a sign pointing him that way), he is finished. He has made it through Texas and into New Mexico. He hasn't seen the gray truck since Sierra Blanca, and he has convinced himself that it wasn't Henry at all. Henry is on the road up ahead. And by tomorrow he will be waiting for Ian in a town called Kaiser, California, and that is where Ian will kill him. Ian will kill him and he will get Maggie back. That is the plan.

But that is for tomorrow.

The orange sun is sinking into the ground for another night. The sky is turning gray, the color spreading in the clear sky like a cloud of kicked-up mud in a once-clear pool of water, and soon the entire dome will be tainted by night.

He is done. Done and done.

He pulls off Interstate 10 and cruises along on an unnamed county road that runs parallel for half a mile before pulling into a dirt parking lot in front of a place that seems only to be called Motel/Food. The sign is hand-painted in white on the front of a rotting wood facade, behind which, he assumes, the food is served. The motel part of the operation looks to be about a dozen mobile homes parked willy-nilly behind the restaurant.

His tires kick up a cloud of dust as he brings the car to a stop. He kills the engine and waits for the dust to settle. With his lung in its current state he doesn't think it's a good idea to breathe it in. But once the air is clear he pushes open his car door and steps out into the hot day. He pulls his soggy cigar from his mouth and spits into the sand. He puts the cigar into the front pocket of his shirt and squints out at the interstate.

It is just empty asphalt.

He straps the satchel containing the Pleur-evac system over his shoulder, takes off his sunglasses, hangs them on his shirt, squints in the suddenly bright light, and heads, past a couple tables with salt and pepper shakers set upon them, into Motel/Food.

A stainless steel counter in a window between Ian and the kitchen. A short-order cook, guy in his sixties with tufts of gray hair sprouting from every orifice like shrubbery, is hunched over the counter, flipping through a titty book with a limp cigarette hanging from his bottom lip. A cloud of smoke around his head.

As the bell above the door rattles—it certainly doesn't ring—the guy stands, straightening the greasy white box of a hat on his head. A couple inches of ash drop from the end of his smoke and fall onto a centerfold model before rolling down into the fold between the pages. He pulls the cigarette from his mouth, blows the ash to the floor, folds the magazine, and stashes it under the counter.

'Howdy. Food or bed?'

'I could use something to drink.'

'Monica's in the shitter and Betsy's stepped out a minute, so that'll have to wait a sec. Not hungry?'

Ian coughs into his hand, then wipes his palm off on his Levis.

'I could have a burger,' he says.

'Cheeseburger?'

'Okay.'

'American, Swiss, cheddar?'

'Swiss.'

'Fries?'

'Yeah.'

'Fried egg on top?'

'Of the fries?'

'Burger.'

Ian shakes his head.

'Sure?'

'Yeah, no egg.'

'All right. Coming up.'

He turns left, peels a patty off a stack of them, and tosses it onto his waiting grill. While that's going, he pulls out a bun, smears it, drops some fries into the fry basket, and gets to humming what Ian thinks is supposed to be 'Under My Thumb'.

Somewhere a toilet flushes, and a moment later a door

opens. A woman walks out, saying, 'We're low on toilet paper, Uncle Hal. A whole roll in a day. Someone needs to change their fucking diet!' Then she sees Ian standing there and blushes. It makes her pretty. 'Sorry,' she says. 'I didn't realize.'

'Quite all right. Monica or Betsy?'

'Monica. Betsy's with a . . . checking on a room.'

Ian nods.

Monica's in her thirties with reddish-brown hair set atop a pale and freckle-spotted face. She is shaped like a twig, no hips at all, and wearing a denim skirt and a T-shirt.

Ian finds her unaccountably sexy. But he has always been attracted to unconventionally pretty women.

'I see Uncle Hal's already cooking.'

'Cheeseburger and fries.'

'Fried egg on top?'

Ian shakes his head.

'Want anything to drink?'

'What do you got?'

She pokes her thumb over her shoulder, toward the small glass-doored refrigerator humming dully against the wall.

'Couple Buds, I guess, and a bottle of water.'

'All at once?'

Ian nods. 'Thirsty.'

'Will you be staying with us tonight?'

'Yeah, if you got the space.'

She lets out a brief laugh. 'Yeah, I think we can squeeze y'in. Just you?'

'Yeah.'

'It'll be seventy-two forty-five,' she says. 'Plus I'll need a credit card on file. We got pay-per-view.'

'I won't use it.'

Monica smiles. 'I don't mean to be rude, but if we trusted

every stranger walked through the door we'd've been broke a long time ago. Ain't that right, Uncle Hal?'

'Sure is, Monocle.'

'I reckon that's true,' Ian says. 'Monocle your nickname?'

'Don't get any ideas.'

'Mean anything?'

Monica shakes her head. 'Just an Uncle Hal-ism.'

He pays with a credit card and puts a five-dollar bill in the tip jar (an emptied tub of red vines with a few loose bills floating around the bottom).

Monica hands him a key.

'You'll be in room four, first trailer on the left, door on the left.'

Ian nods.

Monica turns around and pulls open the fridge. When she turns back, she has his two beers and his water. She sets them on the counter next to a tub of ostrich jerky.

'You can sit wherever. I'll bring your food when it's ready.'

'Thanks.'

He grabs his drinks and walks to a table by the fly-specked window. He sits down and looks out at the desert. A truck hauling groceries rumbles past, and then emptiness. After another five minutes a 747 roars by overhead, shaking the windows in their frames. And then more silence. Ian's eyes sting. He closes them.

'You want some TV?'

Ian is about to say no, thanks, I don't reckon there's anything much on right now, anyway, but Monica doesn't wait for a reply. She grabs the remote from the counter, aims it, and presses a button. The TV comes to life, and a situation comedy flickers across the screen, all set-designed studio and laugh-track laughter. Ian pops a beer and takes a swallow. It is good and cold and soothing on his dry throat. He wonders if he shouldn't be drinking. Alcohol thins the blood. Fuck it. It's only beer and he's only having two.

He nods to himself.

'Fuck it,' he says, aloud this time, and takes another swallow.

'Excuse me?'

Ian shakes his head, nothing, sorry, and turns back to the smudged window. The right half of his body is throbbing with pain.

What if that was Henry Dean pulled over to the side of the road back near Sierra Blanca? Maybe he was arrested and even now is sitting in a Hudspeth County jailhouse. Maybe Debbie is on her way now to pick Maggie up. Maybe there's a message on his answering machine telling him all about it. 'Where the hell are you, Ian? I've called your cell twenty times but it keeps going to voicemail. You'll never believe what great good fortune we've had. Henry Dean was—'

No: that isn't how it happens.

His stomach tightens at the thought of it happening that way. He isn't sure why.

Because you want to run toward oblivion and this gives you an excuse. You know exactly why, Ian, so stop lying to yourself.

He pushes that thought away. He will not accept that.

Even if that were true, it wouldn't—

'You're a million miles away, aren't you?'

Ian jumps and a startled grunt escapes his throat. After a silent moment of nothing, he laughs at himself.

'Guess I was,' he says.

'I didn't mean to scare you,' Monica says, setting down a white plate with a cheeseburger and fries on it.

'I know it,' Ian says.

'Mind if I sit down? Betsy's back so I can kick up my heels a minute.' She gestures toward the counter. Ian didn't even hear the bell above the door rattle, but there she is, Betsy, standing behind the counter, sipping a Cactus Cooler and looking up at the TV in the corner of the room. She's a little younger than Monica, and a little bit prettier, and a little bit curvier, but obviously her sister.

Ian pushes a chair out with his foot. 'Take a load off.'

'Thanks.' She sits down.

Ian flashes her a brief smile, then turns back to the window. The desert stretches on and on, dotted here and there with creosote bushes. Hills float in the distance.

'Nothing out there worth looking at,' Monica says.

'You don't think so?'

She shakes her head. 'Just desert and glimpses of people going to and from places you'll never see yourself. Every once in a while, maybe they stop in, maybe they tell you a little bit about where they've been, but it's just a story you heard, and then they leave again.'

'Is it that hard to pick up and go?'

Monica shrugs. 'Harder than it should be. I've packed my bags a dozen times.'

'Yeah? How come you never went?'

Monica is silent for a long time. Then: 'I guess I don't want to talk about that.'

'Okay.'

Ian takes another swallow of beer.

'What about you?' Monica says.

'What about me what?'

'Where you headed to?'

'California.'

'Los Angeles? Hollywood?'

Ian shakes his head. 'No,' he says, 'not this time.'

'But you been before?'

Ian nods.

'Do you know anybody famous? Is it glamorous?'

'No. It's just a big suburb surrounding pockets of city.'

'No, I bet it's glamorous.'

Ian shrugs.

'I was in a play once. A school play. *Macbeth*, I think. Is *Macbeth* the one with the witches in it?'

'It has witches in it,' Ian says, 'the weird sisters.'

'Yeah,' Monica says. 'I played one of them.'

'Do you remember any of it?'

'Oh, God.' She looks far away for a moment, and then a smile lights up her face. ' "When the hurly-burly's done, when the battle's lost and won." That's all I remember. I always wanted to go to Hollywood and be famous.'

'It's never too late,' Ian says.

'You really think so?'

Ian doesn't answer for a moment. Then: 'I guess I don't.'

'That's what I thought. What are you going to California for?'

'It's my turn to not want to talk about it.'

'I didn't mean to pry.'

Ian shakes his head. 'You didn't.'

He picks up a couple fries and shoves them into his mouth. They taste good. Warm and salty and over-cooked by normal standards, which is how he likes them.

'It's so lonesome, isn't it?'

Ian looks at Monica. She is staring out the window at the desert landscape.

'I guess it is.'

'Do you ever get lonesome?'

'Doesn't everybody?'

'You married?'

Ian shoves a couple more fries into his mouth and holds up his left hand. There are no rings upon his finger. 'I was once. Well, thrice, actually. None of them stuck.'

'You were married *three* times?'

He smiles. 'I believed the vows every time, too.'

'Wow. Do you miss it?'

'What?'

'Being married.'

'Sometimes. Mostly at night.'

'Do you think you'll miss it tonight?'

'I don't know.'

''Cause we could pretend.'

'I'm sorry?'

She puts her hand on his knee. 'We could pretend. I could . . .' she licks her lips, 'we could lie together.'

Ian smiles at her, suddenly understanding. But after laying his hand upon hers and letting it rest there a moment, he pushes her hand away. Gently. 'I don't think that's a good idea.'

'It would only be seventy dollars. We work it out where we charge for an extra room. You could use your credit card.'

'It's not you, Monica. I have a medical condition.'

'What, like herpes?'

Ian is so startled by the question, and the blankly serious look on Monica's face, that he actually laughs. The laugh turns into a cough, but he manages to stifle it early. He clears his throat. 'Sorry,' he says. 'No, not herpes. It's just—it's not a good idea.'

'Okay,' Monica says. 'Do you mind if I still sit with you?'

'No,' Ian says. 'In fact, I'd like that.'

He's just eating the last of his dinner when a local news program comes on. After some talk of little or no import a brunette woman with her hair in a bun, big brown eyes, and a tight-fitting blouse says, 'Just under three hours ago, on Interstate 10, outside the small Texas town of Sierra Blanca, a Hudspeth County Sheriff's Deputy, Deputy Pagana, was killed during a routine stop. The incident was captured by the deputy's dashboard-mounted camera. Police have released the footage to the media in the hopes that it will lead to information on the whereabouts of the perpetrator of this crime. We would like to warn you that the following footage is of a disturbing nature and may be inappropriate for children.'

An awkward pause during which the newswoman blinks at the camera, and then a cut to grainy footage seen through a dirty windshield. The footage is in color, and has audio, though the audio is tinny and hard to hear. Mostly just background noise with the occasional rumblings of a voice you can't understand. It is dated and time coded. For a moment all that's visible is the back of a gray Dodge Ram pickup truck. Ian can see Maggie through the rear window. She is looking back at the car, seemingly at the camera, at him, then a hand, Henry's hand, grabs her and turns her around. A uniformed sheriff's deputy then walks along the left side of the frame. He reaches the truck. Ian's Mustang passes by on the road behind him. There is some talking. Then, without warning, the deputy pulls out his gun. He steps back. He looks scared. He yells. He pulls open the truck's door and yells some more. He wipes sweat off his face with his shoulder. And then a flash from the truck. A red explosion from the deputy's hip. He staggers backwards several steps, out of frame. A red mist hangs in the air. Then another flash from the truck. Henry steps into the daylight, breaks open his sawed-off shotgun and pulls shells from it. He drops them to the asphalt. He reloads, points the gun at something out of frame, and yells. Sounds like he's telling someone to get out of their car. He curses and the curses are censored by beeps. He walks out of frame toward the person at whom he was yelling. A moment later Maggie slides out of the truck and onto the asphalt. There she is, the bravest person he has ever met. She looks around with frantic eyes, and then runs around the front of the truck and disappears. The gray truck wobbles slightly. Perhaps someone getting out of the passenger side. That side is not in frame. A woman's voice tells someone named Sarah to stop. Henry runs across the frame and around the front of the truck. Toward Maggie. The program cuts back to the woman at the news desk. She looks very serious.

'Police believe Deputy Pagana's killer is a man named Henry Dean,' she says, 'who is already wanted for questioning in connection with several kidnappings and murders in Tonkawa County, Texas. He is believed to be traveling with his wife, Beatrice Dean, and a young girl named Magdalene Hunt, who, police believe, Mr Dean kidnapped from her home over seven years ago. If you have any information as to the whereabouts of Mr Dean, please call Detective Roderick with the Hudspeth County Sheriff's Department or Detective Sanchez at the Federal Bureau of Investigation's El Paso field office.'

Phone numbers appear onscreen.

Ian steps out into the dying light. He walks to his car, grabs a duffel bag with clothes in it and the sawed-off shotgun he got from the police station. He squints out at the gray asphalt of the interstate and past it to the desert landscape.

The entire right side of his body throbs with pain. He feels sweaty and sticky and dirty and sick.

After a moment he turns away from the road and makes his way around back of Motel/Food to find his room.

Picture yourself standing on a road beneath the white sun. Sweat trickles down your face. Your skin is overheated and itchy. Your clothes are damp and they stick to your skin. How you got here is irrelevant: you're here. And you are looking to the northeast, toward Sierra Blanca. You're looking that way because that's where it's happening . . .

A blond girl in a dress runs through tall dead grass. She is barefoot, you can see that as her heels kick above the grass, and her feet kick up sprays of dirt as she runs. If the frame included only her bare feet cutting through the grass the scene could be a happy one: a girl running toward her one true love. It would all depend on the soundtrack. But this is a long shot and you see much more than just the feet, and the soundtrack is raspy breathing and feet pounding against dirt. Behind the girl is a fat older man. You've never met him but you know his name. Henry Dean. He runs after the girl. For every two steps she takes, the man requires only one. The distance between them shrinks and shrinks and shrinks, and she screams for help as she nears the town, but help does not come. Then the man is upon her, and he swings with a heavy arm and his fist hits the side of her head like a swinging club, and she is off her feet, in the air, still moving forward, but also sideways with the force of the blow. Then she falls, vanishing into the tall grass.

The ground rushes up at her, oh God how did this happen, I was supposed to get away, and her head smashes against a rock in the ground, and the blow switches off her consciousness like a light—click—and in the dark room of her mind she has only some small sense of what is happening. Warmth against her body: the hot ground upon which she lies. A breeze blows and the tall dead grass rustles around her making sounds like whispers. Hush. Something sticky running into the bowls of her closed eyes. Someone picks her up. A grunt, not her own, for she is silent and silent and silent.

She tries to open her eyes but she cannot. She tries to speak but she cannot. She is locked in the dark room of her mind and cannot see an EXIT sign anywhere, nor a door.

Henry walks back toward Beatrice with Sarah sagging unconscious in his arms. Bee is standing there with dirt on her knees looking at him with her mouth open. Her toes point at one another. Her arms hang at her sides.

'I got her,' he says. 'I got her for you.'

'You shouldn't've hit her.'

'She would've got away.'

'You shouldn't've hit her. You shouldn't've hit her and you shouldn't've shot them people and you shouldn't . . .' Her voice breaks and she stops. Finally she looks up at him once more and says, 'You shouldn't've hit her.'

His first instinct is to tell her to shut her mouth, don't be stupid, I couldn't let her get into town, Bee, but he does not tell her that. He closes his eyes and exhales in a long sigh and opens his eyes and says, 'You're right. I'm sorry.'

'Okay.'

'Now let's get to the truck and get out of here.'

'Her head is bleeding.'

'She fell on a rock.'

'Will she be okay?'

'How the hell should I—'

Several cars are stopped on the interstate. People are talking loudly, panic in their voices, surrounding the dead deputy. A woman is on her phone with the police, practically screaming

Sierra Blanca. News of what happened here will move through town like brushfire. He's lived in a small town all his life and knows how quickly news spreads. He has to get away from here as fast as possible, and there is only one place for him to go. There is nobody he can count on but his big brother.

As he drives onto the interstate he sees the right lane is completely blocked off by flares and traffic is backed up several cars as sheriff's deputies wave cars through one by one.

After everything that's happened, this is where it ends; in some spit-smear of a town in West Texas with the sun beating down on him. He puts on his turn signal and merges into the left lane. He reaches into his shirt pocket and pulls out a roll of antacids and thumbs one into his mouth and chews it.

There are five cars in front of him. Deputies stop each car and ask questions before allowing them through.

This is where it ends.

Henry looks in the rearview mirror as he drives away from the scene of his most recent crime. His chest feels tight, but the further he gets from it, the smaller the scene appears in his rearview mirror, the less his heart seems squeezed. He can barely believe he made it through.

'Where you headed?'

'My brother's place in California.'

'What for?'

'Pick up a car he don't want no more.'

'Brought the whole family?'

'Why not? You don't get to go to California every day.'

'Where you traveling from?'

'Houston.'

'You live in Houston?'

'If you wanna call it living.'

'What kinda car?'

'Fifty-six Buick Special. Gonna restore it.'

'Hobby of yours?'

'Man needs a hobby.'

'All right, go on.'

'Thank ya.'

A smiling salute, and that was it. He was sure they'd ask him for identification. But maybe nobody with authority has arrived yet. Maybe they were just looking for suspicious behavior and if everything seemed cool they'd move on to the next. Doesn't matter.

He slipped through.

The gray road stretches out before them. The cab is silent but for the rattling of the truck itself. Beatrice looks out the window while Sarah leans against her, asleep. Henry glances over trying to read her expression in the reflection on the glass, but it is blank. Her eyes dull, her mouth hanging open slightly. He does not like the silence between them. He is doing all of this for her and he refuses to lose her to it.

'What are you thinking, Bee?'

'Nothing.' She does not even glance toward him when she speaks the word, simply continues to stare out at the emptiness.

'Nothing?'

'Nothing.'

'You must be thinking something.'

No response.

He licks his lips. 'You know I love you, right, Bee?'

'Okay.'

'I know some of the stuff that's happened last two days upset you.'

'It didn't happen. You done it.'

'I had to do it. I did it for you.'

She turns now and there are tears in her eyes. 'Well, you shouldn't've.'

'But, Bee—'

She cuts him off with the silent but vehement shaking of her head. Tears roll down her cheeks. 'You shouldn't've.'

'There was no choice, Bee.'

'There's always a choice.'

'Do you want to go to prison, Bee?'

She wipes at her eyes. 'What would I go to prison for?'

'What do you think?'

'I don't know.'

'Sarah. She's why we had to leave Bulls Mouth. She's why we're on the road now. She's why we needed to get rid of our truck. Why Flint and his woman had to die. Don't you act like you don't know what's going on, and don't you act like it's got nothing to do with you. That ain't fair and you know it.'

'Henry, I—'

'You know what happened to the other Sarahs, Bee. You know what we done. We *both* done it. I did what I had to do to make you happy, but you let me. You knew and you wanted it so I done it. Don't act like you wasn't a part of all this.'

'But . . . I needed—'

Henry nods. 'I know it,' he says. 'That's why I done it.'

'But what you done to that nice couple and to that cop was—'

'Was what I had to do to get us out of a tight spot Sarah got us into.'

'You . . . you killed—'

'I did what I had to to keep our family together.'

Bee sniffles and sits silent a long moment. She licks her lips. Then she looks at him with wide hopeful eyes. 'You *had* to?'

Henry nods. 'I couldn't let nobody tear our family apart, could I?'

'They wanted to take Sarah away?'

'That's right. We couldn't let them do that.'

'Family's the most important thing there is.'

'It is.'

'You didn't really want to stomp on Sarah last night?'

'I was just mad, Bee. I would never hurt Sarah. Not on purpose.'

'Because she's family.'

'That's right.'

'And family's the most important thing there is.'

He nods.

'I love you too, Henry.'

'I know it,' Henry says. 'Now wipe your eyes. I hate to see you cry.'

Ian stands motionless under the hot spray of the shower. His eyes are closed and all he can see is that which exists within his mind and his mind for the moment is empty. These moments are rare and he holds on to them as long as possible, which is never long. As soon as a part of his mind becomes aware of the silence within, it is no longer silent.

The catheter twists out of his chest just below and to the right of his pectoral muscle, and then curls down to the drainage system sitting on the floor just outside the bathtub in which he is standing. It is still in the satchel. He saw no reason to remove it. His body is turned slightly to the right so the shower water does not hit the wounds in his chest.

He opens his eyes and grabs a small bar of single-use soap from the window sill where it was resting. He rips the paper from it and wets it and washes himself.

Outside, through the window, he can see the sun sinking into the ground. A wind blows a swirl of dust across the lot, toward the restaurant in front of which his car is parked. He left it there before coming to his motel room, which is not a motel room at all, but half a single-wide mobile home. Where there should be a hallway leading to the back half there is only a slab of unpainted drywall. His room consists of what would normally be the kitchen and living room, though the kitchen has been converted into a bathroom and the living room into a bedroom. The bedroom consists of small bed, a chest of drawers, a mirror, and a table on which rests a small TV. An ancient fan wobbles in a ceiling decorated by fat black flies, its five blades cutting through the hot air without cooling it in the least.

Ian rinses and shuts off the water.

He pushes the plastic shower curtain aside and steps from the tub, slipping on the linoleum floor and having to catch himself on the counter.

Something in his back tears as he reaches out to catch himself and he curses through gritted teeth, goddamn it, and closes his eyes in pain. Tears stream down his face. After a moment he opens his eyes. The pain begins to recede. It is still there, and severe, but it becomes almost tolerable. He grabs a towel from the counter and dries himself off. Arms and legs and back and fa—

The towel is covered in blood.

There are several drops of it on the linoleum floor. And now he can feel it running down his back. He picks up the satchel from the floor by the tub and walks naked to the living room where a mirror sits upon the chest of drawers. He turns around and looks at himself over his shoulder. Several of the stitches have been torn from the wound in his back—which is larger than he would have guessed, the bullet having taken its pound of flesh with it as it left—and blood is bubbling from it, frothy and seemingly thick as honey.

'Shit.'

He stands motionless for a long time as blood drips to the carpet, and then he walks to the phone and dials the manager's office.

'Motel/Food.'

'Monica?'

'This is Betsy.'

'Can I talk to Monica?'

'I'm sure I can help you, hon.'

'I'd like Monica.'

'Right. Hold on.'

The sound of the phone being set on the counter.

'Mon, I think it's the guy just checked in.'

A long emptiness. Then: 'Hello?'

'Monica.'

'Hey. Did you change your mind? I was hoping you would.'

'Not exactly,' he says. 'Do you have a first-aid kit?'

Ian walks to his duffel bag, which is sitting on the bed, unzips it, and pulls out a pair of boxer shorts. He slips into them.

A knock at the door.

He walks to it and pulls it open. On the other side stands Monica with a white metal first-aid kit hanging from her fist. For a long time she is silent, and he can only imagine what he looks like. Middle-aged and overweight with thinning blond hair and wearing nothing but a pair of boxer shorts, a plastic tube twisting out of his chest and into a black satchel which he is holding by the handle like a door-to-door salesman.

'Hi,' he says.

'Jesus,' she says. 'What—what happened?'

'I was shot.'

'With a gun?'

'With a gun.'

'You should go to the hospital.'

Ian shakes his head.

'I've already been,' he says, and holds up the satchel. 'That's where I got this. I just had an accident, is all.'

'What happened?'

Ian turns around to show her his back. He looks over his shoulder at her. She is grimacing, but she does not look away. In fact, she leans forward, examining the wound.

'You sure you don't need to go back to the hospital?'

'It's not as bad as it looks.'

'I don't believe you.'

'I can probably bandage it myself if you just—'

'Don't be dumb.'

'What?'

'It's in the middle of your back. Unless your elbows bend the wrong way, you're gonna need help.'

Ian stands silent for a long moment, then steps aside to let her in.

He lies on his stomach on the mattress and Monica straddles him. The first-aid kit sits open beside her. He cannot see what she is doing, but he can feel and hear her. He can feel the soft curves of her backside against the backs of his legs. He can hear her tearing the paper from something. He can feel her gently wiping the blood away from the wound with a pad of gauze.

'You're right,' she says.

'What?'

'It's not as bad as it looks. Only a few stitches tore out.'

He has barely felt a woman's touch in two years, not since he went drinking at O'Connell's and picked up one of the coeds from Bulls Mouth City College, and that was an angry drunken fuck, nothing like the gentleness he feels now from Monica. He had forgotten that this kind of gentleness existed.

After she wipes the area around the wound, he feels her

pour something onto it and into it. It stings and he sucks in air in a hiss.

'Sorry.'

'It's okay.'

She wipes at it again, and then lays something over it. She does it with gentleness, a soft touch that makes the pain feel almost pleasurable. Then she pulls something else from the first-aid kit, and he hears a clinking sound, then something like tearing. Medical tape being unspooled and torn away. She tapes a pad of gauze onto his back. After another minute, she tosses everything into the first-aid kit and latches it closed.

'All done.'

'Maybe you could stay a while longer.'

'You're in no shape for that.'

'I know. That's not what I want.'

'What do you want?'

He lies on his back in bed and watches her take off her clothes. She does it slowly, first her T-shirt, and then her bra. She unbuttons her skirt and lets it drop to her feet. She is wearing a pair of utilitarian white panties. She puts her thumbs into the waistband and pushes them down. She has a thick thatch of reddish-brown pubic hair. The bones in her hips are visible. Her breasts are small and her nipples light pink, ghosts of nipples. There is a mole on her left breast. She stands there completely naked before him, looking at his face.

Then she walks to him and lays herself down beside him, on his left side, and he feels her smooth legs against his legs and her warm breasts brush against his skin, her coarse pubic hair against his hip, and her breath on his cheek, and she rests her head in his armpit and she puts a hand on his heart.

'It's beating so fast,' she says.

'I know,' he says.

Ian watches the fan in the ceiling spin. He tries to follow a single blade as it makes its way round and round, but keeps losing track after four or five rotations, the blade dissolving back into a blur with the rest of them. He imagines his life after getting Maggie back. He imagines living in an apartment in Los Angeles with her and Monica. Monica is sweet and gentle and true. He might be able to live with her. He likes the idea of once more having a woman in his life. A partner. He thinks of Debbie, widowed back in Bulls Mouth, but he knows there is nothing left there. Sometimes people have too much history together, history of the wrong kind, and people cannot tear pages from the book of their life. Once something is written there it is permanent. But maybe he could start something new with a new woman and his daughter. Chapter four. Her body feels right against his body. He smiles at the thought, though he knows in the back of his mind that it's nothing more than a childish fantasy. He smiles at the thought and tries to hold on to it for as long as possible.

'Maybe you can stop by again on your way back from California,' Monica says.

'I'd like that.'

'Really?'

'Yes.'

'I would too. I like you.'

'We could have a date,' he says. 'A real date.'

'Yeah?'

'I could buy you dinner and we could ask each other what our favorite color is.'

'We could start now.'

'Okay.'

'You first.'

'Green.'

'Me too,' she says. 'What's your favorite food?'

'Meat.'

'Meat isn't a food.'

'It's a food group.'

'Then mine is sugar.'

'Okay. Filet mignon.'

'That's better.'

'What's yours, really?'

'You're gonna laugh.'

'I won't.'

'Promise?'

'Stick a needle in my eye.'

'Okay. Those little sour gummy worms. You know the ones?'

'Really?'

She nods. He can feel the movement against him, though he sees only the ceiling above.

'That's disgusting.'

'You promised you wouldn't laugh.'

'I'm not. I'm closer to puking.'

'Stop it,' she says. 'You're making me feel dumb.'

'Okay,' he says. 'I'm sorry. You can have sour gummy worms on our date if you want.'

'That's better,' she says. 'What's the worst thing you've ever done?'

Ian swallows. 'I don't like this game anymore,' he says.

'How bad can it be?' she says. 'Did you steal something?'

'Let's skip that question and move on to—'

The sound of a car outside makes him stop. He listens closely. It pulls to a stop out front.

He sits up.

'Could you see who it is?' he says.

'Are you in trouble?'

'Please,' he says.

Monica gets to her feet and walks naked to the window. She pulls back the curtain and looks out.

He shouldn't have let himself relax. He knew better than to let himself—

'Who is it?'

'It looks like a police car.'

He gets to his feet and bends down to pick up his satchel, but suddenly everything goes gray like a thin blanket thrown over him, and the blanket is very heavy, and he's falling to the floor, it pushes him to the floor, and then he's on the floor, and there's nothing.

Maggie opens her eyes. She does not know where she is. She is leaning against something, something soft and warm. A person. Her head is throbbing. Her mouth tastes bad. She sits up and looks around. She is in a truck, Beatrice on her right and Henry on her left. They are both eating hamburgers wrapped in yellow paper. She looks out the windshield. They are in a parking lot behind a McDonald's, and beyond the McDonald's the pink evening sky lined with gray clouds that look almost solid. The descending darkness makes the sky feel very small: it is closing in on her. She feels trapped sitting in the cab of this truck, trapped on either side by the hulking figures of Beatrice and Henry.

She rubs at her eyes.

Beatrice glances over at her. 'You're up,' she says.

Maggie nods, but does not feel like she is up. She feels groggy and gray and caught in a dream. A nightmare.

'How's your head?'

'Hurts.'

'You had a accident.'

She thinks of the ground rushing up at her.

'I know.'

'We got you some food.'

Beatrice leans down between her feet and brings up a hamburger from a white paper bag. She hands it to Maggie and

291

Maggie takes it. She holds it and looks at it. For a moment she thinks she is not hungry, that she will not be able to eat the hamburger, but then her stomach grumbles loudly and she realizes she is starving. It's been a long time since she last ate. She unwraps the hamburger and her stomach clenches and she takes a bite and tastes ketchup and pickle and she barely chews before swallowing and taking another bite.

'What do you say?'

She looks at Henry and swallows. 'Thank you.'

'Not me.'

She turns to Beatrice. 'Thank you.'

'You're welcome.' Beatrice smiles at her.

Maggie takes another bite.

Fifteen minutes later they're back on the road. Maggie sits between Beatrice and Henry and looks out the windshield. Darkness is spreading quickly across the land now that the sun is below the horizon. She is afraid that she will never escape. She wonders where her daddy is.

She closes her eyes and counts to ten.

She opens her eyes. She feels like a person in a snow globe. The sky is so close. Maybe it always was that close and she just doesn't remember. She spent a long time in the Nightmare World. Outside is bound to seem strange to her now.

She wonders what Borden is doing.

He's not real.

Everything will be okay, she thinks. Everything will be okay.

The sky is darkening, but she has her own light inside. Not even the Nightmare World could kill it. Certainly the setting of the sun will not.

Diego parks his car next to Ian's Mustang in what is left of the day's dying light. He kills the engine and steps outside. He squints at the interstate, then sprinkles tobacco into a rolling paper, rolls it, licks it, and sticks it between his lips. He thumbs the end of a match into a flame and lights his cigarette. It's a loose roll and it burns quickly. It tastes good but in four drags it is burned down to his nicotine-stained knuckles. He drops it to the dirt and heels it into submission and walks toward a building fronted with a sign that says MOTEL/FOOD in hand-painted white lettering.

The place is quiet but for the TV on the wall in the corner. It plays a series of loud and obnoxious commercials while a woman and a cook with a cigarette hanging from his lip play a game of cards.

When the bell above the door clinks dumbly, the woman turns around and says, 'Hi there, officer.'

'Howdy.'

'Are you here on business,' the cook says, 'or are you eating?'

'I could eat.'

'What'll it be?'

'What's good?'

'Cheeseburger.'

'Then that's what I'll have.'

'Fried egg on top?'

293

'I'll skip that part.'

'American, Swiss, cheddar?'

'Cheddar.'

'All right, coming up. Fries?'

'Onion rings.'

'Will you be staying with us tonight?' the brunette asks.

'I hadn't really thought about it. I reckon so. I stopped here because I'm looking for—'

The door swings open behind Diego, the bell clinking, and he spins around. A stick of a woman in a denim skirt and a T-shirt, barefoot and with her hair mussed, comes in and her gaze shifts around the room till it finds him.

'Ian wants to see you,' she says.

There is a smear of blood on the front of her T-shirt and another on her cheek.

'Is he okay?'

'I think so. He passed out for a second, but I . . . I think he's okay now.'

Diego nods. 'Where's he at?'

She leads him outside and around to the back of the building where several single-wide mobile homes are scattered across the land, and there is Ian, walking out the front door of one of them in nothing but boxer shorts and a pair of black shoes. He is pale and his skin is almost translucent as cooked onion. His shirtless belly is very white and there is a tattoo on his right shoulder, though from where Diego is standing it just looks like a green-gray smudge. Sweat stands out in beads on his face. A tube runs from his chest and into a black satchel he carries in his right hand like a man spreading the good news.

'Diego.'

'Are you sure you're okay?' the woman says.

'I'm fine. I just lost some blood and shouldn't have bent down.'

'I thought you were dead for a second.'

'I don't kill that easy.'

'You look pretty near it,' Diego says. 'You need to rest.'

'Can't.'

'Why not?'

'Someone might be passing by. I need to be alert. Asleep isn't alert.' Then he looks to the woman. 'Do you mind if I talk with my friend privately a minute?'

'Yeah,' the woman says. 'I'll just be up front. Sure you're okay?'

Ian nods. 'Thank you.' Then he looks toward Diego. 'Let's go inside,' he says. 'I need to sit down.'

Ian sits on the edge of the bed and Diego pulls a wooden chair away from the wall and sits across from him. Diego hasn't seen his friend since right after Henry Dean put a bullet through him and is shocked at how exhausted and sick he seems—somehow worse than when he lay in the gravel bleeding. He shouldn't be up. He certainly shouldn't be driving halfway across the country.

'You killed Donald Dean,' he says.

'He was scum.'

'He was a person. You didn't have the right to—'

'I know. I know that, Diego. But I did it anyway. I don't give a shit about right or wrong. I want my daughter back. Once she's safe, then I'm willing to face the consequences for what I've done . . . and for what I haven't done yet. But until then, nothing is gonna stand in my way. Not Donald Dean, not a bullet, and certainly not you.'

'You try to face off against Henry Dean in the shape you're in, he's gonna kill you.'

'I don't have a choice. He might be coming down that stretch of road in the next hour or two, unless the law catches up with him first, and I can't be asleep if he does.'

'It'll be dark by then. He might drive right by.'

'He might. If he does, I know where he's headed. But if I'm not ready for him and he does decide this is the place he's getting me off his back . . .' Ian coughs into his hand. The sound is wet and comes from a very deep place. Ian's face turns red. When he is done coughing he looks at his hand.

'Let me see.'

Ian opens his palm toward him.

A meaty wad of red in its center like a Christly stigma. Ian wipes it off on his blanket.

'You need to get to a hospital.'

'Not happening.'

'Ian.'

'Goddamn it, Diego. I didn't ask you to come here.'

'At least get some rest. We can park our cars around back so he can't see them from the interstate. You can get some sleep, we can go after him tomorrow and finish this.'

'He still could stop here.'

'I'll watch for him.'

'If I agree to this I don't want you with me tomorrow.'

'We'll talk about that then. What you need now is rest.'

Ian closes his eyes. His mouth hangs open. He looks to be on the verge of falling asleep even as he sits there. Falling asleep or passing out, Diego cannot tell which. He wonders if Ian can. Ian opens his eyes again and looks at him for a long time.

'You're a good friend,' he says finally. 'You could have . . .'

'I'm loyal to my friends. Now get some rest. I'll move our cars around back.'

'And . . . and you'll watch for Henry.'

'I will.'

'Okay.'

Ian watches Diego walk out the door and close it behind him. He will have to convince Diego to go back to Bulls Mouth tomorrow. Ian doesn't want him anywhere near what will have to happen if he's to get Maggie back. But it's good that he is here tonight. Ian is more tired than he can remember ever being. He is tired and not thinking straight. His eyes sting and his eyelids feel very heavy. If he closes his eyes that doesn't mean he doesn't love Maggie. It doesn't mean he won't get her back. It doesn't mean anything. He'll get her back tomorrow. But tonight he can sleep. Blessed sleep. Punishing himself will not get her back, nor will it prove his love. Diego is right. He needs to sleep. Henry will kill him if he doesn't get some rest. He lies on the bed and feels hot and cold simultaneously and slightly nauseous as well. He deserves a little sleep. Who puts a fried egg on a cheeseburger? He is very tired. He had a friend in school who used to put potato chips on his bologna sandwiches. A little sleep now and lot of sleep once he gets Maggie back. Maybe fried egg is good on a cheeseburger. Someone should close the curtains. If anybody ever asks him again if he wants fried egg on his cheeseburger he's going to say yes. Life is short. A person should only say no if they have to.

FIVE

Ian wakes to the sound of a knock at the door. He opens his eyes and sees white ceiling and a fan turning slowly. A few flies hang above him, punctuating the ceiling. His chest aches and throbs. He sits up and grabs the bottle of pain pills and pours a few into his mouth, then punches some caffeine tablets through the foil backing of the plastic sheet in which they were packaged and swallows those as well. There is another knock at the door. He gets to his feet, bending down to pick up the satchel, and he walks to the door and pulls it open.

Diego stands on the other side, looking tired. But he is showered and dressed in clean clothes and freshly shaved, though he missed a patch of hair under his left ear and another just under his chin.

'What time is it?'

Diego looks at his watch. 'Nine thirty.'

'What? Fuck. What did you let me sleep so long for?'

'You needed it.'

'Anything last night?'

Diego shakes his head.

'Not that I saw. Might have driven past, several cars did, but nobody stopped here.'

Ian nods.

'Okay,' he says. 'Guess I catch up with them in California.'

'We catch up with them in California.'

Ian shakes his head.

'I don't think so.'

'Get dressed. I'll buy you breakfast.'

Monica brings them eggs and bacon and bagels soggy with butter. Ian thanks her and takes a sip of orange juice and watches her walk away. He wishes there was more in him. He wishes when he looked at Monica he felt something. But he does not, nor does he think he could. Not now. Even thoughts of the future are oddly emotionless, not like they used to be.

'Distant,' he says under his breath.

'What?' Diego picks up a piece of bacon and takes a bite of it.

Ian shakes his head. Nothing. 'I'm serious about wanting you to go back to Bulls Mouth,' he says. 'I don't want you near this. You have Cordelia and Elias to think about and you shouldn't be here.'

'He'll kill you.'

'Maybe.'

'And if he does, what happens to Maggie?'

Ian looks down at his plate and pokes at his eggs with a dirty fork, but does not eat. After a while he simply sets his fork down again.

'That doesn't concern you,' he says finally.

'You know better than that.'

'There's nothing I can say, is there?'

'Nothing you can say what?'

'To get you to drive back to Bulls Mouth.'

'No,' Diego says.

Ian nods and is silent a long time. Finally he says, 'Okay.'

He picks up his fork again and scoops egg into his mouth. It is flavorless and the texture is somehow terrible and dead in his mouth, but he chews and swallows and takes another bite. They have a long day ahead of them.

A long day during which someone will almost certainly die.

Ian throws his duffel bag into the back seat of his car.

'Why don't I ride with you?' Diego has his own duffel bag hanging from his fist. 'I was up all night. I could get some sleep in on the way.'

'What about your car?'

'I'll pick it up on the way back.'

'Okay. Get in. I'll be right back.'

Ian stands in the doorway and says, 'I'm going.'

Monica looks up from a crossword puzzle she has laid out on the counter before her and sets her pencil down. It rolls to the edge of the counter and falls to the floor, but she only glances at it a moment before looking back to Ian.

'Are you really gonna stop by on your way back?'

'We're leaving Diego's car. We'll have to pick it up.'

'Yeah?'

'Yeah.'

She smiles.

'Good. Maybe we can really go on that date then.'

Ian is silent for a long time. Then, smiling: 'Maybe we can.'

Ian and Diego are on the road by ten fifteen. Diego smokes a cigarette with the window down and looks out at the desert while they drive, and then he snuffs his cigarette out in the ashtray, puts his seat back, and goes to sleep.

Ian drives in the silence.

Today is the day he gets his daughter back. It is strange to think about. Strange and frightening for reasons he cannot begin to understand. Or perhaps for reasons he refuses to understand. But he will get her back nonetheless. He will get her back and he will hold her in his arms.

In a life of failures he will have this.

They pass a sign that says KAISER NEXT EXIT, and Henry puts on his turn signal and merges into the right lane. Maggie looks out at the desert. She feels half in a dream. They drove all night. Almost all night. Henry fell asleep once and the truck rolled onto the shoulder of the road, but he snapped awake as the truck jerked about and grabbed the steering wheel and pulled them back out onto the interstate. Shortly after that he pulled off the road and they slept. But Henry must not have slept too long because the next time she awoke it was still dark and Henry was driving again.

He pulls off the interstate and onto a smaller road, passing a place with a sign that says DESERT CAFE, and Maggie imagines they serve dirt sandwiches. You pick them up and the sand falls out between the slices of bread and into your lap.

How's the sammy?

Oh, it's a bit dry.

Then they're past the cafe and all that Maggie can see is empty desert. The road is filled with potholes. Thatches of dead grass sprout from cracks in the asphalt. Vapor rises in the distance.

They drive by a sign riddled with shotgun holes, rusted and barely readable. It says KAISER 8 MILES, and there is a white arrow pointing straight ahead.

'We're almost there, Bee,' Henry says.

'I can't wait to get out of this truck,' Beatrice says.

Maggie can't either. They have been driving a very long time. She can't wait to get out, but she is afraid of what will happen once they get where they're going. She doesn't understand why she hasn't seen Daddy since yesterday afternoon. Maybe he forgot about her. No, she knows better than that. He did not forget about her. Her daddy would never do that. Maybe Borden got him, got him and killed him for Henry. Borden isn't real. She knows that. Borden isn't real and even if he was real he couldn't leave the Nightmare World. He is like a fish in that way and cannot leave the waters of the dark place where he was born. Even if he was real he couldn't. But he isn't. Her daddy didn't forget her and Borden didn't get him. Daddy is coming for her. She looks back over her shoulder but sees only road: empty gray road: and everything in the distance receding and receding and receding.

They drive through miles of emptiness. Dirt and shrubs and strange-looking trees. There are stretches of road that vanish beneath the windswept sand, but the asphalt always emerges some time later. And after a while they start passing by gray hills like heaps of ash, and the ground looks harder, and then a great gray pit in the earth, carved down and down and down, like stairs for a giant, and the pit is surrounded by broken machinery and at the bottom of it blue blue water, the only water in sight.

'Iron mine,' Henry says. 'Dried up in the seventies.'

Not long after that they arrive at the entrance to a small town surrounded by hills. A lonesome, desolate town, seemingly abandoned. There are buildings here, but they are not peopled. There is not a soul in sight. And it is silent. Not even the barking of a dog to stain the clear, quiet air.

'Goddamn,' Henry says.

He drives up the main street slowly, passing a gas station whose windows have been shattered. A Coke machine out front is lying on its side looking like someone took a baseball bat or a crowbar or a sledge hammer to it. Past that and on the other side is a grocery store, also empty. The middle of the day and not a single car in the parking lot, only a few bushes growing from the cracks in the asphalt. The front windows of the grocery store have also been shattered, and Maggie can see what look like food cans scattered across the lot, maybe things people didn't want like beets and lima beans.

They round a bend and pass an abandoned school, blue buildings left to flake apart beneath the desert sun, a baseball diamond which once had green grass growing in it now dead brown, bleachers sitting empty in the distance. Another turn and they enter a neighborhood of residences, the street lined with telephone poles made gray by the weather. Two out of three houses seem to have vanished. There is evidence that they were once there; the foundations laid out on the ground in the shapes of houses let you see where various rooms should be, but the buildings are gone. In the back yards rusty clothesline poles poke from the ground, usually with the lines long rotted away. Occasionally a T-shirt hangs from a rope like a flag of surrender.

'Are you sure this is the right place?' Beatrice asks.

'This is the right place,' Henry says.

'Where'd all them houses go?'

'Sold. Cut in half and put on trucks and hauled off to be planted in better ground.'

'Your brother lives here?'

'You been here, Bee, about twenty years ago.'

'That was here?'

'Changed, hasn't it?'

Maggie wasn't even born twenty years ago, but she doesn't think it's changed. She thinks it's died. When she was locked down in that basement, in the Nightmare World, she sometimes found the shells of beetles whose insides had been eaten hollow by ants. This town reminds her of that.

Henry pulls the truck to a stop in front of a small single-storey house which was probably once painted white. It now looks about ready to collapse in on itself.

Henry looks at her and at Beatrice and says, 'Wait here.'

Then he pushes open the door and steps from the truck. He walks to the front door of the house. A moment later he knocks.

Henry knocks on the peeling green-painted door and waits. When, after some time, there is no answer he knocks again. Ron hasn't had a phone for several years so Henry could not call him to let him know he was coming. Probably he is at work. Last time the two men exchanged letters—four maybe five years ago—Ron had gotten a job as a guard at a privately run prison about twenty miles away, Joshua Tree Medium-Security Correctional Facility, mostly populated by non-violent drug offenders.

Henry walks around the perimeter of the house, looking for open windows and checking the closed ones to see if he can push them open, but in the end he finds himself back out front with no way inside. He could break a window, but Ron's the kind of man who upon seeing signs of a break-in will shoot first and asks questions later. While there might be some irony in driving fifteen hundred miles only to get shot by the man you came to for help, irony just ain't a thing Henry is willing to die for.

He walks to the truck and looks in the window.

'He ain't here. We'll have to wait. You guys might as well get out and stretch some.'

'I have to pee,' Bee says.

'Just take some of them McDonald's napkins around back of the house and squat.'

He looks out at the faded gray street. He needs Ron to come home. Ian Hunt could arrive at any moment, and Henry has no weapons. He lost both his Lupara and his .22 in Sierra Blanca and has been utterly defenseless since. Ian could drive right up the street and put a bullet in his head and he couldn't do a goddamn thing about it. That ain't no position to be in.

That ain't no fucking position to be in at all.

'Come on, Ron,' he says.

He looks at his watch. It's only noon. If Ron works eight to four, as he used to, he won't be getting home till four thirty at least, and that's if he don't stop off someplace to get lit. That leaves over four hours during which Henry can get his brains blown out. And while this corpse of a town is a good place to finish this, nobody around to call the police about any noise and plenty of places to dump a body where it won't ever be found, the qualities that could work in his favor could also work in Hunt's.

If Hunt shows up in the next four hours or so.

If it weren't for getting pulled over this would have ended yesterday, it would have ended last night. But after Henry lost his weapons, he knew the only thing to do was to get to Ron's as quick as possible and hope when he got here he had time enough to prepare for Hunt. He still doesn't know if he has that time. If it weren't for that fucking cop this would be over. He felt kind of bad about having to shoot him at the time, the man was just doing his job, after all, opposed to Henry though he was, but thinking about the situation it's put him in Henry's glad he killed the son of a bitch.

He looks at his watch again, and he waits.

Ian and Diego cross the state line into Arizona around two o'clock in the afternoon, passing a sign welcoming them to THE GRAND CANYON STATE, though the surrounding desert looks the same as it did ten minutes earlier when they were in New Mexico. Ian has always liked the desert. The harshness of it and the emptiness. If God exists He lives in the desert, of that Ian is certain. None of the masks of civilization here. No grinning handshakes and knives in the back. The desert is honest: it will take you whole and leave a husk and you will know what it is doing while it's happening. It is what it is and makes no apologies.

There is something to be said for that.

Ian coughs into his hand, and the cough becomes a fit.

Between the coughs he manages to say, 'Take the wheel,' in a tight, strangled voice, and Diego does so. His coughing fit is wet and painful and comes from a very deep place in him and when it is over tears stream down his face and the strong taste of metal fills his mouth.

He wipes his hands off on his Levis, rubs at his eyes, and takes the wheel once more.

'Thank you,' he says.

Diego stares at him silently for a long time.

'Do you need to stop?'

'No.'

'Are you okay?'

'No.'

He glances at Diego, expecting him to say something, expecting him to tell Ian he needs to go to the hospital and take care of himself, expecting him to once more suggest that they tell the police what is happening, but he does none of those things. With only a nod he makes it clear that Ian's answer is okay. As long as Ian knows what he is doing to himself, Diego will accept it and help him. He does not turn his back on his friends.

Diego rolls a cigarette and looks out the window. 'When do you think we'll get there?'

'Around sunset.'

Diego grunts in acknowledgment, lights his cigarette, and cracks the window.

The wind blowing through the car is very loud and very hot, but it feels good against Ian's face even as hot as it is.

He looks to the gray road ahead.

In another four and a half or five hours they should be there. In another four and a half or five hours he gets his daughter back.

Maggie hears the car before she sees it, and Henry must hear it about the same time she does, because he gets to his feet from the curb where he was sitting with her and Beatrice and sort of leans forward as if that will help him see it sooner. Maggie feels a burning hope that it is her daddy. It is her daddy and he has come to save her and he will wrap her in his arms and take her away from here forever.

A white Toyota turns the corner and the face behind the windshield is not her daddy's. It is nothing like her daddy's. It is an ancient face into which time has carved great hollows. The eyebrows are thick and bushy and gray. The nostrils flare. The tongue, a colorless piece of meat, pokes out and licks the dry lips and disappears back into the pit of the mouth like some blind burrowing animal that's sensed a predator.

The car slows and, though it is merely a machine, seems to approach them with great caution.

Henry waves.

The man behind the wheel of the Toyota lifts his hand in an automatic return wave, but for a moment his face remains blank and stupid. Then his mouth opens in an ah and he smiles and says, audibly, 'I'll be a goddamned son of a whore.'

He pulls the Toyota into the driveway, pushes open the car door, steps out into the daylight, and holds out his arms. He is wearing a beige uniform and a belt with a black stick and a pair of handcuffs and a can of pepper spray hanging from it and black shoes. His thin gray hair is cut close to his head.

'Henry,' he says.

'Ron.'

They hug.

'How you doin', Bee?'

'Okay.'

'Good to hear it. And you must be Sarah,' looking toward Maggie. 'I can't believe I never met you before. I'm your Uncle Ron.'

Henry grabs Ron's arm.

'Listen, we need to talk—now.'

'Okay,' Ron says, 'let's head inside.'

Maggie sits silent on the floor while Henry and Ron sit on the couch. Henry talks, and though his talk is at least half lies Maggie does not interrupt him. She merely watches and listens. While Henry tells his story Ron's face changes, and his posture. His eyebrows lower on his head and his brown eyes seem to go black as shadows fill the deep pits of his sockets. The corners of his mouth curl down. His large nostrils flare. His loose bones weld together, locking him into a tight robotic posture. His round shoulders square, his c-shaped back snaps straight. His hands open and close in a motion Maggie recognizes from Henry. His tongue licks his dry lips. And when Henry is done Ron nods and says, 'So how long we got, you reckon?'

'I don't know. He could be here any time.'

'And he'll be heading to the house?'

'Best as I can figure.'

'Okay,' Ron says, 'I know just what to do.'

Henry and Beatrice and Maggie pile into Ron's Toyota as Ron said they should before he disappeared into a hallway, and now he emerges from the green-painted front door of his house with two rifles under one arm, boxes of shells in the other hand, and a pistol tucked into his waistband.

He hands the rifles to Henry, who slides them between his legs, butts on the floorboard, barrels aimed at the roof of the car.

Then Ron gets into the car himself and closes the door behind him.

Maggie does not understand what is happening, not exactly, but she knows it is bad. They're going to try to use those guns on Daddy. She wants to do something, but she doesn't know what. She can't even run. This town is empty, and miles from anywhere else. She only wanted to go home. She only wanted to go home to her daddy and mommy and—

Stop it, Maggie. Stop it.

One two three four five six seven eight.

She exhales in a slow breath. She has to be a big girl. She has to stay calm. She has to stay calm and see what happens and if there's anything she can do to help herself or help Daddy she will. But she can't panic. That won't get her anywhere. She closes her eyes and is enveloped by darkness. She opens her eyes, feeling a bit better, though still scared.

'Where we going?' Henry asks.

'High school.'

'High school?'

Ron nods.

'Trust me,' he says and starts the car.

They park in an otherwise empty parking lot. It is strange to be the only car in this vast field of asphalt. They get out of the car. There are several textbooks lying open on the asphalt, the hot breeze like a ghost occasionally turning their pages. Henry hands Ron one of the rifles and keeps the other for himself.

'This way,' Ron says.

They walk toward the front door of a two-storey building. It is a light blue color, the paint chipped and peeling. Not just the paint is peeling—time and weather have taken out chunks of the outer wall itself, leaving behind empty pits guarded only by what looks like chicken wire. They walk up five concrete steps and into a large empty corridor lined with lockers, some open, some closed, several still padlocked. The open ones have pens and pencils and books in them, pictures taped inside some of the doors. Books litter the vinyl floor. There are also occasional animal skeletons.

A rattlesnake lies on the vinyl floor in front of them. It looks to be in pretty bad shape. Ron pokes at it with the barrel of his rifle to make sure it's dead. It is. They step over it and continue walking.

'Beatrice and Sarah can wait for us in one of the class-rooms,' Ron says.

'I'm hungry,' Beatrice says. 'Are you hungry, Sarah?'

Maggie nods.

'You couldn't've said nothing before this minute?'

'I didn't want to interrupt.'

'We was at Ron's house. There was food there. What the fuck do you think we're gonna find here?'

'I just wanted to use the vending machine.'

'What fucking vending machine?'

Beatrice points. At the end of the hallway sits an ancient

vending machine with ancient food in it. Bags of chips, candy bars.

'All right,' Henry says. 'Let's get you some.'

They walk to the end of the hall where the vending machine sits. As they near it Maggie can see that several of the bags have been chewed through by animals—small rough-edged holes in the packaging, and pieces of food visible, usually small crumbs of it littered with even smaller pieces of insect shit.

'All right,' Henry says, 'stand back.'

He slams the butt of his rifle into the glass front of the vending machine and it cracks loudly, sounding to Maggie like God clapping His hands. Then he slams the butt of the gun against it once more, and it shatters and pieces of glass fall to the floor where they shatter further. He knocks more glass away, then hands the rifle to Ron and starts pulling out packages and going through them.

'Most of this shit's been got to, Bee.'

He throws the stuff that's been gotten to to the floor.

But they still manage to find six bags of chips and three candy bars and two bags of pork rinds that seem safe, or at least undisturbed by animals. With Beatrice's arms piled up with food, they head toward the nearest classroom.

'I need to talk to my girls a sec,' Henry says.

'Have to it,' Ron says, 'but make it quick. I wanna get to the roof ASAP.'

Henry nods, and then guides Beatrice and Maggie into a classroom.

The room is bright with daylight. It is empty save about twenty desks stacked in the corner. A tattered poster of the multiplication table hangs on the wall. There are math problems written on the chalkboard, faded white ghosts of what used to be. The floor itself is littered with textbooks and math papers. A row of windows, some of which are now shattered, reveal the baseball diamond. Empty bleachers. A rusty dugout. Plugs where bases used to be. A pitcher's mound. Dead grass.

Henry grabs Maggie by the arm and walks her to the stack of desks. He grabs one of the desks from the top of the stack and pulls it down and puts it on the floor. He shoves her into it.

'Sit here.'

Then he stops, apparently thinking. Turns silently and walks out. When he returns he has a pair of handcuffs, Ron's handcuffs, in one hand and a pistol, also Ron's, in the other. He tucks the pistol into his waistband, and then walks to Maggie with the handcuffs. He puts one of the cuffs on her wrist, tight, and the other he wraps around the desk, around part of the metal frame that curves up from the seat and bends to become the desk-top frame, onto which the slab of wood is screwed.

'What if I have to pee?'

'Squat by the desk.'

He turns away from her and walks to Beatrice. He pulls the pistol from his waistband and puts it into her hand.

'What's this for?'

'Just in case.'

'Just in case what?'

'It's a semiautomatic and the safety's off, so be careful. All you have to do is aim and pull the trigger, Bee. You got that?'

'Aim and pull the trigger at what?'

'Anybody walks through that door other than me or Ron.'

'I don't wanna shoot nobody, Henry.'

'What do we do, Bee?'

'What do we do?'

'We do what we have to to keep the family together.'

She is silent a long time, and then she nods.

'Good girl. Now keep an eye on Maggie, give her some chips or something, and if anybody walks through the door other than me or Ron . . .'

Bee just stares at him.

'Bee?'

'What?'

'If anybody comes through the door other than me or Ron what are you gonna do?'

'Aim and pull the trigger?'

'That's right.'

As soon as Henry is gone Maggie begins trying to squeeze her hand out through the cuff. It hurts, but if she squeezes her hand tight, and folds her thumb into her palm, she thinks she might be able to get free. If she has enough time.

Henry walks out of the classroom and into the corridor.

'All taken care of?' Ron says, pulling himself up from his leaning position against a wall of lockers.

'Yeah.'

'Good.'

He hands Henry back one of the two rifles, what was once their dad's .30-06, an old army job that takes an eight-round *en bloc* clip. When their dad got drunk he would shoot bottles off fence posts with it and tell them, 'Patton used to say this was the finest piece of military machinery ever made, and you know what? That crazy motherfucker was right.' Henry checks to make sure it's loaded, and then nods to himself.

'To the roof?' he says.

'To the roof.'

They climb an access ladder in the janitor's closet, push open a hatch, and make their way out onto the asphalt roof. It is early evening now and the sun is low and red in the sky. For some reason it makes Henry think of cracking a fertilized egg into a frying pan. That yellow yolk, that seed of red upon it cooking and dead. The evening sun. He turns in a circle and looks at the deserted town around them. He stops and looks down the long gray strip of asphalt leading to town. He can see for miles. If he had better eyes he could see all the way to the interstate.

'Good place,' Henry says.

'I know it,' Ron says. 'Only the Jackrabbit Inn's taller, three storeys instead of two, but you can't see the road leading to town as good.' Ron nods to his right and says, 'Let's take a load off while we wait.'

There are two lawn chairs sitting out in the red evening light and between them a styrofoam ice chest. Ron walks over and eases into one of the chairs. The thing protests under his weight. He pulls the lid off the ice chest, reaches inside, and pulls out a Coors. He breaks it open. It foams and he sips at it.

'It's warm,' he says, 'but it's beer.'

'Who's the other chair for?' Henry asks.

'For you.'

Henry sits beside his brother and looks west toward the falling sun. A warm beer rests between his legs. He felt panicky before when he was unarmed and simply waiting to be killed, but now he feels oddly calm. He's here and ready. Beatrice is safe. Sarah is locked up and incapable of doing any harm. And soon Hunt will be dead.

He glances over at Ron. 'It's been a long time,' he says.

'Too bad it's under these circumstances.'

'I think he got Donald. I didn't tell you that part at the house. It's the only way he could've found out where I was heading.'

'Got Donald?' Ron says. 'You mean kilt him?'

Henry nods.

'You think or you know?'

'I think.'

Ron shakes his head. 'No,' he says, 'he didn't kill Donald.'

'I think maybe—'

'Donald's the only one of us who's any good. He couldn't've got killed.'

'I think he—'

'Hush up and watch the sunset.'

'I just—'

'Hush up, Henry. You never did know when to keep your goddamned mouth shut.'

Henry picks up his beer and takes a swallow. He squints toward the sunset, then looks left at the gray road to the south leading from the interstate into town. It is empty.

By the time they each finish their second beer and grab their third Ron is smiling again.

'I missed you, Henry.'

'I missed you too.'

'This kinda feels like fishing, don't it?'

Henry nods. 'It's nice.'

But suddenly the smile is gone from Ron's face and he is no longer looking at Henry but past him. He nods his head.

'Look it.'

Henry looks left, to the south, and sees it. A dirty red car coming toward them. At this distance it looks like little more than a matchbox, a toy you could lose under your bed, but it's Ian Hunt all right. And suddenly Henry's heart is beating very fast in his chest, a percussive blood-drum pounding out the rhythm of his fear. And even now, even up here with his older brother, two rifles, and a couple boxes of ammunition, the sight of Hunt's red car coming toward him does make him feel fear. He does not know why, but it does.

He finishes his warm beer, tosses the can aside, and drops

322

into a prone firing position, up on his elbows, butt of the rifle in his shoulder, legs forming the number four behind him. He leads the red Mustang with the barrel of his gun. It grows larger as it comes nearer. A dusty old beater of a car.

He breathes in and out in tight, jerky fits. He's going to have to get himself under control if he's to make this shot count. A man has only one unexpected shot, and he'd do well to make it count. That means creating a calm in his center. At this distance a small shift can mean putting the bullet off target by a foot or two. The throbbing beat of his heart or a poorly timed inhalation and that is it: he's missed.

Ron remains seated in his lawn chair. He takes a loud swallow of his beer, sets it down, then drops to a knee. Henry doesn't see it, but he hears it, and he knows that's the position Ron likes to shoot from, for some reason.

'You got him?'

'Hush it up,' Henry says. 'Lemme concentrate.'

'So you got it.'

'Yeah, now quiet.'

As the car gets nearer Hunt's face becomes visible. As does the face of the man beside him. He is not alone. He brought someone with him. Henry is sure that he was alone when he saw him on the interstate yesterday. Somewhere along the way he picked someone up. He squints, trying to see if he recognizes the man in the passenger seat. Officer Peña. Diego Peña.

'Oh, fuck,' he says under his breath.

'What is it?'

'I said lemme concentrate.'

'Then stop cursing and start concentrating.'

Did Hunt involve the police after all? No, that doesn't make any sense. Peña's just a city cop and this is way outside his jurisdiction. Peña doesn't even count as a policeman this far west. He's just another *si habla español* with a gun.

He looks past the Mustang and into the distance. There are no other vehicles within miles. Hunt and Peña are alone out here. They're alone out here, and Henry has to make sure they never leave. He has to kill them. Then it's over.

He licks his lips. He inhales and holds his breath. The world is a storm but he is its eye. He lines Ian up in his sights.

The cold metal of the trigger dents the pad of his finger as he puts pressure upon it, then it moves beneath that pressure.

It is nearly seven o'clock when Ian pulls the Mustang off the interstate; the sun is low in the sky and has lost much of its midday polish and the sky itself is reddening. They drive past a place called the Desert Cafe, and then past a shotgunned sign that says KAISER 8 MILES. Beyond the sign there is no evidence of human life save the road itself, the desert stretching out on either side of them dotted only with shrubbery and Joshua trees. A rattlesnake is stretched out on the other side of the road to catch the last of the day's sun before slithering off for the night. The corpse of a jackrabbit half a mile past it.

Neither he nor Diego say anything for a long time.

Then Ian breaks the silence: 'You don't have to be here for this.'

'But I do.'

'You don't. You have a wife and a son and you don't have to be here for this.'

Diego looks at him a moment, and then out toward the desert to his right. Ian glances at him, but he is silent and his head is turned away.

'When I was in grade school,' Diego says after a while, still looking out his window, 'around twelve or so, I was hanging out with these older kids at recess. They walked up to this kid sitting on one of the picnic benches next to the basketball courts, just this kid about my age reading a Stephen King novel or something, and started harassing him. 'Nice shoes,' someone said. They were the cheap plastic kind and the tops were already cracked. 'Thank you,' he said. You could hear the nervous tremor in his voice. I remember that very clearly, that nervous tremor. 'You find 'em in the trash?' That kind of thing. I just stood there. I might have even thrown out an insult of my own, you know, to fit in, but I felt ashamed of myself, Ian. My heart felt sick. I've never forgotten that.'

Ian slows down as they approach the town itself. To the right is an abandoned gas station with a tipped-over Coke machine lying dead in its parking lot. Civilization felled. Dead grass juts from cracks in the asphalt. Then they pass a grocery store, also abandoned.

'Jesus,' Diego says. 'It's like a preview of the end of the world.'

Ian nods. 'Keep a lookout for any sign of them. I don't like driving into this at—'

Thwack.

For a moment Ian has no idea what happened. Then he sees a small hole in the middle of the windshield. He looks to Diego. Diego looks back.

'Your ear's bleeding,' Diego says.

Ian touches his right ear. It stings sharply and his fingers come away red. He glances to his seat's headrest. A hole just big enough to stick your pinky finger into.

'Put your head down,' he says to Diego as he drops his own.

Thwack.

Pieces of the windshield start to fall around them.

Ian puts his foot on the gas, panicking and trying to get them out of the line of fire, but accidentally stalls the engine after only ten or fifteen feet. He reaches out to the driver's side door—he thinks the gunfire is coming from the school to the northeast and wants the car between him and any bullets flying toward him—and pushes it open.

Then he pushes himself out the car door and onto the road saying, 'This way, Diego, and keep your fucking head down.'

He hits asphalt and a terrible pain rips through his chest.

He looks down. Red spreads quickly across his shirt. The tube tore out. He forgot about it and it tore out. It lies across his seat and hangs down the outside of the car and drips pink pus-blood onto the dirty asphalt. On the end of it, wrapped around it, is the black string that was once stitched through his skin, making the edges of the wound pucker like a tulip, and a pink triangle of the skin itself. When he breathes he hears that punctured-tire wheeze. He puts his hand over his chest to stop the air from leaking out that way. The last thing he needs right now is a collapsed lung.

Thwack. Thwack.

Two more bullets hit the car.

Diego drops to the road beside him.

'Are you shot?'

Ian shakes his head.

'I need plastic,' he says.

'Plastic?'

He closes his eyes and grimaces in pain. Then he opens them again. Diego sits on his haunches, ducked behind the Mustang and looking down at him.

'In the car,' Ian says. 'On the floorboard. There should be a small sheet of plastic. Can you get it?'

Diego nods and climbs back into the car.

Thwack. Thwack. Thwack.

Silence from within the car.

'Diego?'

More silence. He's almost convinced himself that Diego was shot when he emerges with a rectangle of plastic about six inches long and three inches wide. It has two stickers on it. The first sticker marks it as a TUNA FISH AND CHEDDAR SANDWICH and the second has the price, $4.99, and a barcode.

'This?' Diego asks.

Ian nods. 'That's the one.'

He unbuttons his shirt with his right hand while holding his left over the hole in his chest.

'Okay,' he says. 'Listen. I'm gonna pull my hand away from my chest. I need you to slap that piece of plastic over the hole.'

'Okay.'

Ian licks his dry lips. 'Okay.'

Ian pulls his hand away. He inhales and hears that terrible whistle. Then pressure and it stops. Diego is leaning over him, hand holding the plastic over the wound in his chest.

'Okay,' Ian says. 'I got it.'

He puts his own hand over the piece of plastic.

'Help me sit up and get this shirt off.'

They get Ian up and then get his right arm out of his shirt; then, after putting his right hand over the wound in his chest, his left arm.

'Now,' Ian says. 'Let's tie the shirt around me. Use it to hold the plastic in place.'

Diego nods. 'Okay,' he says.

He shakes the dust off the shirt, then slings it around Ian's back.

Ian simply sits with his back against the car's left front fender and catches his breath. Tears of pain stream down his face and his heart beats irregularly in his chest. He breathes in and out. He closes his eyes and opens them. The pain is tremendous. He reaches into his pocket, pulls out the bottle of tramadol. He thumbs the cap off the bottle and looks inside. Three pills left. He pours them into his mouth and dry swallows, then throws the bottle aside.

'Are you gonna be okay?'

He shakes his head.

'No,' he says. 'But we're here and we're doing this, so let's finish it.'

'Let's.'

'Get the guns from the back seat.'

Maggie is pulling her hand against the cuff, grimacing, unable to get the metal ring over the meat of her thumb, when she hears the first gunshot. Beatrice jumps at the sound and drops the bag of chips in her hand.

She leaves the chips where they lie and walks to the pistol Henry gave her and picks it up from the floor where she set it. She examines it, a confused look on her face, like she doesn't know how it got into her hand, sets it down again, and walks to the window. The evening light splashes across her face.

Another gunshot sounds and Beatrice jumps again.

'What can you see?'

'Nothing,' Beatrice says. 'Just a baseball field.'

'That's my daddy,' Maggie says. 'Those gunshots mean my daddy's here.'

'Henry's your daddy, Sarah.'

'Henry will never be my daddy.'

Two more gunshots echo through the hollow school building, the sounds bouncing off the walls and repeating and repeating and repeating, but softer each time.

'Henry will never be my daddy,' she says again, 'and you'll never be my momma.'

Beatrice looks at her with wide, sad eyes, half her face lit by what is left of the day splashing in through the windows, the other half covered in shadows and seemingly younger as the shadows hide the lines in her face.

'Why would you say such a thing, Sarah? We're doing all this for you. To keep our family together. Family's the most important thing there is and we're doing this for you.'

'I don't want you to. I want to go back to my *real* family.'

'We're your real family now.'

Maggie shakes her head.

'No,' she says. 'My daddy's here. My real daddy. He's my family. Him and my momma and Jeffrey. My daddy's a policeman and he's going to put you and Henry in jail forever and ever. He's going to put you in jail and take me home and I'll never have to see you again.'

'Don't talk like that, Sarah.'

Tears stream down Beatrice's round face, but her eyes are ablaze with anger as well as sadness. Her hands form fists at her sides. She almost looks capable of violence.

Maggie has never spoken to her this way, mostly out of fear that Henry would find out and put her on the punishment hook, but also because she always felt a little bit sorry for her, she has always seemed so sad, but she does not feel sorry for her now, and she is no longer afraid of Henry. No longer so afraid of him that she is willing to remain silent. She simply wants to be home with her real family. That want burns hot within her chest. She thought she would never feel that again. She thought the sun that burns within her had died, but it did not die.

It was only nighttime.

Three more gunshots echo through the air one after the other in quick succession.

'Henry's probably dead now,' Maggie says. 'You'll be in jail alone and Henry will be dead. No one will even write you any letters and no one will visit.'

'Don't *talk* like that,' Beatrice says, pushing Maggie. The desk tilts, holds a moment, precariously balanced on two legs, and then crashes onto its side. Maggie's elbow slams against the floor and pain vibrates through her body and a strange sensation shoots up her arm and her pinky and ring fingers go numb.

Beatrice rushes to her side and works to pull her and the desk up. It takes some doing, but she manages it. Maggie rubs at her elbow with her free hand. She thinks of pulling out of the handcuffs and grabbing the gun from the floor and running out of here. She knows her daddy is here, but she cannot just sit and wait to be saved. She waited trapped in the Nightmare World for a long time, and it was the longest night she has ever known, the longest night, she hopes, she will ever know, and she will not sit and wait ever again.

'I'm sorry, Sarah,' Beatrice says. 'I didn't mean it. I'm sorry.' She strokes Maggie's hair and pulls Maggie's head to her fat belly and presses her head against it. 'I'm sorry.'

Maggie pulls her head away.

'Just leave me alone.'

'You'll feel better when all this is over,' Beatrice says.

'I don't want to talk to you anymore.'

Beatrice wipes at her eyes. She walks to the window and looks out again.

'You shouldn't say things you don't mean.'

'I *do* mean it.'

Beatrice looks at her once more, and then turns back to the window. She simply stares out into the fading light of evening.

Maggie looks down at her wrist and tries once more to pull her hand through the cuff. It slides fine until the meat of her thumb, and there it stays no matter how hard she pulls, the metal digging deeper and deeper into her flesh.

Frustrated, she hits the top of the desk with her free hand. The other end tilts into the air and slams back down. It is loose. Eyeing Beatrice to make sure the woman is not looking at her, she pushes up on the desk. She lifts the top of the desk as far as it will go. Two of the screws have been stripped from the fiberboard underside. Maybe by the fall. She can almost slide the cuff wrapped around the desk right off. She doesn't have to free her hand. All she has to do is pull off the top of the desk. She just has to get the final screw out, and she can slide the cuff right off.

Beatrice is still staring sadly out the window. Maggie is stung by another pang of pity for her. Her face just hangs there looking so lonesome. Even after everything there is a part of her that wants to give Beatrice the love she so obviously needs. But Maggie cannot love her. Maggie cannot even like her. She can only feel a strange combination of pity and hatred.

She pushes up on the top of the desk, trying to pry it loose.

Henry lies prone on the roof of the high school. He squints down at the car on the street below, but has seen no movement for some time. He has no idea what they're doing back there. His arms are cramping. He's not going to be able to lie like this much longer. And their silence is making him nervous. They cannot just wait there forever. They have to do something. Why aren't they shooting back? If they were returning fire he might be able to locate them and finish them off. Just one or two shots would be enough. Then he would know where they were—and when they popped up to shoot again that would be it.

Maybe he already has finished them off and that's why they aren't moving. Except he knows better than that. That's the kind of thinking that will get him into trouble. If he lets his guard down he'll get himself killed.

'Can you see anything?' he says to Ron, who is behind him, crouched down on one knee, rifle at the ready.

'No,' he says. 'What the fuck are they waiting for?'

'I dunno,' Henry says. 'But I don't like it.'

That's when he sees the driver's seat slide forward and tilt toward the steering wheel.

He sees movement behind it—an arm reaching into the

back seat, he thinks. It's hard to tell for certain. But it is movement.

Inhale. Hold the breath. Take aim. Steady.

The world is a storm but he is its eye.

Exhale.

Squeeze the trigger.

Ian hears the bullet slam into his car and flinches, but Diego does not. Diego simply reaches into the back seat and comes out first with the rifled Remington 11-87 and the sawed-off Remington 870, and then with the .308 and the duffel bag in which the boxes of ammunition are stored. Ian pulls the duffel bag toward him and unzips it. He tosses Diego the shells for the .308. Then pulls out shells for himself and gets to loading the two shotguns.

Once they're loaded he slides to the front of the car and looks around the bumper trying to spot Henry, trying to spot movement of any kind. He knows the shots are coming from across the wide street, and from the north, and from a good distance, by the sound of it.

'Where are you, you son of a—'

He pulls his head back quickly and a moment later there is the sound of a gunshot and the dirt three feet behind the place where his face was kicks up a cloud of dust, and a few pebbles from the ground throw themselves against the right leg of his Levis.

'They're on the roof of the school,' he says. 'About fifty, sixty yards away.'

Diego nods. 'What do you want to do?'

Ian closes his eyes a moment, thinking. He did not want to get Diego involved in this way. He did not want to ask of him

336

what he is about to ask of him. Even now he wishes he had talked Diego into heading back to Bulls Mouth. If Diego was not here he would have to think of something else. But Diego is here. He opens his eyes and looks at his friend. This will change him. What he is about to ask of his friend will change him forever.

'How's your long-distance shooting?' he says.

Ian sits on his haunches behind the Mustang. To his right Diego is readying himself for a run toward what once was a hardware store. If he can get behind it, he can make his way in relative safety to the top floor of a three-storey hotel called the Jackrabbit Inn about three hundred yards further on. From that vantage point he should have clear shots at Henry Dean and his brother on the roof of the school.

'You ready?' he says.

Diego nods.

Ian exhales and his exhalation turns into a deep cough. Liquid gags up from his lungs like muddy water from a well-pump and he spits it to the asphalt between his feet. Tears stream down his face. He leans his head against the car fender before him and spits once more. His chest is throbbing with pain. Last time he tried to do this he was shot. What is it they say about doing the same thing repeatedly and expecting different results?

'One,' he says, looking toward Diego.

'You sure you're—'

'Two,' he says, cutting off the question.

Diego nods briefly. The nod tells Ian that he accepts that as an answer.

'Three.'

Diego takes off running.

Ian jumps to his feet, swinging the shotgun up and into the crook of his shoulder, and he fires at the roof of the schoolhouse. The pain is incredible. Concrete explodes less than a foot below the place where Henry is crouched. A white shell flies from the shotgun, arcs in a blur through the air, and hits the asphalt to his right. He fires again and again and again. Both Henry and his brother drop down, becoming invisible from this angle.

But Ian remains standing, squinting toward the school, watching the flat line of the roof and waiting.

Blood runs down his sweaty belly from the hole in his chest, which is throbbing with pain. His breaths are quick and shallow, as he can manage nothing but shallow breaths any longer. Any time he tries to breathe deep it turns into a painful coughing fit. He knows what is happening. With the tube removed from his lung he is drowning in his own blood. It is beyond a feeling of drowning now; it is the actual thing.

A flash of movement from the roof of the school. He fires. Concrete explodes.

The movement ceases.

Ian glances behind him.

Diego is out of sight.

Good. Black dots are swimming before Ian's eyes and he doesn't think he'll be able to remain standing much longer.

He fires off the last three rounds in the 11-87's magazine, listening to the shells clink to the asphalt to his right between shots, and then allows himself to sink to the ground behind the car, out of breath and in pain. Every shot sent a terrible force through his right shoulder and his wounds are now screaming. Sweat runs down his face and drips from the end of his nose. He blinks several times, and then looks for Diego.

He does not see him, nor does he hear him.

The air is silent and still but for the sound of his own breathing.

And then he does hear him. He hears the rapid rhythm of his boots. He hears running. He is far away and getting farther.

Ian nods. Good.

He grabs the box of deer slugs and starts reloading.

Maggie slides the handcuffs down the length of the arm of the desk, being careful they don't rattle too much. She slides them beneath the wooden desktop, now detached from the frame, and then she is loose. The cuff slides off and dangles from her wrist. It is strange: a tightness in her chest seems to uncoil with the simple knowledge that her arm is free.

Her arm is free.

She looks up at Beatrice.

Beatrice does not look back.

The gun sits on the floor next to a pile of chips and candy bars.

Maggie slides out of the desk, eyes on Beatrice, and makes her way silently across the room. She is barefoot, so it is not difficult to be silent. But Beatrice must see her movements out of the corner of her eye, in her periphery, because she turns to look at her and says, 'Sarah, what are you doing? Henry said to stay here.'

Maggie runs to the gun and picks it up.

Beatrice walks toward her, but stops when Maggie points the gun at her.

'I don't want to shoot you,' she says with a shaky voice. 'But I will.'

Beatrice is silent. She simply stares at Maggie with her wide, glistening eyes. Tears once more roll down her round face. Her chin trembles. Her shoulders sag with defeat.

'We're never gonna be a family again, are we?'

'We never were,' Maggie says.

Beatrice leans back against the wall and slides down it to a sitting position, with her knees up and her arms on her knees. She looks down at her lap. Maggie can see her cotton panties. Somehow that makes her seem very much like a little girl. Tears drip off her face and splash against her dress.

'We never were,' Beatrice says, eyes focused on nothing, and it seems as if she is speaking a foreign phrase for the first time. A foreign phrase whose meaning she does not quite understand.

She looks up at Maggie as Maggie backs her way out of the room.

'We never were,' Beatrice says again. Then: 'But I loved you.'

'I didn't love you,' Maggie says.

Then she turns around and runs out into the corridor, looking for a way out.

The first shot from above thwacks into the roof just to the left of Henry's legs. He can feel the displaced air ripple outward and press itself against his body and he hears the bullet connect with the roof, an almost wet crack like a bone breaking open and spilling its marrow, and several splinters are thrown against his Levis.

'Where the fuck did that come from?'

Ron behind him scanning the surrounding buildings, looking for the source of the gunshot whose bang still echoes through the empty streets of the town.

'I don't know,' Henry says. 'It had to come from above. The angle is wrong for—'

The second shot hits less than a foot shy of the place where Ron is crouched, and splinters fly from the roof and into his face. He falls backwards with a curse, blinking as tears stream down his face, about a dozen bleeding pin-prick holes in his cheeks.

Henry looks back toward the street. The shooter, which has to be Peña because Hunt is still trapped behind his now bullet-riddled car, has to be in the Jackrabbit Inn, it's the only building taller than the schoolhouse, but Henry can't see him anywhere. He doesn't see him on the roof, and while several of the windows on the third floor are open, all he can see behind those windows is darkness. The sun is setting behind the building, lighting Henry and his brother while keeping the east side of the Jackrabbit Inn in shadows. And it's the east side of the hotel he and Ron are facing.

'We have to get off the roof,' he says. 'Ron, we gotta get off the—'

Ron is sitting up, rubbing his eyes, when a third shot is fired. A red dot presses itself into the center of Ron's left hand. He pulls it away from his face and looks at it.

But the bullet continued through the hand, and there is another dot in his left cheekbone and his left eye is filling with blood and a slow trickle runs from his right nostril, down onto his lip, and then along the top of his lip, drawing a red mustache there before dripping from his face.

'Ron?'

Ron looks up from his hand to Henry.

'Something happened to my . . . hand.'

He holds it up for Henry to see, blinks several times, and falls over sideways.

'Ron?'

Henry gets to his feet and turns in a full circle, confused somehow—this isn't how it was supposed to happen. It was supposed to be easy. It was supposed to be easy and quick, a few shots and finished. He glances toward the Jackrabbit Inn and again sees only darkness in the windows there. He turns and runs toward the hatch in the roof as the fourth shot cuts through the air. He drops down the ladder and lands in the janitor's closet and falls backwards against a shelf full of cleaning supplies.

What the fuck just happened?

He tries to accept what he saw, but his mind keeps rejecting it. He cannot have just seen his brother get killed. That's impossible. It's impossible.

It happened.

First his younger brother, then his older brother.

Hunt has to pay for that if for nothing else. He knows Donald would never give him up unless he was forced to. He knows he would never—

He closes his eyes and tries to get his mind right.

He has to finish this.

He opens his eyes and walks out of the janitor's closet and down a wide flight of stairs to the first floor. He walks down the corridor, and is about to pass the classroom that Beatrice and Sarah are waiting in when Sarah runs out of it, into the corridor. A gun hangs from her right hand, the handcuffs still wrapped around her wrist clinking against its barrel.

She looks left and sees him, and there is a moment of terror in her eyes, but only a moment of it. Then she lifts the pistol in her hand and points it at him.

'Don't move,' she says.

He stops and puts his arms up, still holding his dad's .30-06 in his right hand. First his younger brother, then his older brother. Now the one in the middle.

'What are you doing, Sarah? How'd you get out?'

'Shut up,' she says. 'Shut up and put down that gun.'

'You don't even know how to use that gun, Sarah. You're not gonna shoot me.'

'It's a semiautomatic and the safety's off,' Sarah says. 'You told Beatrice. All I have to do is aim and pull the trigger.'

He takes a slow step toward her.

'I said stop!'

He does.

'Put down your gun.'

'You're not gonna shoot me.'

Sarah licks her lips and raises the barrel of the pistol so it's pointed at his face. He stares into it, and then past it to Sarah, and he sees that she will shoot him. If he isn't careful she will shoot him. He thinks of Beatrice's ankle. He never did find out exactly how that happened, but looking into Sarah's face he thinks he knows. Her eyes tell him that she is very much her father's daughter. At least in one respect she is: once she begins something, she does not quit.

'Put down your gun,' she says again. 'Right now.' Her voice trembles with rage.

He thinks of all the times he tied her hands, all the times he hung her from the punishment hook. He thinks of leaving her in the basement. He thinks of hearing her cry when she was younger. He thinks of when the crying stopped.

He nods, then leans down slowly and sets the rifle onto the floor.

'Did you shoot Beatrice?'

'No,' Sarah says. 'I didn't have to.'

'Good,' he says. With him leaning forward she is almost within arm's reach. He wonders if he might be able to lunge at her and get the gun away. 'Good,' he says again. 'You don't want to shoot anybody.'

'I don't. But I will.'

'I know that, Sarah,' he says. 'I know th—'

He jumps at her and just manages, barely, to grab her wrist before the gun goes off. The sound rings in his ears, deafening him completely, if only momentarily, and he staggers backwards, hand still wrapped around Sarah's wrist.

Son of a bitch: she actually shot him. He's faced off against half a dozen cops in the last few days and come out unscathed, only to be shot by a fourteen-year-old girl.

But he will not die like this. He will not.

He struggles to pull the gun out of Sarah's hands.

Ian sits on his haunches and waits, the rifled shotgun in his hands and the sawed-off shotgun tucked into the back of his Levis. He heard gunfire echo its way out the front door of the school and now he waits for something human to emerge.

Silence follows silence.

He swallows and can feel his Adam's apple bob in his throat. His mouth is dry, his lips cracked. His eyes sting.

And then he sees movement on the other side of the doorway, behind the shadows. His first urge is to stand and shoot, but he does not do that. He waits to see what emerges from the shadows and what emerges from the shadows is Henry. Henry carrying Maggie, holding her around the waist and with a pistol to her head. He is pale and glistening with sweat and there is a hole in the middle of his neck like a tracheotomy and blood is running down the front of his shirt and Maggie is trying to pull his arm away from her waist so she will be let loose.

Behind Henry and Maggie is Beatrice. Her head is low and her shoulders slumped. She barely seems to be there at all.

Ian stands, pointing the 11-87 at Henry and walking around the front of the car. He feels wobbly on his legs, but he does not care and he does not move slowly. He cuts the distance between Henry and himself in half.

'Let her go,' he says.

'So you can shoot me?' Henry says, his voice little more than a frog's croak. 'No chance.'

'I'm gonna shoot you anyway, you son of a bitch.'

Henry shakes his head. 'You won't risk killing your own daughter, Hunt.'

'I said let her go.'

'No. You're not gonna risk shooting her. I know it and you know it. So just drop your gun. We're walking to Ron's car and we're driving away and that's the end of it. You lose, Hunt. You tried, but you lose.'

Henry takes several slow steps toward the parking lot where a white Toyota sits. His wife Beatrice walks behind him. Her eyes are wet with tears and glistening.

'Put down your gun, Hunt.'

'Let her go.'

'Put it down or I'll shoot her myself.'

He presses his pistol against Maggie's temple.

Maggie looks at him with eyes filled not with fear but with anger. 'No, Daddy! Don't put it down! Don't let him get away! Don't let him take me away again! Please, just don't let him take me away again!'

'Shut up, Sarah,' Henry says. 'Put it down, Hunt, or she dies.'

Ian's chest throbs with pain. He thinks he could probably get Henry. He could probably get Henry, but even the small chance of hitting Maggie makes him hesitate. He will not do that. He nods, more to himself than to Henry, and leans down to set the 11-87 on the ground. But as he stands, black dots swim before his eyes and the light seems to fade from the sky, as if night were falling all at once, and there is a brief moment during which he thinks he may pass out, just drop like a corseted lady in an old film, and then will come the gentlemen with fans, and all he can think is two words over and over again: not now not now not now not now.

And he manages, barely, to hold on to consciousness. Light runs back into the dome of the sky like liquid over an upturned glass bowl. He regains his balance.

'Smart man,' Henry says.

'No,' Maggie says. '*No!*'

And she slams both her elbows back simultaneously into Henry. The left elbow sinks into his gut, and a strange sound explodes from Henry's mouth, like a large dog letting go a single bark, and Maggie drops to the ground from his loosened grip. She drops to the ground and runs toward Ian. Her face is full of terror and joy.

Henry swings the pistol around toward her, and shouts, 'Stop, Sarah, or I'll—'

But that's all he manages to get out before Ian reaches behind him—with a great tearing pain in his chest and back, as if a hot metal rod were pushed clean through him—and pulls out the sawed-off shotgun and swings it around so it's pointing at Henry, and fires. It seems to happen in slow motion. First everything quickly—the elbow, the drop, the running—and then he grabs the shotgun and time slows like suddenly they were all moving through honey. Maggie seems to hang in the air between running steps and Henry's arm is moving slowly—slowly—and his words sound like a seventy-eight playing at thirty-three and a third. The sound of Ian's shotgun firing is extremely loud, and he can see the buckshot emerge. He can see the last few grains of gunpowder spit from the barrel behind the eight .36 inch pellets before they burn to nothing on the air. He can see smoke blue and thin curl from the barrel. Multiple cracks as the buckshot hits bone and tight groups of holes punch themselves into his face and head, and his skull seems to dent inward like an empty beer can as the contents splatter on the sun-bleached asphalt behind him as well as Beatrice's face and hair and dress.

Then Maggie is jumping at Ian and he leans down to accept her hug. She wraps her arms around him and kisses him and says, 'You're bleeding, Daddy. You're bleeding,' and he kisses her cheeks and her eyes and her mouth and he can feel her heart beating against his stomach, and tears well in his eyes, the first time he has cried in a long time.

Henry falls to the ground and a puddle of blood spreads like a blanket beneath him.

'Maggie,' Ian says. 'My Maggie.'

But then he sees Beatrice lean down and pick up Henry's pistol and he swings the shotgun up, aiming at her. But he does not fire. He sees immediately that she does not intend to continue Henry's fight. She stands and she looks toward them and tears well in her eyes as she says, 'I'm sorry.' Then she puts the pistol into her mouth.

It's a semiautomatic and the safety's off, so all she has to do is pull the trigger.

Diego walks down the street toward them and they wait, Ian and Maggie, with her small hand in his large hand. Ian looks down at her and smiles. She looks up at him and smiles back and her green eyes that could break your heart if she wanted them to smile also. He can hardly believe it is her hand he's holding. His daughter. His little girl. His Maggie. He thinks of holding her on the day she was born. He thinks of standing over her crib and watching her sleep. He thinks of the first time she wrapped her tiny fist around his thumb. He thinks of changing her diapers. He thinks of her cradled in his arm, taking a bottle. No matter what happens next he knows what he's done and what he's become, it was a price worth paying. He would pay it twice and again if he had it still to give. And if there's more to pay he will pay that too.

Diego looks sick. He is pale and sweaty and his eyes are far away.

'I killed one of them,' he says.

'I'm sorry,' Ian says. 'I didn't want you to have to do that.'

'The bullet hit him right here.' He touches his own cheek.

'I'm sorry.'

'Right here,' he says.

They take the white Toyota back to the falling-down house Ron lived in before he decided the world was no longer his home. Diego, Ian knows, would try to talk him into heading to a hospital if he weren't lost inside himself, but he is, and Ian does not intend to go anywhere tonight. He is too tired. If he wakes up tomorrow he'll think about it, but he believes he's earned a few hours with his daughter. He believes she's earned a few hours with her daddy.

They get to the house and open the door and go inside.

Diego finds a bedroom in the back and goes there and sits alone.

Maggie eats and talks and talks and talks, as if she has not spoken to a soul in years. Ian sits with her and listens. She tells him about the Nightmare World, and about counting till her head was filled with numbers so that the bad thoughts could not get in, and about how Henry's brother Donald brought her books and even gave her lessons sometimes, in history and math, and about Borden and how he was her only friend, and about how she tried to escape, how she ran through the woods and how his voice, her daddy's voice, gave her hope and made something in her that she thought was cold burn hot. She asks about Mommy and he tells her that Mommy is waiting for her return. He tells her that Mommy loves her very much. He tells her that Mommy will probably let her sleep in bed with her for a long time. He tells her that she is the strongest, bravest person he has ever met. He tells her that she is a miracle.

The hours they spend together are the best hours he's ever lived and the truest, and when they fall asleep beside one another on the fold-out sofa-bed with Maggie's head leaning against his shoulder and her small hand in his large hand he has a smile on his face and the dreams he dreams are of the future, a bright future full of joy and laughter.

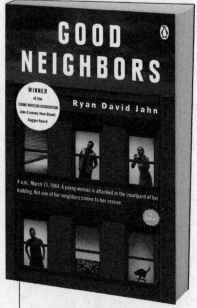